The Cavaradossi Killings

Books by David Dvorkin

Fiction

The Arm and Flanagan
Budspy
Business Secrets from the Stars
The Cavaradossi Killings
Central Heat
The Children of Shiny Mountain
Children of the Undead
Damon the Caiman
Dawn Crescent (with Daniel Dvorkin)
Earthmen and Other Aliens
The Green God
Pit Planet
The Prisoner of the Blood series

- *Insatiable*
- *Unquenchable*

Randolph Runner
The Seekers
Slit
Star Trek novels

- *The Trellisane Confrontation*
- *Time Trap*
- *The Captains' Honor* (with Daniel Dvorkin)

Time and the Soldier
Time for Sherlock Holmes
Ursus

Nonfiction

At Home with Solar Energy
The Dead Hand of Mrs. Stifle
Dust Net
Once a Jew, Always a Jew?
Self-Publishing Tools, Tips, and Techniques
The Surprising Benefits of Being Unemployed
When We Landed on the Moon: A Memoir

The Cavaradossi Killings

David Dvorkin

Editing, print layout, e-book conversion,
and cover design by DLD Books
www.dldbooks.com
Editing and Self-Publishing Services

ISBN: 978-1-7362886-0-3

Dedication

For Leonore
La Prima

One

When he could no longer deceive himself about his guilt, he left, returning to a place few people chose to leave. The person most important in his life had left that place, too, but surely she had not chosen to do so.

He took with him what he considered appropriate pay for the services he had rendered.

Tom could smell the cologne before he opened the door. He looked up at the tall, beefy, middle-aged man waiting impatiently on the doorstep.

"Yes?"

"Tom!" the man boomed. "You haven't changed at all! You look just the same!"

The other man's face and body had changed considerably. It was the loud voice and overbearing manner that identified him. "Jack Tourneau," Tom said. "I didn't know you were still here." After the briefest hesitation, he added, "Come in."

As he led the way to the living room, Tom asked, "Want something to drink?"

"What's that you're drinking? Looks like urine with ice in

it."

"Why, you haven't changed either, Jack." Tom held his glass up to the light for a moment. "You're right." He sipped his drink. "Fortunately, it tastes like bourbon. Want some?"

Jack shivered. "Brr! Alcohol! Never touch the stuff." He slapped his thick middle. "That's how I've managed to keep my schoolboy physique. Got any Diet Pepsi?"

"Nope."

"Okay, then, I'll have a bourbon on ice."

Tom raised his eyebrows.

"*Almost* never touch the stuff. Today doesn't count."

"And why is that?" Tom asked as he went behind the bar.

"Because today I'm greeting an old school friend I haven't seen in over twenty years. So this is a special celebration."

Tom put a couple of ice cubes in a glass and poured bourbon over them. He glanced at Jack, already sprawling at his ease on the couch with the best view.

"You can see the whole damned city from here," Jack said. "Hell of a view. Hell of a drop–off."

"About a hundred feet."

"Better be careful when you mow. But I bet you hire the mowing."

Why don't you go outside and stroll along the edge? Tom thought. Swallow all of your drink first. "I don't have a lawn. I went for the natural look."

Frank snorted. "That figures. I always wanted a house up here. This place must have cost you a fortune."

"Mm hm."

"Quarter mil? Half? More?"

"A fortune."

Jack grinned at him. "Close-mouthed bastard. You haven't changed in that regard, either." He reached up to accept his drink from Tom. It was the gesture of a monarch accepting a drink from a servant.

Tom shook his head in silent wonder at Jack's old talent for taking center stage. "I just moved in yesterday. How did you know I was here? Or is this a coincidence? Maybe you came to my door to sell encyclopedias."

"Nice try, Tom. You went into the license bureau this morning to get a driver's license. The woman who took care of you was Janice."

"Janice?" Tom frowned for a moment, recalling the face. She had seemed familiar at the time, he remembered. "Wait a minute. Not Janice Sheridan? Janice the cheerleader?"

"That's right."

"Jesus," Tom muttered.

"Twenty years," Jack said. "And fifty pounds."

"I didn't move back here to get depressed," Tom said, "but now I am."

"So why *did* you move back here?"

Jack must have thought he was being casual, that he was disguising his interest. But reading other men, seeing through their armor, had become a survival skill for Tom during his twenty-two years in Chicago. "Just looking for peace and quiet, Jack. Early retirement in the old home town."

"Pretty damned early," Jack said. "You're the same age I am, and I won't be able to retire for more than twenty-five years. What've you been doing since you left town?"

"Saving carefully. What have *you* been doing since I left?"

"Why, I've been following in my daddy's footsteps, Tom.

Some of us have reason to want to do that, you know."

I actually looked up to this jerk when I was a kid, Tom thought. Amazing. "So you're teaching at the college?"

"Not *just* teaching at Triple C. I'm teaching English, just like my father. Been there for ten years, now. Ever since I got my Ph.D."

"How is your father?"

Jack shrugged. "Dunno. He got old enough to retire, the lucky bastard. He and my mom are off somewhere in the Pacific. They spend all their goddamned time traveling and squandering their savings. They gave us the house, anyway. You remember the house." He held up his empty glass. "Like another."

"Like, okay," Tom said. He set his own almost full glass down on the coffee table and stood up. He took Jack's glass and went to the bar with it. "I always liked your father," Tom said. He refilled Jack's glass, but this time he put in four ice cubes first. He brought it back to Jack, who had slid lower on the couch.

"More than you liked your own," Jack said. "For which I never blamed you. No fault of yours. I understood why you were always over at our place. Especially after your mom—" He paused and had the grace to look embarrassed. "After you lost your mom."

Tom went to the window and stood looking out over Ransom, his back to Jack. The window extended from floor to ceiling and across most of the east wall of the living room. The builder had assured Tom that he would install glass capable of withstanding the winds up here. How about bullets from resentful people living below, Tom had wanted to ask. "Do you enjoy teaching, Jack?"

Jack grunted. "Most of the time, I hate it. But I like the hours. And the coeds. You should see them, Tom. They don't dress the way they did when we were young. Oh, I'm sorry, you didn't go to college. I forgot."

Tom laughed despite himself. "Sure you did, Jack. So, let's see. You've checked out my house and me and my liquor. We've renewed our dear, close friendship of boyhood days. What else did you come here to do?"

"To invite you to the opera," Jack said.

Tom spun around. "*What*?"

Jack chuckled. "Caught you, didn't I? Well, it's not my idea. I hate opera. It's Ellen's idea."

"Ellen?"

"My wife. The former Ellen Chernikov."

Again, Jack had managed to get him off balance. "Ellen married *you*?"

"*I* married *Ellen*." He radiated self-satisfaction. "You'd know this stuff if you'd kept in touch with the old gang, Tom."

"You have children?" Tom shivered inwardly with disgust at the thought of Ellen Chernikov pregnant with Jack's babies.

But Jack shook his head. "Turned out Ellen couldn't. It used to bother her at first. Just fine with me, though. I hate kids. Anyway, Ellen runs the Ransom and Central Colorado Opera Guild. The name's bigger than their whole damned budget. Or the size of their audiences. Ellen always did love music, but you probably don't remember that."

Tom remembered everything about Ellen Chernikov with painful clarity, and he was sure Jack knew that. "So Ellen knows I'm back?"

Jack drained the last of the bourbon from his glass and set

it on the coffee table. “I told her as soon as I found out. And she insisted I come up here and invite you to the opera they’re putting on.” His speech had become slurred. “Tomorrow night is the first performance. They rent the auditorium at the high school. If you want, I could tell her that you hate opera as much as I do, and you said you couldn’t come.”

“I love opera.”

“Ugh! You do?” He stared at Tom for a moment. “Where *have* you been for the last twenty plus years, Tom?”

“Listening to some of the best singers in the world. I got addicted. However, I do hate amateur opera. Opera’s like ballet—brilliant or awful. There’s no middle ground.”

“Christ, I bet you like ballet, too.”

Tom nodded. “All real men like ballet, Jack.”

Jack snorted. “We have a different definition of real men.”

“Very likely.”

Jack stared again at Tom, then looked around the living room. Then he shrugged. “Your business. Anyway, these folks aren’t really amateurs. Not entirely, I mean. A lot of them are from the music department at Triple C. And the locals Ellen recruited have some background, too. She says they’re pretty good, and I trust her judgment on this. I can’t tell the difference. It’s all crap to me.”

“What opera are they doing?” Tom asked, hoping it would turn out to be a light musical and not an opera at all. Or at the worst, an operetta.

“Tosca.”

Of course, Tom thought. He wondered why amateurs always aspired too high.

“At least it’s being done in English,” Jack said.

Tom groaned inwardly. Of course it is, he thought.

"There are only a few of the old gang still living here." Jack said. "Most of them will stay as far away from this thing as they can, but a couple of them might show up. And some of Ellen's and my friends will be there. This would be a good chance for you to get yourself involved in the social life of Ransom, such as it is. Unless you're rather spend your *retirement*—" he grimaced "—up here by yourself. I know Ellen was looking forward to seeing you again."

Tom looked at him sharply, but this time Jack maintained a bland expression that Tom couldn't see through.

Finally, Tom nodded and said, "Okay, Jack. Tell Ellen I'll be there."

Jack sprang to his feet with surprising vigor, but then he swayed a bit and put one hand on an arm of the couch for support. "Tomorrow night, eight o'clock, high school auditorium. Buy your ticket at the door." He laughed. "There're *always* plenty of seats available. Get there early, so I can introduce you around. You remember how to get to the high school, don't you? Of course you do. Hell, you practically grew up in that place, right? Okay, Tom, see you tomorrow night." He walked to the front door in a fairly straight line and let himself out.

Tom stood watching Jack leave, making no move to accompany him to the door.

After Jack was gone, Tom locked the door, dumped the ice cubes from Jack's glass and the remaining liquor from his own into the sink, picked up the book he had been reading when the doorbell rang, and resumed his quiet evening.

Two

The next morning, Saturday, Tom ate a leisurely breakfast and read both the Ransom *Roundup* and the Denver *Post*.

The Denver paper seemed remarkably shallow after the two Chicago dailies. He could subscribe to those here, of course, but he had chosen to leave his old life behind, and reading the papers that concerned themselves with that life wasn't the way to do it. Even more important, it seemed unwise to him to give anyone in Chicago, even a newspaper subscription department, his current name and address.

Although the *Roundup* was smaller than the *Post*, it was actually the more interesting of the two to Tom, because its news concerned life in Ransom. It echoed the life Tom had lived before Chicago. The names of city officials and other local notables were virtually all different, but the place names were the same. Tom felt an almost physical click of fitting back into place.

Maybe I do belong in Ransom after all, he thought. The previous evening, enduring Jack Tourneau's visit, he had had his doubts.

After he had finished breakfast and the papers, Tom

headed for town.

He spent a couple of hours in the downtown area, marveling at what had changed and what hadn't. Later, there'd be plenty of time to leave downtown and drive past his old house. Maybe.

The sky was cloudless, the air was clean, the temperature was in the mid–eighties, and the humidity was fifteen percent. After twenty–two summers in Chicago, it felt wonderful.

At first, something seemed to be missing. Then he identified it: noise. Traffic was light and the streets were quiet. When he passed people talking to each other, they weren't yelling. He thought the quietness of the place would take the most getting used to.

Toward noon, Tom began to wonder if the license bureau was open on Saturdays. There was a good chance that it was, he suspected, at least in the morning. He knew it was silly of him, but he wanted to talk to Janice Sheridan to see if he could tell why she was watching and reporting on his doings. It was probably natural, he thought, for her to be inquisitive about him. He hoped it was nothing more than that.

He got to the license bureau just in time. According to the hours painted on the glass door, the office closed at noon on Saturdays. An employee, a young man, was turning the sign in the door around to read CLOSED just as Tom entered. "Could you come back on Monday?" the young man asked hopefully.

"I'm just here to talk to someone for a moment," Tom assured him. "No paperwork required." He looked around and spotted the woman he had dealt with the day before. She was standing in front of her desk, cramming things into her purse. Tom stared at her, trying to see in her the lean, tanned cheerleader of his high school days, but he could find no trace, no remaining hint.

He walked over to the desk, not sure how to go about this. Maybe this woman wasn't Janice Sheridan. Maybe Jack had been playing one of his old hostile games. Tom stopped in front of the desk. "Hello," he said.

She smiled widely at him, a smile that exposed strong, white teeth. It was the smile of woman who saw herself as still attractive, and for that moment, Tom could see again the girl of twenty-two years before.

"How have you been, Janice?" he said.

"Hi, Tom. I didn't say anything yesterday because I could tell you didn't recognize me. I was waiting to see if you finally would."

Tom smiled at her. "I recognized you right away, but I was trying to slip back into town without being recognized myself."

Janice whooped with laughter. "Tom, you've hardly changed! Of course anyone who used to know you would recognize you. And of course I've changed. Don't play games with me."

Tom nodded his acknowledgment of her point and her honesty. "Can you spare a few minutes, or do you have to get home right away?"

"Actually," Janice said, "I was going to have lunch before going home. With a couple of the other girls. Just a sec." She looked around and spotted two women, younger than she, waiting by the front door. "Change of plan," she called out. "Gonna eat with an old high-school friend."

The two looked at Tom and then at Janice. You must be joking, their expressions said. Then they shrugged and left the office together.

Tom knew that look of dismissal. Twenty–two years ago, it had wounded him every time. Now it had no effect.

Tom had reached his full height by the time he was sixteen. He was five foot four inches tall, slender, with light–brown hair, an unremarkable face, and an introverted personality. He had never had a date during his adolescence in Ransom. Chicago had been a different matter, although he had been careful not to form any close relationships while there. During those twenty–two years, he had managed to build in himself the self–confidence and self–respect he should have been developing during the preceding eighteen.

Janice looked embarrassed on her friends' behalf. "I guess I just assumed you'd come have lunch with me," she said. "No place expensive. Just a local sandwich shop. Although with your address, I guess you could afford better, right?"

Tom laughed. "I don't remember you being so inquisitive. Of course, I didn't remember that we were such good friends before, either."

"Oh, hell, Tom, twenty years later everyone's friends with the people they went to high school with."

Later, sharing a booth with Janice in a sandwich shop a couple of blocks away from her office, Tom said, "This place wasn't here twenty–two years ago." He looked around the sterile room. The sterility was strictly visual; the place smelled of stale grease. The restaurant was part of a national chain, and it was identical in appearance and even smell to the outlets of the same chain he had seen in Chicago. "The homogenization of America."

"You still talk the same way," Janice said. "Lighten up, Tom.

Our food's ready. I'll go get it."

While she was doing so, Tom tried to remember what had occupied this building's place on Howard Street during his youth, but he couldn't. He hadn't trained himself to remember things in those days, the way he had later. It hadn't been so important to remember details in the old days. I guess it's not important any more, he thought. I could start lapsing into my dotage right away, and it wouldn't matter. I'm safe here, and I'm retired.

Janice returned with their sandwiches and began eating hers immediately. Tom stared at his. He asked her, "Have you been working at the license bureau ever since the old days?"

"Not all that time. Only for the last sixteen years. I went to college for a couple of years, but I flunked out. Then I got married, and that also lasted for two years. He flunked out of marriage."

"Anyone I'd know?"

"Chuck Hathaway. He was a year ahead of us in school. Remember him?"

Tom called up an image of a tall, beefy blond boy with an eternal scowl and a temper as quick and vicious as that of Tom's father. Tom had always been careful to stay out of the way of both of them. He nodded. "Uh huh."

"Exactly," Janice said. "Well, I was twenty years old. What did I know? But I learned. So after trying college and then marriage, I tried working for the state. That one lasted. It's not a bad job, and the retirement package is a good one, so I came out okay in the end."

"No kids?"

"Thank God, no."

"Does Hathaway still live in town?"

"Oh, don't worry about him. He's not around anymore. After I kicked him out, he joined the Army. I hear he's a sergeant in charge of Basic Training in Georgia, now. Can you imagine being an eighteen–year–old kid just joining up and having to deal with Chuck?"

"Easily." Tom took a bite of his greasy sandwich as a way of creating a pause and a transition. He managed to chew and swallow, and then he said, "Jack Tourneau came to see me yesterday. To welcome me back, you could say. He mentioned that you had told him I was back and that you had given him my new address."

Janice looked distressed. "Oh, dear! Was that wrong? I didn't realize you didn't want anyone to know about you. I'm sorry, Tom! I won't tell anyone else, I promise. Although I guess it's too late for that, isn't it?"

"No, no, it's okay," Tom said reassuringly. "I'm not trying to hide here. I was just a bit surprised, that's all." Tom Hamilton wasn't trying to hide anywhere. He had gone by a different name in Chicago.

"That's a relief. Still and all, I am sorry, Tom. You do know that all that license information is public record, don't you? So anyone can come in there and look through our files. You can even fill in a form, and for a few bucks we'll search our database for you and give you the home address of anyone who has a driver's license anywhere in the state."

Tom nodded. "Yes, I'm familiar with that. Although that's changing in some places."

"Violent places where there've been problems," Janice said. "We don't have any real big celebrities around here, and nothing has ever happened to make us change our rules."

Tom concentrated on his sandwich. It was disgusting, but Janice was gobbling hers down, and he felt obscurely that she'd be hurt if he left his, so he forced himself to work his way through it. He was satisfied now that Janice had not been keeping an eye out specifically for him. It wasn't a logical conclusion but rather one based on intuition and his reading of her personality. He had learned to trust that ability.

"You haven't told me what you've been doing for the last twenty–something years," Janice said suddenly, as though she'd been reading him as well.

Tom was momentarily startled, even though he knew her asking him that question at that moment was merely coincidence. "I've been out of town," he said, and took a large bite from his sandwich.

Janice chuckled. "No kidding! And?"

Tom waited until he had managed to swallow. "This and that. Around and about. Supporting myself and not writing home."

Janice's face grew serious. "No happy memories for you here, I guess. So why did you come back?"

"To visit again all the places where I would have spent so many happy summer days with my dog, if I had had a dog. And to take advantage of the fine bargains in the local real–estate market."

"You've just bought one of the most expensive pieces of property in town!"

"It's a bargain compared to prices where I last lived."

"What're you going to do for a living?"

"I'm retired."

Janice waited for more. When it didn't come, she finally said, "You always were a close-mouthed kid. Did anyone ever tell you that?"

"Just recently, although not quite in those words." He pushed his sandwich away from him. Half of it remained on the plate. "I ate a pretty big breakfast."

"Doesn't measure up to what you've been eating all those years in—where did you say?"

"Out of state."

She laughed. "May I?" Without waiting for Tom's response, Janice pulled his plate over and transferred the remnants of his sandwich to her own plate.

"Do you like opera, Janice?"

"Tom, that's just the kind of weird thing you used to say back in high school. No wonder you never had any dates. No, I don't like opera. I only listen to country and western. Do you like country and western?"

Tom grimaced. "I think country and western music is a symptom of the decline and fall of Western civilization."

"Yeah, I thought that's what you'd think. Okay, so you would never want to go to the concert I'm going to tonight, and I would never want to go to that thing the Tourneaus are putting on."

Tom nodded. "Fair deal." He pushed himself out of the booth. "I'm going to spend the rest of the day reacquainting myself with the town before I get ready to go to that thing. Have a good time at your concert."

"And you have a good time at the opera. Even though it won't be as good as the ones in—where was it?"

"Europe."

Tom drove around for a couple of hours, surprised at how poorly his memory of the town jibed with the reality. There had been real changes in Ransom since he'd left, but even things that surely had not changed—such as the direction a given street ran in, or the location of one building in relation to another—were not as he remembered them. Had his memories changed as the years had passed, or had he, as a boy, not noticed the world around him in a clear, precise way?

He had learned since those days to value precision of observation and clarity of memory. More than once, a detail noticed and remembered had saved his life. Only now, though, did he realize just how much he had changed and even recreated himself during his time away from Ransom. To an extent, he seemed to have recreated Ransom as well.

He parked outside the high school and stared at it for a while. This place, by contrast, was exactly as he remembered it. His boyhood self had taken note of every detail and committed each to memory.

If the outside was exactly as he remembered it, then the inside might be unchanged, too. But he felt an enormous reluctance to go inside and see it all again. Well, he told himself, it's Saturday, so it's probably locked up. The janitor will have locked it up.

The janitor.

Tom started his car again and drove down the streets he had walked down every school day.

The house was a mile from the high school. "The house," he still called it in his thoughts, even though it was now somebody else's house. Well, it had always been someone else's house. Tom had never felt that it belonged to him in any sense, or that he belonged in it.

133 North Elm. An address he was unlikely ever to forget. It sounded so peaceful and idyllic. It sounded like gracious homes shaded by huge trees, big houses where trouble never intruded, where people lived peaceful and happy lives undisturbed by loud noises or violence.

Tom parked a block away and walked slowly down the sidewalk.

The neighborhood had been a poor one twenty-two years earlier, and it seemed still poorer now. Like so much else that seemed to have changed, he thought, it might really be his viewpoint that had changed with the passing years and his growing wealth.

He passed the house Nick Jaruzelski had lived in and stopped on the sidewalk in front of number 133.

He had once read that people revisiting the scenes of their childhood found everything smaller than they remembered, because their memories were of things as seen from a child's perspective. It didn't seem to be quite true in this case, though. The trees had grown with the passage of time, and the buckled sidewalks were buckled more than he remembered.

And the house looked even bigger.

The house still had about it an aura of pain and danger. Tom walked even more slowly as he passed by it.

It's my imagination, he thought. It must be.

How could the dead material of which the house was built have retained his boyhood suffering? How could it radiate that suffering? Why hadn't that changed when new people moved in?

Perhaps they're the same as the man who lived in it before, Tom thought. Perhaps another man lives here now who terrorizes his family and fills their days with violence and dread.

Well, Tom told himself, enough of this. You're being self-indulgent.

He turned to head back toward his car.

Two young men were coming toward him on the sidewalk. One was white and one was black. Both were much taller than Tom, and both wore tank tops displaying impressive muscles. They filled the sidewalk, and they exuded a familiar menace.

The neighborhood thugs were all white in my day, Tom thought. Social progress.

Back in Chicago, he had never had to worry about this sort of thing. He was known in all the dangerous parts of town. Rather, it was well known who his protectors were. He had grown too used to that protection; it had made him incautious. And he had not realized just how much his old neighborhood had changed.

Tom turned and walked rapidly away from the two young men. He walked as though he had urgent business and was about to turn into one of the houses he passed. He didn't look back to see whether they were drawing closer. He wasn't sure what he would do—what he could do—if they were to catch up with him.

He reached a corner, turned to the right, and kept walking.

End of the block. Turn to the right again.

This time, he was able to check the sidewalk behind him from the corner of his eyes as he turned the corner. The two were still following him, still keeping their distance. Maybe there was nothing to this. Maybe they were innocent kids out for a walk, no violent intentions at all. Or maybe not.

Third corner. Another turn to the right. Tom took his car

keys from his pocket as he turned, selected the right key by touch.

He sprinted suddenly. He sensed the two young men breaking into a run at the same time. He reached his car, key held out, thrust it into the lock, turned it, jumped inside, closed and locked the door.

The two were right behind him. They pounded on the closed windows of his car, furious at him. There was no doubt now about their intentions.

Tom smiled at them and then reached calmly toward his glove compartment. The two young predators backed away, hands up placatingly, and disappeared.

Tom sat in his car for a while before starting it. He was sweating, his heart was pounding, and his hands were trembling. "Damn," he muttered. I don't belong here anymore. I haven't changed at all since I was a teenager. I never did belong here.

Maybe I should have a real gun in the car, he thought, not just a pretend one. What if my bluff hadn't worked?

But he hated guns and always had. He hated violence of all kinds.

Violence, he thought. It makes some men feel more alive.

It had always made him feel dead.

When he got back to his house in the foothills above Ransom, he stood outside for a long time on the narrow rocky strip between his picture window and the drop-off, looking down at the town. He thought he could pick out his old neighborhood. He was now on the opposite side of town from that cramped neighborhood, that cramped house, that cramped life—across town and high above it all. The stony edge of the cliff at his feet separated his new world from his old one and kept the old world at bay.

He hadn't bought this house with any attention to that symbolism, but now he decided he liked it.

Three

Tom looked at himself in the mirror and decided that he was very nicely dressed to go to an opera performance he was dreading and which he feared would probably sound much more like country and western than Puccini.

Maybe I should have tried again to get Janice to come with me to this thing, he thought as he adjusted his tie. Maybe she would have enjoyed it after all. And then I could tell myself that I'd finally had a date with Janice Sheridan. He had dreamed of that throughout high school—that, and acceptance by Jack Tourneau and his crowd.

He paused as a thought struck him. Had Ellen Chernikov changed as much as Janice had?

Ellen Tourneau, he corrected himself.

Tom reached the high school at seven. There were cars outside and a few people standing outside, smoking. Ransom had recently passed a law forbidding smoking in all public buildings and most restaurants and workplaces—something that would have been unthinkable during Tom's boyhood. Tom took a deep breath and held it as he walked past the smokers and into the building. Many of them looked angry. It was an expression Tom had seen before on the faces of smokers exiled to the outdoors.

The auditorium entrance was opposite the main door, and the lobby between the door and the entrance to the auditorium was occupied by more people, not smoking, standing in groups and chatting. What struck Tom most was how unfamiliar it all seemed. He had half expected to be catapulted back into the past by the sights and smells of the place. He had expected to think of the other opera attendees as parents visiting his school. Fortunately, he felt none of that.

The box office was a folding table set up just inside the door. An attractive woman of about Tom's age sat behind it selling tickets. Tom drew out his wallet and stepped up to the table.

A very attractive woman, he decided.

She finished selling tickets to a middle-aged couple and turned her attention to him with a pasted-on smile. The smile suddenly grew real, and Tom recognized her at the same moment.

"Tom! Jack said you'd be here, but I was afraid you'd change your mind."

He remembered how much he had liked her voice. "Hello, Ellen. Pardon me: Mrs. Tourneau."

The smile turned mischievous. Tom remembered that, too. "You never proposed to me, Tom."

"I propose to enjoy your opera."

"And you will, too." Ellen turned and gestured, and a young man came over. "Take care of the ticket selling," Ellen told him. "I'll be back in a few minutes. Tom, let me introduce you to our crowd."

"Just your crowd? Not the whole crowd?"

"Everyone here is our crowd," Ellen said, standing up and taking his arm. "It's not the way it used to be," she said. "We grew up."

He had not forgotten that she was a couple of inches taller than he, nor that that had been one more thing about her that had excited him. She looked even stronger now than then. Her grip on his arm was certainly strong, and that was arousing to him.

She obviously still took charge of things. She steered him over to one of the groups of chatting people and interrupted the ongoing conversation. "Listen up, everyone."

They stopped talking and listened respectfully. Ellen Chernikov had had a lot of presence even as a teenager, but Tom didn't remember that she had been quite so commanding.

"This is Tom Hamilton. He's an old high-school friend of Jack's and mine, and he's been away from Ransom since we all graduated from dear old RHS. He's just moved back, and we want him to feel at home again. So make him welcome."

They all said hello and smiled in a welcoming way, as ordered. Ellen squeezed Tom's arm and said, "Talk to you later, Tom. Too busy now."

A few of the group told Tom their names, which he committed to memory, even as he told himself that he could now afford to divest himself of that carefully acquired habit.

Most of them turned out to be academics connected with Colorado Central College. Jack joined the group briefly. His breath smelled of alcohol and his face was flushed. He complained of being hot and took his suit jacket off and folded it over his arm. He spoke too loudly and seemed overly ready to argue. When Jack ambled away, Tom had the impression that the group was relieved.

A new couple arrived in the lobby and joined the group. The man was tall, slender, and darkly handsome. He wore a charcoal-grey suit, expensively tailored. The women in the group seemed far happier to see him than the men. Without even knowing the newcomer, Tom sided with the other men. The woman was blonde and a match for the man—taller than average, considerably prettier than average, and much more self-confident than average. She wore a scoop-neck, collarless white blouse, a grey blazer, a string of pearls, small pearl earrings, a grey skirt, and low heels: the yuppie uniform of the nineties. They both said hello to the group in general. The woman's voice sounded familiar to Tom, but he couldn't imagine why.

Someone introduced Tom to them, and the woman said, "Tom Hamilton!" She held out her hand. "I'm Julie Pressler."

That explained the familiarity of her voice. She was the real-estate agent through whom Tom had bought his house.

Everything had been done by telephone, with Tom making all the calls. He had been forced by circumstances to go by her description of the house, which had fortunately been honest as well as complete. He hadn't wanted to risk so much as giving her an address to which to send photographs of the place because he didn't want her to know what city he was calling from. For the final closing, he had made his complete and sudden move to Ransom, rented a room in a motel, paid his first visit to the house, and signed the papers. Julie had been out of town that day and Tom had dealt with an assistant.

Julie's handshake was brisk, firm, and professional. It

offered nothing, hinted at nothing. It was simply a handshake. Tom decided he liked that.

She said, "I've been meaning to drop by and see how everything's going with the new house. When would be a good time?"

"No need for that," Tom said quickly. "Everything's fine. The house is perfect. You got me exactly what I wanted."

She smiled with pleasure. "Oh, this is my husband, Mark. I think you two know each other."

The two men nodded at each other and made no attempt to shake hands. Mark Pressler, Tom thought. I should have made the connection. Still a supercilious dickhead, aren't you, Mark? "Nice seeing you again, Mark," he said aloud. "I hadn't realized you'd stayed in Ransom." Did the wider world not share your high opinion of yourself?

"No need to go anywhere else, Tom. Some of us have found our happiness in this town and don't have to go searching all over the place hoping to find it."

Not bad, Tom admitted to himself. The boy's wit has improved. Mark had been one of Jack's hangers-on in high school and had exhibited a strong talent for sycophancy and little else. "What are you doing with yourself nowadays, Mark?"

"I'm a lawyer, Tom. I'm pretty well-known in this part of the country. And you? No one's heard a thing about you since you left. We're all curious as to what you've been up to."

"No good," Tom said with a smile. "I've been accumulating worldly wisdom. And money, of course. I'm retired."

The duel seemed to end at that point. Mark retired from the field, but Tom couldn't tell if he did so because he knew himself defeated or because he was bored. Tom turned his attention to the people he didn't know from the old days.

The non-academics were professional men and women from Ransom and Denver. So, Tom thought, Ellen and Jack's crowd isn't really everyone. The class distinctions the two of them had observed so scrupulously in high school still regulated their choice of friends. What makes me acceptable to them now? he wondered. Probably the amount I paid for my house.

Despite his cynicism and the old resentment toward the wealthy that Tom had never managed to rid himself of, he found himself getting along quite well with the group. He assumed that they shared Jack and Ellen's snobbery, but the conversation never touched upon that. Rather, they seemed to be interested in talking about the opera itself and about the previous performances put on by Ellen's organization—none of them very successful, apparently. Most of all, the group talked about who at the college was sleeping with whose spouse. On the last subject, they were remarkably frank in the presence of a stranger. Tom concluded that the gossip was all common knowledge on the campus already. Or that speaking about it in front of a stranger was one way of making sure it became common knowledge.

The man who had been standing to Tom's right moved away, and Tom found himself next to a tall, slender woman with short black hair. She had a pale complexion and wore bright red lipstick and a black, form-fitting dress.

"Arlene Pernowski," she said, holding out her hand. "I told you that when Ellen introduced you, but I don't expect you to remember it."

Tom smiled and took her hand. He didn't mention that he remembered each of the names he had been told, or that he probably would have remembered hers even if he had forgotten all the others.

"Fred Pernowski," a man said, and Tom and Arlene let go of each other's hands. "Arlene's husband," the man added. He was shorter than his wife—only about an inch taller than Tom—and as light as she was dark. He radiated energy. He shook Tom's hand vigorously. "Arlene's crazy about short men like you and me, but be careful, because she'll rip your heart out."

"Oh, Fred," Arlene said, raising her eyes to the ceiling.

Tom laughed. "Has she ripped yours out?"

"Of course," Fred said. "Years ago."

Arlene said, "I keep it right here in my purse for convenience." She opened her purse and rummaged about in it. "Now where did it go? Oh, dear, I've lost it, Fred."

"So what did Ellen say you do, Tom?" Fred asked.

"I think she said I'm retired."

Fred shook his head. "No, I'm sure she didn't say that. In fact, I'm sure she didn't say just what you do."

"Oh, Fred," Arlene said again. "Why can't you just be straightforward?"

"What do you do for a living, Tom?" Fred asked.

"I'm retired."

"From what?"

"Consulting. Elsewhere."

"Oh," Fred said. "Okay." He seemed to tire of the game. His eyes wandered.

"He's waiting for you to ask him what he does," Arlene told Tom.

"What do you do, Arlene?" Tom asked.

Fred looked offended. Arlene chuckled. "I keep house for

the brilliant Dr. Pernowski. He really is brilliant, Tom."

"She's right," Fred said. "I run the human-factors lab at Cee Cubed. Testing the limits of the human body. You know—treadmills, exercise bikes, a giant centrifuge. The lab used to do a lot of work for NASA, stressing astronauts to the limit. Lots of fun. Come by some day, and we'll see how much stress you can take."

"I think this conversation has already stressed me to my limit," Tom said.

Fred laughed loudly. The masculine competitiveness vanished, and he seemed genuinely friendly. "Hey, Arlene, this guy's good. I like him."

"Oh, Tom!" It was Ellen, calling him from one of the entrances to the auditorium.

Tom excused himself and walked over to her.

"Sorry," she said. "I assumed you'd like Arlene. Every man does. But I thought you'd want to get away from her husband. He's such a bore."

"He's brilliant," Tom said.

"So I've heard. Repeatedly. Come on. There are more people I want you to meet."

Tom sighed. "If you insist."

"I do. You're back in your hometown, and you're going to be part of the life of the town. You're not going to sit up there on your hillside in your fancy house and remain apart from us."

"I could build a moat and a drawbridge."

Ellen ignored his reluctance. She pulled him over to a small, slender woman, mid-forties to judge by her face but with entirely grey hair. Tom was struck by the sweetness of her smile. "This is Diane Snow. Be nice to her. Her husband's a cop.

Diane, this is Tom Hamilton. We were high school buddies. He's just returned to live in Ransom again."

Diane's handshake was surprisingly firm given her size and seeming fragility. "Oh, you were away for some years?"

Tom nodded.

"Where?"

Before Tom could come up with a vague, noncommittal reply, Ellen said, "Oh, don't even bother asking him. He's being mysterious. Personally, I think he's an international drug dealer. Or arms trader."

"How exciting!" Diane said. "My husband would love to hear all about it."

Tom laughed. "Your husband the cop? I'm sure he would."

"So which is it?" Diane asked. "Arms or drugs?"

"Both. I trade one for the other."

"Well, I'd certainly like to introduce you to my husband. He was here a moment ago."

"Perhaps later," Ellen said. "Right now, I want to take Tom backstage to meet some of the cast and crew." As she pulled Tom away, Ellen said in a low voice, "She's sweet, but her husband's a boor. I met her through a friend, and she turned out to be an opera fan. That's the only reason she's here. I have no wish to socialize with her jerk of a husband, I can tell you."

She led the way down one of the auditorium's aisles. Here was the shock of memory Tom had expected but had not encountered earlier. He had spent uncountable hours in those uncomfortable seats, squirming through hectoring speeches by one school official or another.

"Do you ever wonder why our society has such a need to torture its young?" he asked Ellen. "Probably because we resent their youth."

Ellen stopped and turned to face him. "Tom, I enjoyed high school. Those were the best years of my life." She turned and walked rapidly away toward the stage.

Tom said nothing more. He followed her up the steps to the stage and across it to the rear, dodging frantic crew members. Ellen seemed remarkably cool and collected given that she was in charge of the entire production and that curtain time was drawing near.

They walked single file down a short corridor and into a noisy room too full of people.

One wall was lined with lighted mirrors. Most of them were being used by people applying stage makeup—sloppily, for the most part. The rest of the people in the room were milling about and talking too loudly. In Tom's experience, backstage areas just before a performance were scenes of controlled madness. Here, there seemed to be precious little control. He foresaw disaster.

They're going to ruin Tosca for me, he thought. I'm going to have to listen to hours of recordings just to get the memory of tonight's performance out of my mind.

But I'll tell Ellen that I enjoyed it, no matter what.

"Here they are!" Ellen said proudly, holding out her arms as if to embrace the entire room. "Aren't they great?"

"They're...young," Tom said.

"Well, of *course* they're young," Ellen said. "They're college students, most of them. Come on, I'll introduce you to Mario."

She went to the one of the mirrors. A young man sat in front of it. He was staring at his reflection and making faces at himself.

"What are you doing, Jerry?" Ellen said sharply.

Jerry jumped to his feet and spun around guiltily. "Mrs. Tourneau! Hi!"

"What were you just doing?" Ellen repeated.

Jerry looked at the floor. "Practicing looks of pain," he mumbled. "For when I get shot."

Ellen poked a finger into his chest, hard. It looked painful. "I told you before, Jerry. When you get shot, you drop. Instantly. Like a marionette with its strings cut. The only thing you do at all is squeeze the bulb in your right hand to make the food dye ooze out on your shirt, and the audience isn't supposed to see you do that."

"Yes, ma'am," Jerry muttered.

"Remember to fall on your left side, facing the audience, with your right hand behind your back. I don't want them to see you squeezing that bulb."

"No, ma'am."

"If you make any faces, this will be your last performance."

"Yes, ma'am."

"Now say hello to Tom Hamilton. Tom is an old friend of mine. Tom, Jerry Angleton. He's our Mario."

The two men shook hands. Jerry Angleton was extraordinarily handsome and, Tom judged, extraordinarily aware of that fact. Angleton redeemed his male vanity, wounded by Ellen's intimidation of him, by puffing out his fairly large chest and looking down at Tom over it.

"Tom," Ellen said, "wait till you see the blood in the final scene. Jerry wears a white shirt, and it'll be covered with blood. Gushing blood. Washable, of course. We have a very small costume budget. Anyway, it'll be great. Everyone will be blown away."

"I can hardly wait to see Jerry get shot," Tom said truthfully.

"Jerry," Ellen said, "remember: no faces."

"Yes, ma'am."

"Good." Ellen grabbed Tom's arm and pulled him across the room. "Isn't he gorgeous?" she whispered. "And a great voice. He should be at a school with an opera department instead of here." She stopped in front of a young woman who was staring vaguely into space, muttering to herself, while two other young women worked on her costume. "This is our Tosca. Karen Franks."

Karen broke out of her reverie for long enough to say hello and then returned to wherever she had been.

"Karen's way of preparing," Ellen explained. "I've asked her what she's doing, but she refuses to say."

They walked away from the muttering soprano. "I'm running out of time," Ellen said, checking her watch. "I wanted to keep my hands off everything at this point, but I just can't. So you'll have to go back out front, Tom. But first, tell me what you think so far."

"It's just like a real backstage at a real opera, Ellen."

"This *is* a real opera!" Ellen snapped.

"I meant, a professional company. A big, famous house."

Ellen relaxed. "Yes! Isn't it exciting?"

"This auditorium doesn't have an orchestra pit," Tom said. "Where are you putting the orchestra?"

"On a tape recorder," Ellen said. "I didn't want to try to deal with the egos of a conductor and a concertmaster in addition to all of these."

"Makes sense." Tom glanced over at Karen Franks. "Golly, gee, she's really gorgeous."

Ellen chuckled. "Touché. Wait till you hear her sing. She'll really win your heart then. You'll be back here after the performance asking her for a date."

"Ellen, she's half my age."

Ellen sighed. "And Jerry Angleton's only a year older than she is. Ain't it the pits, Tom? Doesn't stop some men, though. Well, it's a lot worse for a woman to hit forty. Okay, Tom, go out front now and let me whip this mess into order."

Tom didn't see Ellen again until it was almost time for the performance to begin. The ushers—a group of extremely serious kids from the local high school—were circulating through the lobby and urging everyone to take their seats when Ellen entered the lobby from a side door, breathing heavily. She came up to the group including Tom and Jack and said, "They're ignoring me. It's going to be a disaster."

"Who's ignoring you?" Fred Pernowski asked her. "We're paying attention. *I'm* paying attention."

Arlene Pernowski raised her eyes.

"All of them," Ellen said. "The cast and the crew. Everything was going so well during rehearsals. Including the dress rehearsal. Remember how well that went, Jack?"

"Yeah, yeah," her husband said. He looked at his watch. "We'd better be—"

"But now it's suddenly out of control," Ellen said. "I shouldn't leave them alone, but I couldn't stay back there any longer. I just know I'd have started to scream at them. Well, let them ruin it. I've done my part. I've given everything I could."

"Oh, Christ," Jack said, "will you stop? You go through this crap every time, and it doesn't matter. The kids do okay. They probably do better with you out here than back there, constantly on their backs." At some point, he had put his jacket back on. Now, as he grew angry, he took it off again. He still smelled strongly of alcohol. "What difference does it make, anyway?" he went on. "Look around you, for Christ's sake. The place is almost empty. It's always almost empty for these damned operas of yours. Hardly anyone ever shows up, so what does it matter what the performance is like? Do you really think anyone cares, except for you and people like Tom, here? I'm going in to get my seat. I promised you I'd suffer in silence through your operas, but I am no longer going to suffer in silence through your complaining about them. Okay?"

Tom's glance flicked from face to face. Jack was glaring at his wife, and she was glaring back at him. His face was red, hers was white. The Pernowskis were both looking at the ceiling. The others in the group were looking in various directions to avoid looking at each other.

Jack Tourneau broke the tension by turning away and going into the auditorium. The others in the group started a jagged, nervous conversation and followed him, leaving Ellen and Tom momentarily alone.

Ellen breathed deeply a few times, and the color returned to her cheeks. She forced a laugh and said, "Jack always gets so tense before these performances. You remember how uptight he always was."

"High strung," Tom said. "Delicate. A tender blossom."

Ellen glared at him. "Don't you give me trouble, too, Tom. I was looking forward so much to seeing you again."

"Sorry."

She examined him. "You still judge people, don't you? I

remember you as being very judgmental. You judge and you watch, but you don't get involved. You're watching us from the outside, just like in the past." She turned away angrily and followed the others into the auditorium.

After a moment, Tom forced himself into motion and went into the auditorium himself. Spending the rest of his life in Ransom had begun to seem a very bad idea.

Four

There was, as Jack had said, plenty of room in the auditorium. In spite of that, Tom somehow did not end up with an empty seat to either side, as he would have preferred, but with Ellen Tourneau on one side of him and Arlene Pernowski on the other. Jack was to Ellen's left, looking bored and long suffering, and Fred Pernowski was on his wife's right, looking energetic. It was an uncomfortable position for Tom, who found himself increasingly aware of his attraction to both women. He was determined not to let either the attraction or his discomfort show.

He was also determined not to show the contempt he expected to feel for the performance. He gritted his teeth, pasted on a smile, and paid attention.

And enjoyed himself immensely.

The singers lacked the vocal maturity of the professionals he was used to hearing, but he was charmed by their youthful freshness and enthusiasm. How pleasant it was to see singers who were as young and physically attractive as their characters were supposed to be! Nor was there any bored walking through a part or contempt for the audience. These kids threw themselves into their roles with all their hearts and all their energy. Sometimes a bit too much energy, and the opera teetered on the brink of chaos at times, but Tom found himself willing to excuse all of that. He, and much of the rest of the audience, responded warmly to the enthusiasm of the players.

Jack Tourneau seemed unaffected, however. He showed considerable interest when Karen Franks was on–stage, but he seemed on the verge of falling asleep the rest of the time.

Fred Pernowski and the other men around Tom seemed to share Jack's enthusiasm for Karen's Tosca. Or perhaps just for Karen. Tom had thought her very pretty when he met her backstage, but now, as Tosca, she was beautiful and commanding—quite a change from the distracted and very young woman Ellen had introduced him to.

The women in the audience did not seem to share the men's enthusiasm.

The sexes reacted in the opposite fashion to Jerry Angleton. The men's attention drifted when he was singing, but the women listened raptly. Tom was willing to admit that Angleton was an extremely handsome young man, with a very good physique, although the way the young singer swaggered about the stage implied that he thought himself even better than he was. But what really mattered to Tom was Angleton's voice, which was magnificent. Ellen was right. Jerry Angleton should be studying somewhere else. It was a shame to waste such potential.

When the first act ended and the audience was milling about, stretching, moving out of their seats and into the aisles for the intermission, Ellen turned to Tom and said, "Well? Meet your exacting European standards?"

My, my, Tom thought, how quickly word does get around. It was Janice Sheridan whom he had misled into thinking he'd spent the past twenty years in Europe, and that had been that same morning. "Get that boy a scholarship somewhere if you have any connections at all. He's a conceited young twerp, but his voice is superb."

Ellen grinned happily. "Jealous, are you? And Karen?"

"She's superb, too, but her voice is a bit light for this role."

Ellen laughed aloud. "She's got the hots for Jerry. She's been throwing herself at him all through rehearsals. Ain't opera fun? Grand voices and grand passions!"

"I suppose it's appropriate for Tosca to be in love with Mario, even offstage."

"Except that this Mario is married," Ellen said, "and his wife is both jealous and even better looking than Karen. But never mind that. You liked it? You really liked it, you're not just saying so?"

"I really liked it. Very, very much. You've done a remarkable job, Ellen."

She beamed and turned to her husband. "Hear that, Jack?"

"What do you expect from a man who likes ballet?" Jack growled.

"Don't nit pick," Ellen told him.

Tom could have picked plenty of nits with the production had he cared to. The baritone playing Scarpia, the evil chief of police, was utterly inadequate for the role; he had neither the voice for the singing nor the air of physical menace for the acting. The policemen accompanying Scarpia carried rifles that were imitations of modern weapons rather than imitations of the weapons of 1800, when the opera was set. Tom thought he remembered an explicit reference to muskets somewhere in the libretto. And the backdrops depicted Roman ruins—ancient Rome, with no trace of the Rome these characters would have known.

Never mind, Tom thought. I'm enjoying it, and that should be all that counts. Have to work at being less of a snob if I'm going to spend the rest of my life in this town.

The young singers had more trouble with the second act. Its welter of melodrama got out of hand a few times. Mario's cries of pain from offstage while he was being tortured by the agents of the dreaded Baron Scarpia somehow struck the audience as funny, and giggles erupted from various parts of the hall with every scream. Scarpia's attempt at leering at Tosca brought more giggles.

In the play, Scarpia suggests to Tosca that he will free her lover, Mario. Tosca asks his price. Scarpia makes it clear that she is the price. He praises her beauty and says that he has vowed to possess her.

At this point, a male voice called out from the audience, "Get in line, Baron!"

Ellen ground her teeth audibly. Jack guffawed. Ellen leaned toward Tom and whispered, "I bet you don't have people like that in the audience in Europe."

Tom whispered back, "We do, but we put out contracts on them."

The idea seemed to cheer Ellen up considerably.

Karen Franks brought the audience back under control with her depiction of a woman bowed by grief and helpless in the face of evil. "I have lived for art and love," she sang, her voice filling the auditorium effortlessly. Suddenly, the melodrama became real, and even the inept Scarpia seemed believable. How could Tom have thought Karen's voice too light? Everything about her was perfect.

The audience burst into loud applause when she finished the aria. It caused a long interruption. Scarpia looked annoyed at the delay, but Karen basked in the response.

Tom leaned toward Ellen and said, "Do you know if she dates older men?"

Ellen giggled.

The audience was quiet and attentive for the rest of the act.

Tosca agrees to Scarpia's terms. Scarpia explains that he must stage a fake execution. Mario will be placed before a firing squad, but the guns will be loaded with blanks. Tosca must instruct her lover to die convincingly. After everyone has left, Mario can come back to life, and he and Tosca can flee to safety. Scarpia calls in an underling and tells him to see to it that the prisoner is shot "as in the case of Palmieri." The audience knows what Tosca does not: that Palmieri was really shot, and that Scarpia means that Mario Cavaradossi is to be shot with real bullets. After the underling has left, Tosca insists that Scarpia write out a safe-conduct pass for her now, before she sleeps with him. Scarpia writes out the pass and approaches Tosca for his reward. She stabs him. Scarpia dies, and Tosca leaves with the safe-conduct pass. Curtain.

The audience shuffled out for the second intermission.

"Whew," Ellen said. "I thought we were about to lose it. The rest is duck soup. Tom, if you thought Karen did a great job, just wait till you hear Jerry's final aria."

"He gets shot at the end," Jack said. "That'll be the best part of it."

"But then Tosca jumps off the top of the castle," Tom told him.

"Yeah, I know. Off a kind of step-up thing at the back of the set. There's a pile of pillows down below. I offered to stand down there and catch Karen instead, because it would be safer, but Ellen vetoed that idea."

Ellen laughed unconvincingly. She stood up. "Jack, would you go backstage and check the prop guns one more time? I really want this to look good, and I'm feeling nervous about the bang-up ending fizzling."

"Oh, for Heaven's sake," Jack said. "How many times do you have to have the damned props checked? Send Tom. Or do it yourself."

Ellen said, "I have to go calm everyone down. The kids are all pretty tense right now. I won't have time for the props. Tom doesn't know where everything is, whereas you do. And you're familiar with those guns." She looked at her watch. "This is the short intermission, and we don't have much time left. Come on, Jack."

Jack kept grumbling, but he got up and left with her.

Tom watched them go, thinking that the unpleasant traits in the personalities of both had intensified over the years. He couldn't tell yet whether the good qualities had also grown stronger.

Ellen must have done a good job of calming everyone down. The cast seemed relaxed and self-confident during the final act.

Tosca tells Mario that the bullets will be blank and that he must be convincing when he pretends to die. The firing squad appears.

Jerry Angleton sauntered ahead of them to the wall, as though he were the greatest tenor in history and the bullets would respectfully decline to harm him. He stood in front of the fake wall, legs apart, turned his face to the audience, and smirked. The firing squad lined up facing Jerry, sideways to the audience, raised their rifles, and aimed.

Flames and noise belched from the rifles. The audience gasped in surprise. Jerry Angleton jumped a foot in the air, fell to his knees grimacing madly, and then collapsed onto his left side, as instructed. However, he landed with his right arm in front of him.

The front of Angleton's white shirt was covered with blood, just as Ellen had promised, and it was spurting out of him satisfactorily. But the audience could see Angleton's hand clutching a large rubber bulb from which a tube ran up his shirtsleeve. He raised his head and looked down at his chest, as though to make sure the special effects were working properly. After a moment of stunned silence, a ripple of laughter moved across the audience. Ellen put her head in her hands and moaned, "I'll kill him!"

Fortunately, Angleton let his head drop backward and lay still. The firing squad trooped off the stage. Karen Franks sang that her lover should not move yet.

Not for the first time while watching a performance of Tosca, Tom thought that Scarpia's supposed plot would never have worked in real life—first, because the body would not be left alone after the execution, and second, because of the tradition of the *coup de grâce*.

Now Karen went to Mario's body and urged him to rise. At this point, Tosca is supposed to discover that Scarpia has fooled her and that Mario is really dead. Karen sang, “Get up, Mario!” Suddenly, she yelled, “Jerry, get up!” She grabbed his shoulders and began shaking him.

Getting carried away, Tom thought.

But then Karen screamed, turned to the audience, and shrieked, “Oh my God, he’s really dead!”

Five

Tom pushed his way up the aisle toward the stage, squeezing between the other members of the audience who were headed the same way.

The others stopped at the edge of the stage, gawking at the blood on Jerry Angleton's shirt and Karen Franks' hands. They wanted to see as much as they could, but they didn't want to become overly involved. The stage was an infected area, and the disease was death.

Tom climbed the stairs at the side of the stage and ran to the fallen tenor. Before he could reach Angleton, someone grabbed his shoulder and yanked him back.

"Keep your hands off him, damn it!" The speaker was only an inch or two taller than Tom but seemed a few feet wider, and little of that was fat. Even after the man released Tom's shoulder, Tom could still feel his grip.

"Are you a doctor?" Tom asked.

"Police."

"ID, please?"

The other man hesitated as though Tom's cool, assured manner had made him think that Tom might be some sort of official, and one he should be wary of. He pulled a wallet out of his jacket pocket and flipped it open to reveal a badge and photo ID card.

"Lieutenant Andrew Snow," Tom read aloud. Snow had fading blond hair, still thick. The man in the photograph looked much the same, but his hair was brighter, more definitely blond. "Ransom Police Department, and you're a detective. And an opera lover. How nice. This man needs a doctor, Lieutenant."

Snow glanced at Jerry Angleton. "Hell, this man needs an undertaker. Now it's your turn to show ID."

Tom handed Snow his new driver's license.

Snow glanced at it. "Oh, yeah, heard about you. All right, Mr. Hamilton, get off the stage. If you want to be useful, go find a phone and call this in for me." He fished in his jacket and produced a business card. "Call this number. Tell them what the situation is. They'll know what I need." He turned toward the watching audience members and yelled, "You people keep away from the stage, but stay here in the auditorium. We're going to want to question all of you."

The audience dashed for the exits.

"Crap," Snow muttered.

Good voice, Tom thought. Too bad he's a tenor; he'd make a fine Baron Scarpia. "Are you sure we don't need a doctor, Lieutenant?"

"I'm telling you, that guy's dead. When you've seen as many bodies as I have, you recognize it. Hell, just look at the blood."

"It's food dye, Lieutenant. Just part of the opera. The boy might have had a stroke or heart attack. Happens to tenors—even young and healthy ones. He could just be unconscious." And we should compare body counts some day, he thought with some bitterness.

"Oh, crap," Snow said. He dropped to his knees and felt for a pulse. After a few seconds, he relaxed. "Nope, he's dead. And this sure smells like real blood to me. Now get off the stage and make that phone call like I asked you."

Despite having let things get out of hand at first, Snow did a good enough job once more manpower showed up. Tom watched him directing his underlings and decided that Snow must have had experience in a bigger town than Ransom. Please don't let it be Chicago, Tom prayed silently.

It was hard to think of Snow as the husband of the sweet woman Tom had met earlier in the evening. What could two such people have in common? Other people's choices of mates almost always astonished Tom.

A few members of the audience had lingered, and they were questioned thoroughly and their names and addresses taken. The scantiness of the audience was a blessing for the police. Ellen and Jack were able to give Snow the names of those who had scurried away before Snow's reinforcements arrived.

The members of the cast and crew were likewise questioned and their names and addresses recorded. They too had little to contribute. Most of them were in no shape to answer questions anyway. The police department doctor handed out tranquilizers with abandon, and bottles of whiskey and related liquid tranquilizers circulated rapidly backstage.

Ellen was busy trying to keep the level of panic and hysteria backstage under some sort of control, so Tom didn't interrupt her. Instead, he asked Jack, "Isn't there a state law forbidding alcohol on school property?"

"What?" Jack had been staring into space. "Oh, right. Well, we just ignored that. Ellen was planning a little party back here to celebrate the successful first night." He shook his head. "Christ, poor Angleton. Did you know he was married?"

Tom nodded. "Ellen mentioned it."

"And his wife's pregnant. What a mess!"

It was much more understanding and sympathy than Tom was used to hearing from Jack Tourneau. It was unfortunate, he thought, that it took something so terrible to bring out that side of the man, but it did improve his opinion of Jack.

Tom went back through the narrow passage to the stage. He could just go home now, and he thought he ought to, but after twenty years of the kind of work he had done in Chicago, he found that he couldn't tear himself away. So this is retirement, he thought.

Snow was still on the stage, listening to a report from a uniformed policeman. Behind him, a man and a woman knelt on either side of Jerry Angleton's body. They had maneuvered it into a thick plastic bag and were now zipping the bag closed. Tom stood quietly watching, not wanting to draw attention to himself, but not wanting to leave, either. He could hear nothing from where he stood. He stepped closer and heard Snow say, "...been fired from the audience. SOB's gone by now."

Tom spoke involuntarily. "Fired?"

Snow turned. "What're you doing up here? No one on the stage except on police business."

"Humor me for a moment, Lieutenant. What did you mean by 'fired'?"

Snow hesitated for a moment, then said, "I guess it's not a secret. The kid was shot in the chest. More than once, it looks like to me. We'll know more after the autopsy. Bullets entered through the front, exited rear, and he was facing the audience, so someone fired from the audience."

"The killer aimed and fired from the audience, and no one noticed him?"

"You got a better idea?"

"I have two better ideas. Look out there." Tom pointed out into the auditorium. "See the beams running across the hall, under the roof, where the lights are? A gunman could hide up there, fire his shots, and then leave without anyone noticing any of it. You could check the angle of the bullets' path in the boy's body."

Snow looked where Tom was pointing. "Crap," he said.

"My other idea is probably too obvious. Jerry Angleton wasn't facing the audience. You're misremembering. His face was turned to the audience, but he was looking at us over his shoulder and his body was turned toward the firing squad. Check those rifles."

"They're props."

"They looked real to me. Lieutenant, people have been killed on the stage and in the movies by blanks that weren't blank. I don't mean just in fiction. I mean in real life. It even happened fairly recently to a tenor singing Mario Cavaradossi. Fortunately, that tenor was hit in the foot. However, if you really don't think that's a possibility, I'll just go have a look myself." He looked around the stage. "I wonder where those rifles are."

"Christ," Snow said, "this is just great." He barked orders, and men and women in uniform scurried about the stage looking for discarded rifles. They found none.

"I'll ask Ellen about it," Tom said. He headed for the

passageway leading to the dressing room. Snow pushed ahead of him.

"I'm not going to be able to get rid of you, am I?" Snow said.

"I'll stay out of your way," Tom promised. "It's just that I have this problem: I read too many Agatha Christie novels as a boy."

Snow looked him up and down with open contempt. "Yeah, you look like the type." He sighed melodramatically. "Okay, come on."

They found Ellen in an emptying dressing room. The cast and crew had finally changed into their street clothes and were drifting out, still looking stunned. "Ellen," Tom said, "Lieutenant Snow would like to have a look at the rifles the firing squad used."

Ellen collected herself with a visible effort and said, "Jack's taking care of that. He's the one who got them for me."

"Where is Dr. Tourneau?" Snow asked.

Ellen raised her hands. "I don't know." She called out, "Jack! Jack, the police want to talk to you!"

Jack Tourneau appeared suddenly from behind a stack of equipment. "They want to talk to *me*? Oh, all right."

Karen Franks was with him. She brushed past Tom, Ellen, and Snow and headed for the exit. Ellen's eyes narrowed.

"Very upsetting for her," Snow said, watching Karen leave. No one else said anything.

Snow turned his attention to Jack. "Dr. Tourneau, your wife says you were in charge of the prop rifles. I'd like to see them, please."

Jack led the way to a metal table in the same area from which he had appeared a few moments before with Karen

Franks. The rifles were piled on the table. "Be careful with them," he said. "They belong to friends of mine."

Snow said, "Hey, these are real!"

"Well, of course they are," Jack said. "They're hunting rifles. Bolt-action, because I thought that would look better. One of them is mine. I got a bunch of friends to contribute theirs, too, but I had to promise I'd take good care of them."

"That explains why they aren't muskets from 1800," Tom said.

"You noticed that from the audience?" Ellen said. "Oh, dear. I was hoping no one would pick up that detail. I guess I should have spent more time looking for stage props, after all. Maybe I could have found something from the right period."

Snow ignored the two of them. To Jack, he said, "The rifles were loaded with blanks?"

"Hell, of course!" Jack said. "What do you think—we'd have those kids shooting live rounds on-stage? I loaded them myself, backstage. A blank in the chamber of each one. I made sure they could all handle 22 Long Rifles, so that I'd only need one kind of blank ammunition." He seemed proud of himself for having thought of that detail in advance.

"Where did you get the blanks?"

Jack named a gun shop in Ransom. "My usual place," he explained.

"You're absolutely sure those were all blanks?" Snow asked.

Jack affected a look of disgust. "I know what I'm doing around firearms, Lieutenant. I double checked."

"These rifles are now evidence," Snow said. "Nobody touch them." He said to Tom, with obvious reluctance, "Keep an eye on them for a few minutes, okay?"

Tom suppressed the urge to salute and nodded.

"Just stand here," Snow said. "That's all."

"That's all," Tom agreed.

Snow headed back toward the stage.

"What's going on?" Jack asked.

"In a moment, Jack," Tom said. "Ellen, the firing squad wouldn't have been actually aiming those things at Jerry Angleton, would they? I mean, there was no real reason for them to do so, right?"

"Of course they were aiming at Jerry," Ellen said. "I told them to. Verisimilitude. You'd have been able to tell from the audience if they hadn't."

"Hell," Jack said, "Ellen's such a stickler for those details that she even had me take some of the kids to a rifle range a few times. The ones who'd never fired a rifle before. They used those same rifles with real bullets so they'd know how to look convincing and what the sound and feel are like. Even the blanks will startle you if you don't have a bit of experience."

Snow returned with a couple of uniformed policemen and pointed at the rifles. The policemen gathered the rifles up and left with them.

"Hey!" Jack said.

"Evidence," Snow said.

"Damn," Jack muttered. He turned to Tom. "Promised you an exciting evening, didn't I?"

Tom forced a smile. On the bright side, he thought, that was the most convincing death scene I've ever watched on any opera stage.

He regarded his own cold-bloodedness with interest. A

legacy from the last twenty years, he decided. It was a legacy he had thought he would have no need of in Ransom.

Six

There had been six men in the stage firing squad. All six guns had been fired, and apparently all had fired live ammunition.

Two of the bullets were found embedded in the rear wall of the auditorium at the back of the stage. Those shots had missed the tenor entirely. Of the remaining four bullets, two were found on the floor, just behind the fake wall Jerry Angleton had been standing in front of, and the final two were still in his body. The two found on the floor had passed through the fake wall after passing through Angleton. The four entry holes in Angleton's chest were quite close together.

Tom read these details in the *Roundup*, which carried the story on the front page of Monday's edition. Jerry Angleton's death had been reported on radio and television on Sunday, but with little detail and seemingly little interest. The newspaper, though, seemed to be fascinated.

The main editorial was devoted to the subject. It expressed shock and sadness at the loss of such a promising talent, even though it was clear that the editorial writer had never seen an opera performance and knew nothing about Jerry Angleton or his kind of singing. One of the paper's regular columnists, long an upholder of the virtues of home, family, patriotism, and gun ownership, praised the fine marksmanship of four of the extras in the firing squad and agonized over the threat to the future of the country if the poor aim of the other two indicated the average level of gun knowledge among today's young people.

Tom had spent Sunday morning organizing his new home. The telephone had rung a few times, but he had let the answering machine answer the calls, and he had not yet listened to the messages. It grated a bit to do this, but he kept reminding himself that this was the beginning of his new, slower-paced life. There was no need to rush to pick up the telephone as soon as it rang, no reason for his sudden tension at the sound.

He could tell himself that, but he couldn't stop his heart from speeding up every time. He could, however, begin trying to react more calmly.

On Sunday afternoon, he had gone out and driven around town again, relearning the old parts of the city and learning the new ones.

On Monday morning, after finishing the paper and his breakfast, he listened to his telephone messages.

There were ten of them. Nine were from people trying to sell him something, and all of them promised to call him back in hopes of catching him in. Tom had not foreseen this aspect of buying a new house, but he realized that he should have.

The remaining call was from Ellen Tourneau, asking him to call her and giving her number. She became the first entry in his new Rolodex. As soon as he had completed that task, he called her.

"Took you long enough," she complained. "I bet you would have returned my call immediately in the old days."

"In the old days, you never would have called me."

Ellen laughed, suddenly cheerful. "All sorts of things change with time. Can you meet me for lunch?" She named the sandwich shop where he had eaten with Janice Sheridan.

"Surely there are better places in town than that," Tom said.

"Yes, but that's the most public one around. No one will jump to conclusions."

Not that they would anyway, Tom thought. "Okay, then. Noon? High noon on Main Street?"

"Howard Street."

"I was speaking metaphorically."

"I wish you wouldn't. Yes, high noon on Howard Street. And since you're so rich these days, bring enough money to pay for both of us."

"I can scrape together enough for that," Tom said.

Later, driving downtown, he wished he could travel back in time and tell his teenaged self to be patient because eventually he would have dates in a sandwich shop on Howard Street with both Janice Sheridan and Ellen Chernikov—and within only a few days of each other. Nah, he thought, the kid would never have believed me.

When they were sitting at a table with their greasy sandwiches, Tom said, "You're looking better than I expected, under the circumstances."

Ellen paused with her sandwich halfway to her mouth. "Is that supposed to be a compliment? I guess I'll take it that way." She shrugged and took a small bite.

"Could have been smoother, couldn't I? I meant, after what

happened on Saturday night. I can imagine how close you must be to all your performers."

Ellen put her sandwich down and wiped her hands on her napkin. "Last time I'll ever order a hot sandwich here. Everything's microwaved these days, but they still manage to give you a plate of grease. Tom, singers are replaceable. I had some understudies ready in case something happened—although I never expected anything like this, naturally. Anyway, I had a kid named Mike Berens practicing as Jerry Angleton's understudy. Nowhere near as good a voice as Jerry's, but adequate. Tall blond kid. Nice looking. You may have noticed him. He was playing the officer in charge of the firing squad on Saturday night."

Tom stopped chewing and stared at Ellen.

"Oh, don't be ridiculous!" she snapped. "You're thinking that he loaded the guns with real bullets just so he'd get his big break in a starring role? No one would commit murder just to star in a small-time production like this."

"Hmm," Tom said.

"For God's sake, don't suggest that silly theory to that creep Snow. He's running around town accusing everyone he can think of as it is. I told him it was just a terrible accident, but he told me I don't have the training to recognize a murder, the way he does."

"You're convinced it was an accident?"

"Of *course* it was an accident!" Ellen said. "Someone loaded the guns with live ammunition by mistake. Probably someone did it without even realizing, because so many of the people involved are hunters. It could have been automatic, something you don't even think about. I don't know, maybe it was my fault.

I was in charge. I should have given the guns one final check before that scene."

For the first time, Tom began to take seriously the idea that Jerry Angleton's death had not been an accident. Ellen was wrong in thinking that an experienced hunter would be likely to load the rifles used on-stage with live rounds without being aware of what he was doing. On the contrary, an experienced hunter would be among the least likely to make that mistake, among the most likely to check and double check that the rifles were loaded with blanks and the barrels were free of any debris that might be fired out of the muzzles by the blank charge.

"Sounds like you're ready to get the production up and running again," he said.

"I am ready," Ellen said, "but it's final exams week for the summer session, so I'm putting the reopening on hold for a couple of weeks. In the meantime, I'll be working with Mike Berens and the rest of the cast so they'll be ready to go. Which is kind of why I asked you to eat lunch with me."

"I was wondering."

She reached across the table and squeezed his hand briefly. "I need someone I can talk to about all of this, someone who'll give me some support. Jack never has sympathized with my love of opera and my running the Guild, and now he's really turned negative. He wants me to just drop the whole thing. He's become more preoccupied and distant than ever since Saturday night."

"It's only been two days," Tom pointed out, "and it's finals week, as you just said. Give him time." He was surprised by how much Ellen's touch had disturbed him. He didn't want to have to deal again with emotions and drives as strong as those which had plagued him when he was eighteen, but they seemed to be alive and powerful again.

When Tom didn't respond, Ellen withdrew her hand. "This isn't something new," she said. "Jack and I have had a lot of problems."

A peaceful retirement in the old home town, Tom thought. Away from all the old emotional storms and the more recent physical dangers. Maybe I ought to sell my fancy new house and move on. Go someplace entirely new. Tasmania, maybe. "I'll go talk to Snow. See if I can redirect his attention."

"I'd appreciate that," Ellen said. "Although he'll probably be as rude and dismissive with you as he was with me. The man's a real jerk. So different from his wife. You can tell that he's been a social loser all his life, and now that he's got some power, he's taking his resentments out on the kind of people who treated him with contempt when he was young. You know the kind I mean."

"I suppose I do," Tom said.

Tom left his car parked in front of the sandwich shop and walked the two blocks to the building housing the administrative offices of the Ransom Police Department. It was the same building the RPD had used in Tom's youth, but grimier and dingier than he remembered. He assumed the inside was also unchanged, but also dingier and grimier.

He was right on both counts. Fortunately, air conditioning had been added since his boyhood.

He was eight or nine, as far as he could remember, when he had been brought here a few times by sympathetic policemen. His mother had disappeared around that time, and the policemen had been doing what they could to save him from his father's brutal rages. Which was not all that much, because in those days the police had lacked the legal power to do anything more for Tom than take him away from the house for a day or two. A couple of times, the police had come because of a call from Nick Jaruzelski, who lived next door at 135 North Elm.

Tom had realized early how little the police or the neighbors could help him despite their sympathy. He had then taken to leaving home under his own power whenever he detected the signs of approaching fury in his father. He would stay away, sleeping where he could and eating what he had managed to take with him, until he judged that it was safe to return home.

There were no photographs of his mother in the house, and his memories of her had grown steadily vaguer, less distinct. For a long time, what remained with him most powerfully was his resentment toward her for abandoning him, leaving him behind to deal with his father's savagery. Years had passed with no word from her before a more terrible explanation had occurred to him.

The period of Tom's life in which he had spent a few nights every month away from home, hiding from his father, had lasted for close to ten years, until he was eighteen. He had continued to go to school—partly as a gesture of defiance toward his father, who had always made his contempt for learned men clear. After Tom graduated from high school, he had left Ransom. He had chosen Chicago at random, moved there, and changed his name, trying to cut himself off utterly from his past. And yet, after all that time and all those changes, he still felt a glow of warmth and safety when he entered the police building.

He was intrigued by how much more relaxed the

atmosphere inside the building was than that inside any Chicago police station he had been in—and he had been in quite a few of them. There was no security that he could see, and when he asked to see Detective Snow, the sergeant manning the reception desk pointed down a hallway and said simply, "Second door on the left, sir."

Tom's warm glow vanished as soon as he entered Andy Snow's office.

Snow looked up from his desk. "Yes, can I help—Oh, it's you. Tom Hamilton, native son."

"Prodigal son," Tom said. He sat down in the chair in front of Snow's desk. It was the same sort of sturdy old wooden chair he had spent so many hours in as a child in this building. Then those chairs had been comforting. Now this one was uncomfortable. The office itself made Tom feel uncomfortable. Some of that discomfort was due to the presence of Andy Snow, but some of it was caused by the random clutter in the place, the air of tumult and lack of control. Papers were piled on Snow's desk and the floor. A metal filing cabinet stood open, with a dark tie draped over the door. A coffee cup sat insecurely atop a pile of papers. Another cup was on the floor, near Tom's chair. "I've come here today to make your job easier," Tom said.

"Yeah, right."

Tom was annoyed at himself for making such a bad start, but it was surprisingly difficult to be friendly with this man. How had Snow managed to get this far professionally? Didn't his superiors in the police department react to him with the same instinctive dislike as Tom did?

"Someone once told me," Tom said, "that a murder generally has to be solved within the first twenty-four to forty-eight hours, or it never will be solved. The trail grows cold, and new cases start demanding their share of police resources. Which, as we all know, are never as great as they should be, thanks to short-sighted city governments and voters."

Snow grinned. "As attempts at winning a policeman's sympathy go, that one wasn't too bad, Mr. Hamilton. But whoever told you that was talking about big cities. In a dump like this, we get two murders a year on average. Three, if we're lucky."

"Lucky? Dump?"

"Did I say that?" Snow shook his head. "You must have misheard me. Unlucky. Fine, peaceful, law-abiding city. I'm still waiting for you to help me."

"I was going to help by suggesting that you announce that what happened was an unfortunate accident and close the case."

Snow snickered. "Yeah, right."

"So you don't think it was an accident?"

"Mr. Hamilton, I have so many possible murderers, I almost don't know where to begin. Instead of too few suspects, we've got too many."

"Interesting. For example?"

"Do you really think I'd share that kind of information with you? This is a police matter."

"I might know something of use to you. We could discuss the case. Maybe I'd have something helpful."

"You want to help me?" Andy Snow said. "Tell me you're willing to sign a confession that you murdered Jerry Angleton."

"I was sitting in the audience, Lieutenant."

"I know. I saw you. But all that means is that you didn't pull the trigger. You could still be the guy who went backstage and switched the blanks for live bullets."

"I didn't go backstage after the performance had begun. I can prove that if I have to. So I'm an unlikely suspect. You don't strike me as an opera buff, Lieutenant."

"It's crap," Snow said. "I hate it. But my wife loves it. She made me go with her."

"At least you got to see a murder actually being committed."

"Yeah, that's the bright side of it," Snow said. "Seen that before, though. Plenty of times."

"Even though Ransom only gets two murders a year? Three in a good year?"

"I've worked in the big city, too, Mr. Hamilton. Just like you, right? Where have you been living for the past twenty-two years?"

"Elsewhere."

"You're not really in the clear, you know," Snow said. "Just because you were sitting in the audience, that doesn't put you above suspicion. You could be in league with someone."

"Good Lord," Tom said, "why would I want to shoot a promising young tenor who might have had a great career ahead of him?"

"I don't have the motive," Snow said. "Yet. I need to know a lot more about you and your history. Which I will find out."

The hell you will, Tom thought. And yet the thought of Snow prying into his past made him uneasy. The man might conceivably stumble onto something by sheer luck.

"I still think it was an accident, Lieutenant," Tom said, "but if you really think it was a murder, it shouldn't be that hard to solve this case. You have the weapons that fired the bullets, you have the bullets, you have the boys who fired the guns. You can question the boys, and you can check the shells for fingerprints. If with all that you still can't prove it was a murder and say who was responsible, then you'll just have to admit it was an accident and give up."

Snow sighed theatrically. "Civilians always think our job is simple. Look, Mr. Hamilton. All kinds of people handled those rifles all evening long. Even the casings weren't much use. A couple of partial prints, that's all. Fingerprints are much rarer at crime scenes than most people think, especially really useful prints. Hell, there were people running around backstage constantly, and they didn't have any one person in charge of the rifles. Too small an operation for that. So almost anyone could have passed by and reloaded, and probably no one would even have paid any attention. Even if you just concentrate on the people who we know fooled around with the weapons a lot, you have a very nice pool of suspects to look at."

"You're really saying that even if *was* a murder, it's going to be impossible to find out who was behind it. Meaning, again, that you might as well call it quits."

Snow glared at him. "There's still motive. If I can find the person with the motive, then I'll be on my way back to the big city."

"You said you have too many suspects instead of too few. I think you may have the same problem with motive."

"No such thing as too much motive," Snow said confidently. "And there are some very good ones in this case. You're going to be staying in town, aren't you, Mr. Hamilton?"

"Probably," Tom said. "Unless something comes up unexpectedly. You could try to get a judge's order to keep me here."

"I will if I have to," Snow said. "Have you satisfied your Agatha Christie urgings yet?"

"Almost. I don't suppose the bullets used in this case were some kind of rare brand that can only be mail-ordered from a supplier in Wisconsin that keeps scrupulous records?"

Snow laughed. "Life should be that easy. Nope. Winchester Long Rifle 22s. You can pick them up anywhere around here, including the place in town that Professor Tourneau mentioned. Lots of local hunters use them."

"I guess that covers my Agatha Christie urgings, then," Tom said. "For today." He stood up. "Thank you for being so open with me, Detective. Very generous of you."

Snow stood up too. "Mr. Hamilton, you're an idiot, but I felt like humoring you. This was my coffee break. Now I have work to do, so goodbye."

Walking slowly back to his car, Tom told himself that he really should stay out of this matter, that he should leave Snow alone and let the policeman either find the killer or give up on the case. But he could feel the old urges drawing him further in, and those urges did not come from reading Agatha Christie novels.

Jerry Angleton's shooting presented an interesting intellectual puzzle. This was something Tom could look into without having to worry about emotional stress or ethical questions.

And now there was the element of challenge to it as well.

The hell with it, Tom thought. Who needs retirement? I bet I can beat Snow to the solution.

Seven

Dealing with grieving widows had always been the part of his work that Tom had hated the most. But the information they had was often essential, and it was vital to get that information from them while their memories were fresh.

He drove home and called Ellen Tourneau. Jack answered the telephone. Ellen wasn't home, he said. His tone was suspicious and hostile.

Tom hesitated. He had assumed that Jack would be on the campus and that Ellen would be at home. He was unsure about how helpful Jack would be. But he'd probably become more hostile and would certainly be less helpful in the future if Tom were to say that he'd call later and talk to Ellen. Finally, Tom said, "I was calling to get the address for the Angletons. I thought I'd go speak to Jerry Angleton's wife."

If anything, Jack seemed even more hostile at this. "Why do you want to do that?"

"Because, Jack, I just spoke to that police detective, Andy Snow, and I have an uneasy feeling about the direction he's going in. I think he wants to make a name for himself with this death, and I don't think he's too interested in finding out what really happened so long as he can get someone convicted of murder. I got the impression that he even considers you and Ellen suspects."

"Jesus!" Jack said. "That's ridiculous, Tom! Hell, you were sitting with us when it happened."

"Someone put live bullets in those rifles," Tom said, "and both you and Ellen had the opportunity to do it. As well as lots of other people, of course. Now Snow is trying to dig up a motive for murder, and if he can do that, then he'll go after the person he thinks had the most reason to kill Jerry Angleton."

Jack muttered a string of profanities. When he had calmed down enough, he said, "So what does this have to do with you speaking to Kathy?"

"Kathy?"

"Kathy Angleton, Jerry Angleton's wife. Widow, I mean."

"You know her?"

"Everyone knows everyone in this town, Tom. You've forgotten. I suppose you've spent all this time in a big city, right?"

"Pretty big." It was nonsense that everyone knew everyone else in Ransom. What Jack really meant was that everyone who mattered in Ransom knew everyone else who mattered.

"In Kathy's case," Jack said, "I know her because she was in one of my classes last semester. Bright kid. You still haven't explained why you need to talk to her."

Tom could have pointed out that it was none of Jack's business, but that would only make Jack completely uncooperative. "Information gathering. I know a little bit about investigating crimes, and I've decided to help out in this case. Maybe I can uncover something that will point Andy Snow away from you and Ellen."

"What are you saying, that you've been a policeman for the last twenty years? Given the house and car you just bought, you must have been a pretty crooked cop."

"There are a lot of other kinds of people who investigate crimes, Jack. Stop prying. You know by now that I'm not going to tell you anything. Just tell me where Kathy Angleton lives."

"I'll do better than that. I'll come up to your place and we'll drive over there together. But first I'll call her and make sure she's in shape to talk to us."

"I don't operate that way, Jack. I need to talk to her alone."

"You're a stranger," Jack said. "She'll be much more cooperative if I'm there. She trusts me."

"Out of the question, Jack."

After a moment's hesitation, Jack said, "Oh, all right. They rent a house over on Lincoln." He gave Tom the address. "You know where that is?"

"I'll find it."

"At least let me call her first and prepare her, okay? The police have already been questioning her, and she's not going to want to talk to you unless someone she likes and trusts asks her to. Okay?"

"Okay, Jack. Call her now. Ask her if I can come over around—" he checked his watch "—four. Call me back and let me know."

The Angleton house was near the college campus. Tom thought he remembered the neighborhood as stable and blue collar, an area of small, single-story, well-maintained houses. It looked a lot more run down now. Tom parked in front of the house and hesitated, remembering his experience a few days earlier in the neighborhood he had grown up in. He took a deep breath and left the car.

There was no one around, although there were toys scattered in front of some of the other houses. The front yards tended to be dirt, with occasional clumps of dried-out grass. Most of the houses had trees in front of them—cottonwoods and honey locusts—and all of the trees looked in severe need of watering and pruning. Trees rarely grew very tall here at the foot of the Rockies because of the thin air, the dryness, and the poor soil. Chicago had always seemed like a forest in contrast. These trees, which Tom would once have considered huge, now seemed stunted and meager to him.

A young woman answered his knock. She was small and blonde, and Tom could tell that she was normally very pretty, just as Ellen had said. Now her pregnancy was beginning to show, she looked drawn and exhausted, and her eyes were red. She was small enough to have to look up at Tom, which he found made him feel strong and protective. She stood in the doorway staring at him and saying nothing.

"I'm Tom Hamilton," he said. "Dr. Tourneau was supposed to have called you about me."

"Oh. Yes. Please come in." Her voice was small and weak, and she spoke in a vague and detached way. She was looking at Tom but not really seeing him.

The front door led directly into the living room, which was furnished with a small, worn rug on a scratched wooden floor, an old couch, and two old armchairs, in one of which sat Jack Tourneau. Jack held a beer in one hand. He raised the other hand limply. "Hi, Tom." He sounded nervous.

There was something weirdly familiar about the scene. Tom froze, staring at Jack. He bit back the angry words that first sprang to his tongue. "I'm extremely surprised to see you here, Jack."

Jack looked embarrassed for no more than a couple of seconds. "Thought I'd better be here after all," he said. "Help out. Smooth the troubled waters."

You're an oily bastard, all right, Tom thought. He turned to Kathy Angleton. "Mrs. Angleton, I realize this might be painful for you, but I do need to ask you a few questions. It may be the same questions the police asked, but I'm not with the police. Is that all right?"

She nodded. "Please call me Kathy." She gestured toward the empty armchair. "Can I get you anything? Tea? Coffee?"

"No more beer," Jack Tourneau said. "I got the last one."

Tom ignored him. "No thanks, Kathy. I'll be as quick as I can, and then I'll stop bothering you." He sat in the chair she had indicated.

Kathy sat on the couch. Jack Tourneau lurched to his feet and plopped down on the couch next to her.

Tom tried to keep ignoring the other man. "How long were you and Jerry married?" he asked Kathy.

She looked at the floor and said in a low voice, "Two years, almost. I met Jerry during my freshman year. We got married a couple of months after we met." She looked up at Tom and smiled suddenly. "I would have married him even sooner, if he'd asked."

Tom found himself responding to her smile. "You were happy?"

"Oh, yes!"

Jack Tourneau snagged one of Kathy's hands. "Of course they were. Wouldn't you be if you were married to a wonderful girl like this?"

Kathy withdrew her hand and looked at the floor again. "We were happy," she said quietly.

"Did Jerry ever mention anyone who didn't like him?" Tom asked. "Anyone he had trouble with?"

Kathy said, "The police asked if he had any enemies."

"Yes, I suppose that's what I'm really asking, too."

She shook her head. "Everyone liked Jerry. No one would want to murder him."

"What about the other tenor, Jerry's understudy in the opera?"

"Mike Berens," Kathy said. She sniffed. "He doesn't have a voice like Jerry's. I guess he might be jealous because he'll never be the singer Jerry is. Anyway, they were friends, sort of, and Mike wants to be a music teacher. He's not aiming at a career singing opera, like Jerry."

"So no one ever threatened Jerry's life, to your knowledge?"

Kathy started to say something, then apparently thought the better of it. She glanced at Jack Tourneau, then away.

Jack? Tom thought. Jack threatened the boy's life?

But Jack said, "What is it, Kathy? *Did* someone threaten Jerry? It's best to just tell us everything, you know."

She sighed. "It's silly. It was last semester. A guy who was in your Shakespeare class with me. Fred Christianson. You remember him, Ja—Dr. Tourneau?"

Jack frowned. "Christianson," he muttered. "Don't think so."

"He sat next to Sharon Langley, the brunette girl."

Jack's face cleared. "Oh, yeah, I remember him now. Piss-poor student."

"Well, he kept asking me out. I kept telling him I was married, but it didn't help. Finally I told Jerry about it, and I guess he went to see Fred. I don't know what Jerry said to him, but Fred stopped bothering me. Except for one time. He told me he was going to get Jerry, and that I'd be sorry for sending Jerry after him."

"You told the police about this?" Tom asked.

She shook her head. "No. It just seemed so silly."

"Doesn't seem silly to me," Jack said. He put his arm around Kathy's shoulders. She acted as though she were unaware of the weight of his arm. "Don't worry about it," Jack said. "I'll pass the word to that detective about Christianson."

"Let's talk about Mike Berens again," Tom said. "He was Jerry's understudy, and now he gets to sing the lead role. In spite of what you said, did you see any indication that Mike resented Jerry getting the lead instead of him?"

Unexpectedly, Kathy laughed. "Poor Mike! All he can think about is being on the same stage as Karen. He's so completely crazy about her, he doesn't care what role he sings. We used to laugh about it sometimes, Jerry and me. Jerry even tried to fix them up, but I guess Karen wasn't interested in Mike at all."

"I think I'd better talk to him anyway," Tom said. "Do you have his number?"

"I'm sure Ellen does," Jack said.

Kathy said, "You could check around in the music department at Triple C. They only have five or six practice rooms. Mike might be in one of those, working on Jerry's..." Her voice trailed away and she stared into space for a while. Then she said, "On Mike's new role." Suddenly she turned pale.

"Excuse me!" she gasped. She jumped to her feet and rushed from the room.

A few seconds later, Tom heard the sounds of violent retching. He stood up. "Does she need a doctor?"

Jack shook his head. "Morning sickness. Except that in her case it goes on all damned day." Jack looked queasy for a moment himself. He added, "I advised her to get rid of it, under the circumstances."

"She probably doesn't want to, especially because of the circumstances. The poor kid!"

"She'll get over it," Jack said. "You'd probably better go now." He looked at the doorway through which Kathy had vanished. "I suppose I'd better check to make sure she's all right," he said, although he stayed where he was.

"Don't overexert yourself," Tom said.

"Thanks, I won't," Jack said absentmindedly, his thoughts obviously elsewhere.

Tom had learned little, but he doubted if he would learn much more if he stayed, especially with Jack present. He let himself out and headed for the campus.

Eight

It had been foreign territory during his boyhood. It wasn't just that college students had seemed amazingly grown-up and worldly to him in those days, and it was more than his not having had reason or desire to visit the place back then. Most important of all had been his father's antipathy to the college and to all those connected with it. In retrospect, Tom suspected that his friendship with Jack Tourneau had persisted mostly as a way of defying his father's hatred of people like Jack's father, who taught at the college. The friendship had also given Tom the chance to visit the Tourneau house often and spend time with Jack's father. Thinking back, Tom could come up with no other reason for his having endured so much condescension and contempt from Jack and his friends.

Friendships, Tom thought. Kids base them on so many false foundations, and adults can't find anything to base them on at all.

Colorado Central College had almost 12,000 students. If one included faculty and staff, the population of the campus was almost as big as that of the town of Ransom itself.

That was misleading, since most of the faculty and staff

lived in the town and were part of its population and economy. And yet there was still a division, the kind of barrier between town and gown that Tom had been so aware of in his youth. It was out of place in the modern world, he supposed. It reflected an earlier stage of American society. But it persisted here nonetheless. Seems to me, anyway, he told himself. Which, he thought, probably says more about the state of Tom Hamilton than the state of American society.

The campus was on the west side of town, up against the foothills. Water had not been spared, so there were lush lawns and healthy trees everywhere. The college's use of water was a constant irritant to elements in the city government who resented such profligacy in an arid climate, but the result was a campus of restful beauty.

Tom parked his car in a city pay lot on the other side of the street which formed the eastern boundary of the campus. He crossed the street and passed from the noisy, hot sunniness of the town into the cool, shaded peace of the campus. Metaphorically speaking, anyway. He paused for a moment beside a concrete pathway to watch coeds hurrying by in shorts, tank tops, and sandals, and felt less at peace.

He stopped one of them to ask for directions to the Music Department. The girl's instructions were vague and terse. She was taller than he and she looked through him as well as down at him. Tom ignored her manner and concentrated on what she was saying.

He meandered across the campus, following the directions as best he could, but for the moment not really caring where he was going. Why, it's beautiful! he thought. Why had he never come here as a boy? His father would never have known, and

Tom would have gained some measure of peace from this place.

But it was getting late. He focused his attention on his task, asked another passing student for help, and found the building he wanted.

The sign outside the building read PSYCHOLOGY, but the second student he had stopped had forewarned him. Music was of small importance at CCC—just another department within the School of Arts and Sciences, and a small department at that. It had to be content with the basement of this building, and if the Psychology Department continued to expand, then Music would have to find some other basement.

The stairs from the front door led down to a hallway lined with doors on either side. Folding chairs and parts of music stands and other music-related odds and ends stood against the walls. The doors were conveniently labeled PRACTICE ROOM 1, PRACTICE ROOM 2, and so on. The walls had once been white. Now they were smudged, gouged, and graffitoed.

Tom put his ear to the first door and held his breath and listened, but he could hear nothing. Either it was empty, or the soundproofing of these doors and walls was of much better quality than the paint job. He had no idea what the protocol was in this place. Knock? Open the door and interrupt the practice session that might be underway within? Wait for someone to come out?

A young man carrying a guitar case came charging around the corner at the far end of the hallway and rushed down the hallway past Tom.

"Excuse me!" Tom called out.

The guitarist stopped. "Yeah?"

"I'm trying to find someone who may be in one of these

practice rooms. Is there any way of telling which ones are occupied and who's inside them?"

"Sure. Who you looking for?"

"His name is Mike Berens. He's a singer."

"Okay." The young man grabbed the handle of the door Tom was standing in front of and yanked it open.

There was a single flute note, cut off in the middle, and a woman's voice yelled, "Hey! In use!"

The guitarist closed the door again. "Nope." He stepped to the second door and pulled that one open.

"Hey! I was here first!" This time it was a male voice, but the guitarist shut the door and said to Tom, "Another guitar player. I know him."

"One of those people is going to attack you," Tom said.

"Nah," the young man said. "They're used to it."

When he yanked the third door open, the person within yelled a string of curses at him in a voice that seemed to fit the bill. The guitarist looked at Tom, eyebrows raised. Tom nodded. He stepped to the door. "Mike Berens?"

The young man inside the room, seated at a piano, glared at him over the instrument. "Mike Berens practicing like crazy. Close the door and go away."

Tom thanked the guitarist and stepped inside the room, pulling the door closed behind him.

"I said, *go away* and close the door," Berens repeated.

"Eventually," Tom said. "I'm investigating the murder of Jerry Angleton."

"Oh," Berens said. He looked down at the piano keyboard. "Christ." He looked up again. "Look, I've already talked to you people, okay? I told you guys all I could remember, which wasn't very much, except for poor Jerry falling down and bleeding all over the stage."

"Do you remember the recoil of the rifle as you fired it?"

Berens rose to his feet, his face reddening. Like Jerry Angleton, he was unusually tall for a tenor. Unlike Jerry, he was very heavily built. Some of that was fat, but most of it seemed to be muscle. Tom put one hand on the door handle in case a quick escape became necessary. "You accusing me of murder?" Berens said.

"It's not my job to accuse anyone of anything," Tom said. "I'm interested in eliciting memories."

"Doing what?"

"Helping people remember useful details. Sometimes witnesses don't realize themselves that something will be important. I'm just gathering data. Tell me exactly what you remember, how it all looked from your point of view."

Berens sat down again. "I told you, I don't remember much. I was concentrating on not bumping into the other guys. We were all kind of crammed together when we came on-stage. I was watching the guys around me."

Tom remembered the entrance of the firing squad in the last act. They had been crowded together. He also remembered Mike Berens among them. Berens had not really been concentrating entirely on the other members of the firing squad. Tom had noticed him shooting glances at Karen Franks, standing downstage. "Did you handle the rifle before you had to take it on-stage with you?" Tom asked him.

"Of course," Berens said. "I mean, it's my rifle. I brought it with me to the auditorium. Say, when are you guys going to give it back? It's my favorite. Deer season's coming up. You better get it back to me in time, and it better be okay!"

"I'm surprised you'd let the opera guild use your favorite rifle."

Berens shrugged. "I like holding it, so I decided to use it. Besides, I was the only one who was going to touch it during the performance. Now you guys are getting your hands all over it," he added bitterly.

"You must be very familiar with that rifle," Tom said.

"You bet. Know it like the back of my hand."

"Did it seem strange in any way to you when you picked it up before going on–stage? Didn't you notice a difference in the weight?"

"You mean, like the difference between a blank and a live round?" Berens said. "Come on, that's too small of a difference. No one can tell that just by picking up a loaded rifle."

"It wasn't loaded when you brought it to the auditorium, was it?"

Berens looked at Tom scornfully. "Hell, no. Of course not. You think I'm stupid? I know better than that."

"So you put a blank shell in it before you carried it on?"

Berens shook his head. "Dr. Tourneau took care of that. The rifles were all ready for us. I told you, I was mainly worried about tripping over some other guy's feet."

"When did Jack Tourneau do this?"

"Hell, I don't know. I got there about an hour before curtain time, so I'd have plenty of time to get in costume, get the makeup on, and listen to Jerry singing. I brought my rifle with me, and I put it on the table backstage with the others. Next time I saw it was when I picked it up to go on in the last act. Sometime in there, I guess."

"You wanted to listen to Jerry Angleton singing?"

"Of course. He had a great voice. I enjoyed listening to him. Also, I was his understudy. I wanted to be ready, just in case."

"In case of what?"

Berens waved his hands. "In case Jerry had some kind of problem and I had to take over, of course."

"A problem like being shot, you mean?"

Berens jumped to his feet again. "Jesus Christ!" he yelled. "Are you stupid or something? No! A problem like with his voice, you know? Anything that would keep him from singing. That's what understudies are for. Don't you know anything about opera?" He got himself under control and sat down. He put his hands on the keyboard and played an approximation of the opening bars of *E lucevan le stelle*. "Look, I really need to work on this stuff, okay? I've got to learn the role in between studying for my finals *and* getting ready for my junior recital. I'm really stressed, okay?"

"I thought you already knew the role. Because you were the understudy, I mean."

Berens looked exhausted all of a sudden. "Yeah, I thought so, too. Guess I was wrong. I tried to run through parts of it with Karen yesterday afternoon, and I kept screwing up. She was really angry with me, and so was Mrs. Tourneau."

Tom felt a wave of sympathy for the young man. "All right, Mike. You get back to your practicing."

He left feeling he had wasted his time. The boy had been so open and honest about using his own rifle on-stage, and he had seemed so frank in his admiration of Angleton's voice, that it was hard to envision him as the murderer. Moreover, he seemed none too bright. A baritone had once told Tom that all tenors are stupid because the resonance of their voices in their nasal cavities destroys their brains. Tom wondered if there could be any physiological basis for that slur.

But stupidity was no barrier to committing murder. In fact, most of the killers Tom had encountered had been stupid. Few even of the mob's professional killers whom he had known were intelligent. Most of them avoided capture through a combination of luck, bribery of the police, and a lack of interest on the part of the honest policemen in solving the murders of mob insiders.

There were exceptions. Tom had known a couple of professionals who had planned their hits carefully so as to avoid implicating themselves. They would make the deaths look like accidents, to divert suspicion entirely. Briefly, he wondered if those two were still in the business, or if they had managed to escape from Chicago as he had. In any case, Mike Berens was nothing like them.

He was getting nowhere, he knew. This was not the sort of investigation he had trained himself to do. In the past, he had followed mostly paper trails, and that experience seemed inapplicable in this case. Often, a personal visit had been sufficient to resolve a problem, because those he visited knew whom this seemingly insignificant man represented—what kind of power stood behind him. That too was no longer applicable. Now, back home in Ransom and living under his own name, he represented no one and carried no aura of power, no ability to induce fear.

He told himself that he no longer wanted to induce fear in anyone.

What about inducing respect? he asked himself. Well, he had always wanted that.

Nine

Tom called Karen Franks the following morning. She agreed to speak to him but insisted that they meet in a cemetery.

Specifically, an old cemetery, dating from before the turn of the century. It was located east of the city, on the banks of South Tournant Creek. More up-to-date bodies were buried within the city limits, in places with pastoral names and filled with dark green lawns and stately trees. The old graveyard was called simply Ransom Cemetery. It had been the city's only burial ground during the nineteenth century.

There was one other car in the dirt parking lot, a Neon. Tom parked his Lexus next to it.

The cemetery was surrounded by a sagging fence with an opening where there had once been a gate. A gravel path led from the opening into the cemetery. It was a hot, barren place, devoid of romance or pathos, and of interest only to historians. And, apparently, to sopranos.

Karen was waiting in front of the largest monument in the place, a tall structure of white stone. She stood perfectly still, staring at the monument as though deep in thought. She was dressed in black—black blouse, black skin-tight jeans, black high-heeled shoes. Perhaps it's a mourning outfit for the hip young of the nineties, Tom thought.

He climbed the slight rise toward the monument. He had no hat, but fortunately he had sunglasses. Despite the dryness, he was sweating by the time he reached her. He was breathing hard, too. For the first time since moving back, he was aware of just how little oxygen there was in Ransom's air.

Because of the arid climate, the monument was only slightly weathered. Tom could still read the dates. "Thaddeus L. Hughes," he read aloud. "1834 to 1882. Probably not that young for those days. Local big shot, I suppose."

Karen turned slowly toward him. He could see no hint of tears on her face and no redness in her eyes. "Doesn't it just tear you up to think of all these people buried here?" she said to Tom. She spread her arms wide, as if to embrace all of the dead. "I mean, they were all alive, and they had lives and relationships, and now they're all dead."

"At the moment," Tom said, "I'm more concerned with the more recently dead."

Karen put one hand on her chest. "Jerry. Poor Jerry. You have no idea what he looked like, lying on that stage, dead."

"Actually, I do. I was probably the first person from the audience to reach him."

"You were?" Karen said. "I didn't notice. Oh, but I shouldn't be surprised." She stared intently at him. Tom was sure it was a studied effect, but combined with her striking looks, it affected him anyway. Karen added, "Mrs. Tourneau told me you're connected with an opera house in Europe."

"She told you that? Misunderstanding on her part. I'm an opera buff, but I have no connection with any opera house."

"You don't? Oh." Interest faded from the lovely eyes, and Karen looked around her as though realizing for the first time that she was in a hot, dusty, neglected old graveyard. "Then why am I here talking to you?"

Tom thought her honesty commendable. "I'm gathering information about Jerry's death. I'm investigating it, you might say."

"Are you a reporter?" Her gaze intensified again.

Tom shook his head. "Not a policeman, either. Just an interested...well, fan of the opera, I guess."

Her eyes drifted back to the weathered tombstones. "It was just a stupid accident. There's nothing to investigate. Someone was careless with the rifles, that's all. If you really want to help, then you can volunteer to double check the rifles the next time, when we start performing again. Make sure the same thing doesn't happen to...whatever his name is."

"Mike Berens."

"Yeah. Him."

"I understand you were romantically interested in Jerry Angleton, but he was faithful to his wife."

Karen stared at Tom. There was no artfulness in her gaze now. "Who told you that?"

"That doesn't matter."

"It matters to me! *Tell me*!"

Quite a voice, Tom thought. Raised in anger and at close range, it was hard to resist. He resisted. "As I said, it doesn't matter who told me. What does matter is that your interest in Jerry and his lack of responsiveness seem to be common knowledge, and they make you a suspect in his death. Floria Tosca, the dangerously jealous soprano—a lot of people accept that stereotype."

"Jesus, you're crazy!" Karen said. "Anyway, I was on-stage when it happened."

"For the conclusion of that scene," Tom acknowledged. "But you were offstage only a bit earlier in the act, while Mario Cavaradossi is singing about his rapturous last night with you. For that matter, you could have had an accomplice taking care of the guns for you."

"Oh, right. You think someone would commit murder for me, just because I was angry at Jerry for not responding to me?"

"I suspect a lot of men would be willing to commit murder for you, Karen."

She smiled happily. "You really think so?" Then she grew angry again. "This is all a bunch of shit. I have a career to worry about. Yes, I was hot for Jerry Angleton, but now he's dead." She turned and stalked away toward the gate. The effect was spoiled by the combination of high heels and gravel path, which made her wobble a few times.

Tom watched her go, admiring her despite himself. She probably did have a career ahead of her, conceivably a great career. Since Tom couldn't risk going to Chicago or New York or any other great city again, he would probably never have the chance to see her perform live once she left Ransom. Too bad, he thought. He would like to see and hear her in a few years, when her beauty and voice matured.

Perhaps when she's famous, he thought, she'll come back here to do benefit performances for the Ransom and Central Colorado Opera Guild, which gave her her start. He smiled at the idea. Don't hold your breath, he told himself.

Karen reached the parking lot. She opened the door of the

Neon. She hesitated for a while, standing beside the open door, while she gave Tom's new Lexus a careful once-over. For a moment, he thought she was about to come back to continue their conversation. But then she climbed into her car and drove off.

Tom turned back to the imposing monument to Thaddeus Hughes. "So, Thad," Tom said, "what do you think about all of this? Of course you can't say very much. You're dead. But you know, some of my best friends are dead."

Not a few of them because they had become his friends. During his last years in Chicago, he had been a dangerous man to be friends with, and he hadn't even known it. Throughout his years of working for Trager and his mob, Tom had tried to protect the good from the consequences of their carelessness or foolhardiness and make sure that retribution destroyed only the evil. That had been his major justification to himself of the position he held in Trager's organization. But by the end, simply knowing Tom too well could be cause for a death sentence. The net was closing in on him, and others swimming too near had been caught in it. Far from protecting the good, he had caused their deaths. His discovery of that fact was one of the final factors in his decision to flee.

Although, he admitted to himself, I would have had to run for cover even without any of that. The discovery that the net was tightening around me after Trager died would have been enough all by itself. I thought I was clever, but my enemies were almost cleverer.

So, Thad, with all my cleverness, what have I learned so far about Jerry Angleton's death?

Not very damned much.

Let's consider the possibilities, he told himself.

First, what happened to Jerry Angleton could have been an accident. If so, it was tragic, but everyone will now be very careful when the opera resumes, and there's no need to worry about it any longer.

Or it was not an accident, it was a murder. In that case, let's consider all the suspects.

I have to include Angleton himself on that list, he realized. Not murder, but suicide.

What reason would Angleton have to kill himself in such a complicated way? His wife was pregnant, and they weren't living high on the hog. Insurance money for his widow, perhaps? But what insurance policy would pay off under such circumstances? Apart from all that, Jerry Angleton hadn't struck Tom as the sort to sacrifice himself. Moreover, the boy had had in front of him the very real promise of a lucrative career, so such a sacrifice would have been pointless.

Scratch Jerry Angleton, Tom decided. I'll proceed on the assumption that it was indeed a murder.

First suspect: Fred Christianson, the boy Kathy Angleton said made threats after she rebuffed his advances and told her husband about them. And after Jerry had confronted Christianson and warned him off. Have to look him up, Tom decided.

Second suspect: Mike Berens. Lots of opportunity and lots of motive. After interviewing Berens, Tom was intuitively inclined to dismiss him as a suspect. Better not do that, though, he decided. Keep him on the list. Must approach this intellectually, not emotionally.

That had been his mechanism for doing his job in Chicago.

Over and over, his emotions had rebelled against what he was required to do, but he had managed to get through it by distancing himself from the people involved, by treating it all as an intellectual puzzle.

That intellectual defense had started to weaken, though. Even if Trager hadn't died...

Tom yanked his thoughts back to the problem at hand.

Next suspect: Karen Franks. No. Not that much opportunity, despite what Tom had said to her, and little motive. A woman scorned, perhaps? So angry at Jerry Angleton for rejecting her and remaining faithful to his wife that she arranged for his murder? The method of murder fit with what little Tom had seen of her personality, but she also seemed to be too focused on her own promising career to endanger it. However, that judgment was based on her behavior here in the graveyard, and that could have been an act. She was a stage actress, after all, and a good one. Keep her on the list, he decided, just like Mike Berens.

What about Kathy Angleton as a suspect? No opportunity. There was always confusion backstage, so she might have been able to sneak in, unload the blanks and put in live rounds, and then sneak out, but that image stretched Tom's credulity too far. No matter how confused and chaotic the backstage area had been, the lead tenor's wife could hardly manage to sneak in and out without being noticed. So, no opportunity. And no motive, except the most clichéd—for example, that Jerry actually was being unfaithful to her, and she was getting revenge. But if she did murder Jerry, then she was also widowing herself while she was pregnant, and she was cutting herself off from the income Jerry's probable future success would have brought.

Her eyes had been red with weeping when Tom visited her. In his mind, that was the deciding factor. He removed her from his mental list.

That seemed to be it. A surprisingly short list, despite Snow's claim to have too many suspects. Tom's next step seemed to be to find Fred Christianson.

He took one last look at the old cemetery before leaving. He wondered what it was like to know where those you had lost were buried and to be able to visit their graves. Would he find that more comforting than the way things actually were for him? Or more disturbing?

The most disturbing thing of all, Tom had always felt, was not knowing the truth.

The next morning, Tom called Andy Snow to tell him about Fred Christianson. To Tom's surprise, Jack Tourneau had already called Snow with the information. And Snow had already tracked Christianson down.

After the end of the semester during which the threats had been made, Christianson had moved to New Jersey to spend the summer with a sister and her husband. Shortly after that, he had been killed in a traffic accident.

"You're absolutely sure about that?" Tom asked.

"Of course I'm sure!" Snow growled. "The kid's dead, Hamilton. He drank most of a bottle of whiskey and then drove down the turnpike at eighty miles an hour, missed a curve, and buried his car and himself in the concrete support of an overpass. In the process of which, he also cleared himself of suspicion in the murder of Jerry Angleton. Nice work on Jack Tourneau's part, though," Snow added grudgingly. "That stupid little bitch didn't tell us about those threats, and she should have. Good thing Tourneau got that out of her. You want to be a detective, you should stop reading Agatha Christie novels and ask Tourneau how he did it."

"Thank you, Lieutenant," Tom said. He hung up and moved Mike Berens to the top of his mental list.

For reasons that had nothing to do with logic, he added Jack Tourneau to the bottom of it.

Ten

The two weeks before the reopening of Tosca flew by. Tom felt he had accomplished nothing during that time—neither in his personal life nor in his supposed investigation of Jerry Angleton's death.

Regarding his personal life, he told himself that that was the whole idea of his escape to Ransom. He was supposed to accomplish nothing from now on. His days were supposed to be spent savoring life and freedom. It would take him some time to get used to what seemed like inactivity and laziness, though.

As for Jerry Angleton's death—well, he had no idea what to do next.

He spoke to Kathy Angleton again but learned nothing new.

He caught Mike Berens on the campus again, but the young tenor provided no new information. He was so nervous about a final exam later that day and about his inability to remember large chunks of the Mario Cavaradossi role that his hands were shaking. At the same time, he was furiously angry at Andy Snow, who had apparently just come very close to accusing him of murdering Jerry Angleton. "He said I was trying to get Jerry out of the way and advance my career!" Mike said, scarcely able to speak intelligibly. "As if I would've gotten myself into this mess on purpose!" Tom took pity on him and let him go.

Tom telephoned Karen Franks and requested a second interview, but she refused, and he had no power to force her to speak to him—and clearly no reason to force her even if he could, given her uncooperative attitude.

He had lunch twice with Janice Sheridan. Now that he no longer yearned for her physically, he found that he enjoyed her company. She asked him to accompany her to another concert and give country and western music a try. He refused. He asked her to come to the reopening of Tosca and give opera a try. She refused. Their new relationship seemed firmly established on a comfortable and safe plane.

He had lunch three times with Ellen Tourneau. He was beginning to find her company just as disquieting as he had twenty-two years before. What made it especially so was that Ellen was behaving toward him in a way she never had in those earlier days.

The first time they had lunch, it was in the same sandwich shop on Howard Street. The second time, they met at a small restaurant in Cherry Creek. This was an expensive area of Denver, filled with small boutiques. It was about forty-five minutes away from Ransom.

Their third lunch was at a restaurant in the mountains, a few miles to the west of town. It was Friday, the day before Ellen's second attempt at staging Tosca.

After the waiter had taken their order and left, Ellen said, "Only one day to go. I think it's going to be okay. I just wish Jack were more reliable. He did manage to beg and borrow more rifles for me. Give him credit for that. But still...Maybe I should load the rifles myself instead of leaving it up to him this time. I don't want to take any chances at all."

"It hardly seems likely that the same thing will happen again," Tom said. "The same accident two times in a row?" He shook his head.

"What if it wasn't an accident?"

"That was supposed to remain an unspoken thought," Tom said.

"Filling the pregnant silence between us, you mean?"

"Wow, that sounds like a line from a badly translated aria. All right, if it wasn't an accident, then presumably the intended victim is already dead, so why would the killer risk getting caught reloading the rifles a second time, especially knowing that the rifles will be more carefully watched this time?"

"You're assuming that Jerry Angleton was the intended victim," Ellen pointed out. "You don't know that. No, never mind," she said before Tom could answer. "That was dumb of me. Mario Cavaradossi is the only character in the story those rifles are fired at. So Jerry must have been it."

Too bad it's not equally clear who the perpetrator was, Tom thought. With Fred Christianson dead, Mike Berens was at the top of Tom's list of suspects, but Tom didn't feel comfortable having the boy's name there. If Cavaradossi *does* get shot again tomorrow evening, Tom thought, that would certainly exonerate Berens.

"If you're really worried about the same thing happening again," Tom said, "why are you still using real rifles?"

"Because I still want that realistic flame and noise, that's why," Ellen answered. "You noticed the audience's reaction the last time, didn't you? I mean, before anyone realized that Jerry had really been shot. The way everyone jumped and looked horrified when the firing squad's rifles really fired—that's the kind of audience reaction and involvement I always dream of. I'm not going to give it up. Besides which, I looked around for some good props and couldn't find any, so I would have had to use toy rifles from the dime store. Talk about ruining the audience's willing suspension of disbelief!"

Better than ruining another tenor, Tom thought. "If you're seriously worried, I could stay backstage with Jack. One more pair of eyes."

"Oh, no," Ellen said. "I wouldn't want to deprive you of Arlene Pernowski's company."

"Arlene's happily married to a genius. What would really bother me would be missing even a moment of Karen Frank's performance."

Ellen reached across the table and patted Tom's hand. "But she's so much *younger* than you, dear."

Their waiter appeared beside their table with their food. When they had arrived at one o'clock, the place was already emptying. Now they were the only customers left in the place.

When the waiter had left again, Tom said, "I'm amazed they can afford to keep this place open. This should be the busiest time of year for them."

"With their prices, they don't need many customers," Ellen said. "Wait till you see the bill."

"You must have a high opinion of my income."

"I'm sure it's high enough to pay for our meal," Ellen said. "That's all that matters to me. I bleed men dry and use them up and throw them away. Didn't you know that? Hasn't Jack told you that yet?"

Their conversation had been light and cheerful up to that point. Tom contemplated his food for a long time. What the hell was he supposed to say in reply? "Jack hasn't said anything negative to me about you at all. He gave me the impression that the two of you are very happily married."

Now it was Ellen's turn to stare at her food. "On the whole," she said at last, "I guess we are. God knows I try. I do the right thing by him, in spite of the way he is. In spite of everything, I do love Jack, and I know that he loves me. It's more than just a matter of doing my duty or not having an alternative. But it's not the same as it was at first, when I was young and beautiful."

"You're still beautiful, Ellen."

Ellen looked up at him with a half smile. "Exactly. And the girls in Jack's classes are young." She waved her hand. "Oh, it's more than that. I suppose every wife has to deal with that problem once she reaches my age. At the beginning, Jack and I seemed to have a lot in common. At the very least, Jack seemed to respect my tastes and opinions. But you saw how he acted about my operas."

Should he tell her that Jack had always been a boor and she had been mistaken in those early years? It might be true, but saying so would accomplish little—except to end their lunch on a disastrous note. "I guess I'm not much help in this," Tom said. "I've never been in a relationship for more than a few months, so I don't really know anything about how people change toward each other after many years."

"But if you were married," Ellen said, "I bet you'd continue to respect and support your wife. Wouldn't you?"

Tom nodded. "I hope I would."

"It could have been very different for both of us, Tom. If

only you'd been as strong and forward back then as you are now."

For just a moment, it worked. Briefly, Tom believed she meant every word and he felt dangerous old emotions growing. But then he stepped back psychologically and looked at Ellen, weighing her expression, analyzing her, and he shook his head. "Nothing has really changed, Ellen. We're all much the same as we were. We'd better finish and get back to town."

Later, he wondered if he had been unfair to her. Perhaps the dismal state of her marriage had caused her to recreate the past in her memory as it should have been rather than as it really had been—both with respect to the young Jack Tourneau and the young Tom Hamilton. Perhaps her unhappiness explained it all.

Then he replayed the lunch in his memory and decided that his first instinct had been right. Ellen had been putting on an act and trying to manipulate him.

She might have been doing so as part of a desperate attempt to escape from an unhappy marriage. If so, then Tom could forgive her for grasping incautiously at what seemed to be an opportunity. But he still resented anyone's trying to manipulate him—or thinking they could. He would help Ellen with her opera if she asked him to, but he was not available to help her solve her personal problems. Those had begun when he was in Chicago, building a different life for himself, and they had nothing to do with him.

Eleven

"Second opening night," Tom said.

Jack shook his head. "Reopening night."

The other people in the group standing in the lobby added their own suggestions.

"Second performance," Ellen said firmly. "We had one virtually complete performance, and this is the second performance. Think positive."

"–ly," Jack said. "Zombie night. Frankenstein night. The opera's dead, but the evil Dr. Ellen Tourneau has zapped it with a zillion volts and given it the temporary appearance of life. Beneath that evanescent vitality, however, lies the sweet stench of death."

Once again, Jack had destroyed the conversation and made everyone uncomfortable.

"I'm going to check on the cast," Ellen said and walked away.

Jack snorted. "Just what those poor kids need." He fiddled with his tie and the buttons of his jacket. "What do you think of this suit, Tom? Better than anything my father used to wear, isn't it?"

Clothes don't make you the man he was, Tom thought. "Very nice."

"Scottish woolens place in Denver, on 17th Street. I'll give you the address."

"Good place," Fred Pernowski said. "I've bought a couple of suits there, too."

"I thought academics were supposed to be above such gross material things," Tom said.

"Only concerned with the finer things, you mean?" Fred asked.

"Yeah, like alcohol," Jack said. He glanced at his watch. "Half an hour before curtain time. Fred, I bet we could get ourselves a quick drink somewhere and still be back in plenty of time. Tom, you too."

"I'll pass, Jack," Tom said.

Fred Pernowski checked his own watch. "Well..."

"Don't be ridiculous," his wife said.

"Sure, let's go," Fred said to Jack.

The two men walked away quickly.

"Son of a bitch," Arlene Pernowski muttered.

Marriages are so solid and secure in small towns, Tom thought. Not like the big city, with all its stresses and strains.

Arlene recovered and put on a cheerful smile. "I'm going to go inside and find my seat. Want to come with me, Tom?"

"I'll stay out here for a bit longer. Stretch my legs."

Arlene looked him up and down, a calculating, weighing sort of look. "Perhaps you should have gone out with the guys for a drink," she said at last.

After she left, Tom walked over to Andy and Diane Snow. He had noticed them before, standing apart from everyone else.

Every time Tom glanced at them, they were talking to each other, and Andy Snow was even smiling. What an unlikely pair they were, and yet they seemed to be the happiest married couple in the place—possibly the only happily married couple there. Tom's curiosity was piqued.

"Hello, Diane," Tom said. "And Lieutenant."

"Hello, Tom," Diane said. "You've met my husband already, haven't you?"

She was smiling at Tom, but her husband was scowling. His wife stared at him until he responded to Tom's greeting. He pulled his chin in and rounded his shoulders like a boxer preparing to face a hard hitter. "Hamilton," he grunted, looking at the ground.

Diane said, "Andy." Her tone was mild, her smile was sweet, but her husband straightened his shoulders, looked at Tom finally, and held out his hand.

As they shook hands, Tom said, "I'm a bit surprised to see you here, Lieutenant. Are you hoping for some more excitement?"

"Oh, Ellen gave us a couple of complimentary tickets," Diane said. "She knows how much I love opera. And of course Andy didn't want me to have to go by myself, so he came with me."

A young man walked by lackadaisically swinging a hand bell up and down.

"I suppose that means we're supposed to take our seats," Tom said.

Diane grabbed her husband's hand and pulled him toward the entrance to the auditorium. "Come on, Andy! I don't want to miss a single note."

Andy Snow resisted for long enough to say to Tom, "Yeah, I *am* hoping."

Some breasts, Tom decided, are so savage that not even music has enough charms to soothe them.

He wasn't sure how it happened, but Tom found himself once again seated between Ellen and Arlene. The difference this time was that the two seats on the other sides of the two women were empty. Jack and Fred had not yet returned. The two abandoned wives chatted brightly with each other and with Tom and pretended to be unaware of their tardy husbands.

There was another difference between this performance and the disastrous first one. Tom noticed that the auditorium was packed this time. He assumed that it was morbid curiosity that had overcome the citizens of Ransom, not a sudden love of opera.

Unfortunately for Mike Berens, Mario Cavaradossi appears onstage early in the first act. He is supposed to appear striding briskly, but Mike came in hesitantly, looking at the audience instead of the painting he was supposed to be heading toward.

"They ought to shoot him now," Arlene whispered to Tom, "instead of keeping him in misery until the third act."

Mike launched into his first great aria, *Recondita armonia*, a bit too quickly, as though he shared Arlene's desire to get his misery over with. By the end of it, though, he was doing an adequate job. The opera fans in the audience gave him a generous hand, and the non-fans, those who were there only because of curiosity or persuasive spouses, took the cue and applauded loudly. The result was a longer and louder spate of clapping than Jerry Angleton had been awarded on his opening night.

Mike blossomed. He stood up straighter, puffed out his chest, and grinned at the audience. His new–found confidence lasted until later in the act, when Karen Franks' voice came from offstage, calling out, "Mario! Mario!" Mike froze in place, his mouth hanging open, as though he had only at that moment fully realized that he was about to share the stage and some love scenes with the girl of his fantasies.

When she came on–stage, Karen analyzed the problem immediately. While singing about her jealous suspicions, she walked up to the paralyzed tenor and added an improvised and very real slap across the face. Despite his size, Mike staggered back a step.

"Oh, er," Mike said. Then he earned Tom's admiration. He drew in a breath, let it out, drew in another, and reentered his role.

Unfortunately, at this point Jack and Fred came stumbling into the auditorium. They walked down the aisle talking to each other loudly as though unaware that the performance was already underway. They pushed their way down the row of seats toward their wives, stepping on toes all the way. Tom stood up to let Jack by, but Jack managed to step on the toes of both of Tom's feet anyway. The smell of alcohol as Jack passed by was almost suffocating. They collapsed noisily into their seats and Jack asked loudly, "Wod we miss?"

The audience erupted in laughter, and Mike Berens froze again.

Ellen sat with her eyes closed. Her face was white.

Karen Franks signaled offstage. The music stopped. Then she stalked to the front of the stage and stood facing the audience, hands on her hips. She stood quietly, unmoving, staring out into the auditorium until the laughter had died down. Then, her voice carrying to every corner of the room, she said, "You can laugh, or you can listen. If you want to laugh, go out into the parking lot. Now."

The members of the audience looked down at their shoes, transported back in time to their school days when they had sat in these same seats being admonished by the principal. No one chose to go out into the parking lot.

Karen nodded in satisfaction, walked back to center stage, and signaled to someone offstage. The music squealed in reverse for a few seconds and then started up again. Karen waited patiently until it reached the point where the audience, goaded by Jack and Fred, had interrupted the opera. Then she nodded to Mike Berens, and the performance resumed smoothly. Worship suffused Mike's face.

Ellen's too. "Wow," she muttered. She grinned at Tom, ignored her husband, and concentrated on what was happening on the stage.

The rest of the first act improved by the minute. When the curtain came down, the applause was long and sustained.

Tom walked out with Ellen and Arlene, leaving the two husbands semi-dozing in their seats. In the lobby, Ellen said worriedly, "Jack promised he'd do his part backstage during Act Three, but I'm wondering if he'll be able to stand up by then."

Arlene said, "He'll probably have metabolized it all by then. He's such a big guy, after all."

Ellen narrowed her eyes and looked at the other woman.

"Mike Berens is doing really well," Tom said quickly.

"And Karen?" Ellen said. "I'm sure you think she's even

more wonderful tonight than last time."

"I didn't notice," Tom said. "I was too blinded by Mike's singing."

"Blinded by singing," Ellen repeated. "That doesn't make any sense."

Jack and Fred came out of the auditorium. They stood in the doorway, swaying from side to side, while they squinted at the milling crowd. Finally they saw their wives and managed to navigate to their sides.

"Hi," Jack said, not meeting Ellen's eyes.

"You promised to be backstage during the third act," Ellen reminded him. Her tone was unemotional, her face expressionless. "Better be sober by then."

"Oh, Jesus," Jack sighed.

"Go get some coffee."

He shuffled away on a zig-zag path.

"Fred can help if Jack isn't up to it in time," Arlene said. "Fred recovers quickly, don't you, Fred?"

Fred looked far from recovered, but he managed an almost perky grin. "Ever Ready Freddy, that's what they call me."

"Who calls you that?" Tom asked.

Fred gestured vaguely. "They do."

"Thanks, Arlene," Ellen said, "but I want Jack to do it. It's his punishment."

The second act continued the improvement that Tom had noticed at the end of the first. By the second intermission, the crowd was delighted and Ellen was walking on air. Even Jack, who seemed almost sober again, was uttering an occasional grudging compliment.

Jack's sobriety was temporary, though, and it was fading again when the intermission drew to an end. "You gotta help me with this, Tom," Jack said. "Come on."

"You're going to do it by yourself," Ellen snapped. "And you'll do it properly."

"Fuck you," Jack muttered, but he said it so quietly that Tom doubted if Ellen heard it. Jack grabbed the arm of Tom's coat and pulled him away. "Stay with me, Tom. Which way is it?"

Tom resigned himself to the inevitable and led the way up the stairs to the stage and then across it. Jack followed, stumbling occasionally and cursing the dim lighting of the passageway they had to pass through.

When they got backstage, Jack seemed to be managing well enough at first. The two of them stood by the table holding the rifles, trying to keep their eyes on the weapons but also to keep out of the way of the backstage pandemonium. After a few minutes of this, however, Jack began to sway. He grabbed the edge of the table to keep himself steady. Fortunately, the table was heavy enough to bear his weight without tipping over.

"Kee–rist," Jack said. "Tom, get me a chair, wouldja?"

Tom found one that no one seemed to be using and brought it back. Jack collapsed into it with a loud groan.

"Keep the noise down," Tom whispered.

Jack waved his hand. "Yeah, yeah. How much longer?"

Tom listened to the voices from the stage. After traveling down the narrow passageway from the stage to where he and Jack waited, the voices were muffled and unmusical. It sounded so different from the opera Tom was familiar with that he had to listen intently for a while before he knew what was happening. "They've just started. At least twenty minutes yet."

Jack moaned and put his arms and head on the table, shoving the rifles aside. Tom grabbed wildly at the guns and barely managed to keep them from tumbling to the floor. Idiot, he thought, but he kept quiet and busied himself with rearranging the rifles on the part of the table that was still available.

Ellen showed up. Miraculously, Jack managed to be upright and alert just before she appeared, as though he had some sort of built–in radar that told him when she was coming. "Time to load up," she whispered. "Jack, you've got them?"

Jack nodded and patted the side pocket of his suit jacket. Metal clinked against metal. Tom wondered if Ellen was too preoccupied to see how vague and unfocused Jack's eyes were.

Perhaps she did, for she raised her voice slightly and said, with a sharp edge, "Blanks, right?"

Wounded dignity gave Jack the momentary appearance of sobriety. "Of course!" He took out the six cartridges and dropped them noisily on the table. "See?"

Ellen frowned. "If you say so."

Tom glanced at the cartridges and then away again. "They're blanks, Ellen," he said.

"Okay," she said. "Jack, you do it while we watch. And make sure there's nothing in any of them other than the blanks you're putting in. Quickly, please."

Jack went through the motions smoothly and quickly. Years of practice seemed to be compensating for any lingering effects from his earlier drinking. By the time he was finished, though, he was flushed and sweating. He struggled out of his jacket and let it slide to the floor.

Ellen grabbed it before it landed and draped it over the

back of the chair. "Damn it, Jack," she muttered.

How many drinks did Jack manage to cram down in that short time? Tom wondered. Maybe it doesn't take much. When he was at my house, he was affected pretty strongly by two drinks. He looked well sloshed at Kathy Angleton's house, too.

"All right," Ellen said. "Now you two guys stay here and keep your eyes on those things until the firing squad picks them up and takes them on-stage. Okay? Good."

She turned to go, then snapped her fingers and turned back again. "Damn, I just remembered something! Mike told me has to have his special lucky pen for the final scene, where he's supposed to be writing his last letter to Tosca."

"Special lucky pen?" Tom repeated.

"Are you shitting me?" Jack said.

Ellen shook her head. "This is for real. Opera singers can be very superstitious. If he isn't holding that particular pen, he won't be able to sing his final big aria."

"Jesus," Jack said.

Ellen looked at him, seeming to notice his glassy eyes for the first time. She turned to Tom. "He left it in his truck in the parking lot. He asked me to have someone get it, but I forgot. It'll just take you a couple of minutes, Tom. Please? We don't have anyone else to spare. It's an old Chevy pickup, painted blue. The door's not locked. It's just an old ballpoint. Mike said it's in the glove compartment, right on top of everything else."

"Right." Tom left through the rear stage entrance. He ran around the building and out into the parking lot. The vehicles parked there were illuminated by the flood lamps set along the walls of the auditorium, just below the roof, and the waning half moon high in the sky. Tom stopped in amazement. Had there always been this many old pickup trucks in Ransom?

Fortunately, only two of them matched Ellen's description, and one of those had both its doors locked. Unfortunately, there was no ballpoint pen in the glove compartment of the other one.

Tom checked the parking lot again as quickly as possible, but he couldn't find any other old blue Chevrolet pickup trucks. Mike's truck must be the locked one, he thought. Have to get the keys.

He ran back around the building and arrived backstage, panting and feeling dizzy, just in time to see the firing squad leaving with the rifles. Jack was half lying on the table, dozing.

Means I took too long and missed the aria, Tom thought. Damn! At least Mario doesn't actually use his pen on-stage.

He followed behind the firing squad, watching them carefully. He could see only the last man in the squad clearly. That man was doing nothing with his rifle other than carrying it. But what about the others, the ones partially blocked from Tom's view? In the few seconds their trip down the narrow passageway took, it would be possible for one of them to replace the blank cartridge with a live one he had brought with him. But if one of the men did that, then the man behind that man would surely see what was happening, so *that* man would have to be in on the plot.

Whatever the plot is, Tom thought. I don't even know what I'm really looking for.

He stopped in the wings and watched the squad go on-stage. He was stage right, and Karen Franks was on-stage not far from him. She was pretending to be waiting for the mock firing squad to finish its work, so that she could rush to her lover and escape with him.

Again the firing squad's rifles belched realistic flame and noise and the tenor fell to the stage with convincing blood spurting from his shirt front. "How well he acts!" Karen/Tosca sang.

Almost as well as Jerry Angleton, Tom thought. Of course, Jerry had a built-in advantage that one time.

The firing squad and the other actors trudged away, exiting stage left, leaving only Mike and Karen on-stage. Karen ran toward Mike and called out, "Get up, Mario!" She bent over him and gripped his shoulder.

Mike lay unmoving, but his eyes followed Karen's every move. Ellen would no doubt berate the boy later for not having kept his eyes closed after his supposed death, but Tom, seeing Mike's eyes open and moving, breathed a sigh of relief.

Karen stood up, looking at her hand. She sniffed at it. A look of disgust filled her face. "Oh, shit!" she yelled. "It's happened again!"

Twelve

This time, Andy Snow was the first member of the audience to mount the stage. He dropped to his knees beside the wounded tenor, then stood and faced the audience and yelled, "Shut up!"

Tom had reached Mike just moments after Snow. He listened appreciatively to the way Snow's voice filled the auditorium—better than Mike's during the performance so suddenly ended, and with a nicer tone. Then Tom gestured one of the members of the firing squad over. "There's a phone back stage?" he whispered.

The boy nodded.

"Get to it, and call for an ambulance."

The boy raced off. Tom turned to find himself staring up at Snow's red face.

"Oh, Christ, it's the Agatha Christie bad penny!"

"Ambulance is on its way."

Snow grunted. The sound could have been the word *thanks*, but it was hard to be sure. He turned back to the audience and yelled, "Christianson, Frasier, up here, quickly!"

A man and a woman in police uniform ran down the aisles from the auditorium entrance and climbed on-stage. They were carrying metal boxes. They pushed everyone else aside and knelt beside Mike Berens and set their boxes next to him. They began doing mysterious things to him. The woman pulled Mike's shirt open and worked on his chest while the man forced Mike's teeth apart. The man opened his metal box and drew a tube from it and inserted the tube into Mike's mouth. Tom turned away at this point.

"You were prepared for this," Tom said to Andy Snow.

"I used to be a Boy Scout." Snow raised his voice again. "Everyone, stay where you are! We'll be taking statements from all of you."

Just as had happened the first time, the audience made a mass rush for the exits. This time, though, the doors were blocked by uniformed policemen and women, and no one got away. Snow grinned happily. He turned to Tom and said, "You, too, Miss Marple. Get down there and act just like everyone else."

Snow and his men questioned each member of the audience. The stage and the backstage area were off limits to everyone except the police and medical personnel. Audience members who had not yet been talked to had to stay in their seats, like students being punished for the misdeeds of a fellow student. The interviews took place in the lobby, after which the interviewees were allowed to leave through the main entrance.

Snow saved Tom and the Tourneaus till the end. The other interviews had been fairly brief, but theirs weren't.

Snow spoke to them separately—Ellen first, then Tom, then Jack at the very last. When he questioned Tom, Snow asked him over and over to describe what he had done backstage during the opera. Tom told the same story each time in much the same words—the simple, boring truth. Before finally telling Tom he could leave, Snow said, "See, this is how it really works. It's not like Poirot sitting everyone down and explaining what happened."

"But he actually solved murders."

Snow glared at him. "I'll solve this one. It just takes some time. You sure as hell won't be able to snoop around. This place is going to be locked up after I'm finished here, and I'll be the only one with a key."

It was after midnight before Snow finished with Jack. Ellen had waited in the parking lot for her husband, and Tom waited with her. When Jack finally showed up, he was sober. Time and tension, Tom supposed, had burned off the alcohol. Instead of being drunk, he was now belligerent.

Jack had kept his anger under control while Snow was questioning him. Now he vented it at Ellen and Tom in the parking lot. "What has that guy got against me?" he yelled. "He's out to get me!"

"It's the nature of police work, Jack," Tom said. "Snow needs every detail he can get, from every possible viewpoint."

"So why did he keep asking me the same questions over and over? Trying to see if I was lying? Trying to make me say something different? God damn it, why are you defending him?"

Jack grew still angrier and more agitated. He was shifting from foot to foot restlessly, almost bouncing, reminding Tom of Fred Pernowski. It was fury, though, not energy that was making Jack move.

The parking-lot lights had been turned off, but the moon still hung above the mountains to the west, flooding the parking lot with its pale light. The moonlight made Jack's face look white and at the same time emphasized every fold and wrinkle. Watching him opening and closing his mouth and frowning and glaring, Tom thought that Jack looked like the reanimated corpse of an old man who had not been entirely sane when alive.

Tom said, "Sometimes when you describe a place or an event for the umpteenth time, you suddenly remember something you left out the first however many times." Why *am* I defending Snow? Tom asked himself. It's true that he's doing his job methodically, but it's also true that he seemed to enjoy inconveniencing us.

"I'm sure Tom's right," Ellen said. "I'm sure that's all it is. Where's your jacket?"

"What the fuck are you talking about?"

"Your jacket. It's part of your suit. Where is it? And your tie's gone, too."

"Fuck my fucking jacket!" Jack screamed. "It was hot in that fucking building! I took it off. I don't know where it is." He was already getting hoarse from shrieking, and he was almost incoherent.

I wonder if any of Jack's students are standing out there in the darkness watching and listening to all of this, Tom thought. Or the head of the CCC English department.

Ellen must have thought of the same thing. She said, "Let's confine the screaming and cursing to inside the house as usual, shall we? Come on." She started to walk away. Bellowing at a slightly lower volume, Jack followed her. They both seemed to have forgotten about Tom.

Tom watched them for a moment, glad to have drifted out of their joint attention. He caught himself thinking that Ellen could have done much better. He shook his head in annoyance at himself, and then turned away in the opposite direction and walked rapidly toward his own car.

Mike was luckier than Jerry Angleton. Or perhaps not, according to what he said to Ellen when she visited him in the hospital.

"Whispered, I should say," Ellen told Tom, "not said. He'll never be able to speak properly again, let alone sing. You should see the way the nurses up there at Max Health fuss over him, though. That should be some compensation."

That struck Tom as unlikely.

The firing squad had been less accurate than when they were shooting at Jerry. Perhaps that was due to their memory of what they had done to Jerry and their fear—justified, obviously—that it would happen again. Perhaps their good marksmanship the first time had been a fluke. Whatever the reason, all but one of the very real bullets had missed Mike. That one, however, had been sufficient. It had passed through his diaphragm and then his spine. Conceivably, he might have been able to pursue his original career goal of voice teacher while confined to a wheelchair if the damage had been limited to his spinal cord. As it was, his diaphragm would end up more scar tissue than muscle.

"I hope you didn't tell him he's lucky to be alive," Tom said. He felt a vast sadness for the boy's loss, more than he had felt for the loss of the far more talented Jerry Angleton. "At least he wasn't married. I don't mean to sound heartless, but that's a good thing in a case like this, don't you think?"

Ellen shrugged. "Depends." She glanced at her husband, who was lying on the couch barely conscious. "In some instances, what happened to Mike might make a wife very happy."

This conversation took place during and after dinner on Wednesday evening. It was supposed to be dinner for three, but it hadn't turned out that way. Jack had swayed visibly when he had answered the door, and he had kept drinking after the obligatory cocktail period and through dinner. Instead of dinner for three, it had started out as dinner for two and a half. It was down to two by the time Ellen brought out dessert.

Am I here to prove to Jack that my occasional lunches with Ellen are innocent? Tom wondered. No need for Ellen to bother. Jack had never shown any sign of jealousy.

Not because he trusts Ellen that much, Tom realized, but because he can't envision me as a rival. Tom was annoyed by that—and annoyed that it annoyed him.

Tom and Ellen sat in armchairs in the Tourneau living room drinking coffee and talking about the second shooting as though they were alone. It was almost like the lunches they were now in the habit of having together once a week.

Tom wished they were together in a restaurant instead of in this house with Jack managing to make his presence felt despite his lack of consciousness. Driving over here, Tom had let himself imagine that the evening would turn out all right. Applewood, the neighborhood the Tourneaus lived in, was a pleasant part of town, an upscale neighborhood near Colorado Central College, and it had pleasant associations for Tom.

Most of the residents were connected with the college—most of them in the higher levels of the administration, given the cost of the houses. The prices were considerably below what Tom had paid for his house, but nonetheless, by Ransom standards, those who lived in Applewood were among the blessed of the earth.

Tom had driven slowly through the curving streets of Applewood on his way to the Tourneaus' house this evening. As a boy, he had always walked here. Crabapple trees were planted everywhere. As an adult, he wondered if they were the source of the name. He wished it were May. He remembered that it was beautiful here when all the trees were in bloom and the smell of their blossoms filled the air. Now, in summer, he smelled the crisp, dry smell of pine needles.

This evening is starting out well, he had assured himself.

Now he felt like an idiot for having let himself fall into that delusion.

"It was good of you to visit Mike in the hospital," Tom told Ellen.

"It wasn't good *for* me. Anyway, I'm not the woman he wants to see there. I asked Karen to go see him."

"And she refused."

"How'd you guess?"

"Easy enough," Tom said.

Despite appearances, Jack wasn't quite asleep yet. He spoke suddenly, with surprising clarity. "Hey, Ellen, bet if you slid into the hospital bed with that kid, he'd be able to use his lower body again."

Ellen put her cup down on the saucer with a loud clatter. Her face was white with anger. "You bastard! That boy's life is ruined! He'll never sing again. He'll never make love to a woman again. How can you joke about it?"

Jack began to snore. He was smiling, though—a victorious smile, as though he'd just won an obscure battle.

Tom sat quietly, watching the two of them. It was, he thought, a bit like attending an Albee play but without the snappy lines.

Ellen looked down at her cup. Coffee had spilled from it when she'd set it down so hard, and it had run out of the saucer and into her lap. She stared from the spreading stain on her slacks to her husband as though unable to decide which needed to be removed first. "What a terrible accident," she said.

Tom set his cup and saucer on the table beside his chair and stood up. "I'll get you some paper towels."

"Oh, not this accident. I meant what happened to poor Mike Berens."

"Once is an accident. Not twice. My God, who would do something like this? And why?"

"A madman," Ellen said. "It has to be. I guess this lets Mike off the hook, anyway, doesn't it?" She stood up too. She gestured at Jack. "He's out for the night. Common pattern." She patted her thighs. "Why don't you get those paper towels and come upstairs with me and help me clean this up?"

They stood still, staring at each other for quite a while. Whether I say yes or no, Tom thought, I'll hate myself for it afterwards. Finally, he said, "It's not a good idea, Ellen. I'd better leave now."

Driving home, he thought, I was right about one thing: I said no, and now I hate myself.

Awaiting him at home was a message on his answering machine from Andy Snow. Would Mr. Hamilton please stop by Lieutenant Snow's office as soon as possible, but no later than the following afternoon? Just a few questions.

The mills of Snow grind slow but exceeding fine, Tom thought. He was surprised it had taken Snow this long to get around to him.

Tom had planned to visit the county building the next morning, so he decided to go to Snow's office on the way. He didn't mind answering whatever questions Snow had, and he would be happy to see the inside of the police building again, with its old feelings of safety and shelter. In addition, he had to admit to himself, he had a sudden desire to see just how far he could push Snow and how the detective would react to being pushed. Snow was an interesting psychological puzzle in and of himself, almost as interesting as the question, Who Is Shooting the Great and the Adequate Tenors of Ransom?

Snow was on the telephone when Tom walked in his door. Snow twisted in his chair and looked up to see who had entered, and he groaned. He finished his conversation hurriedly and hung up. "Glad you could make time for me, Mr. Hamilton. So kind of you. Have you solved the whole case yet?"

"Not quite yet, Lieutenant. I should have it all wrapped up by lunch time, though."

"Yeah, right. Poirot would know all the answers already, wouldn't he? Sit down, Hamilton."

Tom sat down in the same uncomfortable wooden chair he had sat in on his previous visit. "Lieutenant, before you start asking me questions, I'd like to ask you something. Do you think it's possible that both shootings were accidents?"

Snow paused—not to consider the question, Tom knew, but to consider whether to reply at all. When he spoke, his reluctance was obvious. "Of course not. Someone deliberately switched the ammunition before the kids playing the firing squad went on-stage. Now it's my turn. The way I reconstruct things, with this second shooting, two people had the maximum opportunity to fuck with the ammo—you, and Jack Tourneau. I've spoken to Professor Tourneau, and he says he was so drunk, he doesn't remember what was going on around him. Any comment?"

"Jack was pretty drunk, yes," Tom said, nodding. "I'm not sure he even knew where he was. I saw him put blanks in the rifles. I don't think he was in any shape to change the loads later on."

"That's commendably honest of you, Hamilton. So that leaves you."

"Opportunity, but no motive."

Snow stared at Hamilton thoughtfully and scratched his cheek. "Missed a spot. Don't you hate that—you shave carefully, but then you find you've missed a spot?"

"Maybe you could arrest someone for it," Tom said.

"I'll have a motive once I find out where you've been for the last twenty-three years."

"Twenty-two," Tom said reflexively.

Snow grinned. "Right you are."

Tom laughed. "Now that you've won the game, can I go?" He had planned to push Snow, but the pushing had been in the other direction. He must not underestimate this man.

He remembered the scene on-stage just after Mike Berens had been shot. Paramedics were working on Mike. They were there because Snow had had them stationed outside the auditorium, ready. Snow was ignoring them, trusting them to do their job properly, while he scanned the stage and the audience. Snow had radiated alertness, intelligence, and eagerness. At that moment, Tom had realized that Snow had the kind of ambition that had made some policemen Tom had known in Chicago so vulnerable to corruption, open to the offers Tom had passed on from the men he worked for. That sort of environment was Snow's natural one, not a town like Ransom. And that had been the sort of place Snow had worked in before. Tom wondered what Snow had done to get himself exiled from those urban opportunities—and how much he'd do to get back to them.

"I think maybe you're my prime suspect now," Snow said. "I don't have to tell you to stick around, do I? I've been having a hard time finding out where you lived before you came here. Which makes me suspicious all by itself. But it also tells me you have ways of vanishing when you want to. Don't try to do it now."

At least Mike's not his prime suspect any more, Tom thought. Maybe I should test that. "You know that Mike Berens had a strong motive for getting Jerry Angleton out of the way, don't you? Professional opportunity and romantic jealousy."

"Yeah, I know all about that," Snow said. "And he was high on my list until he got shot."

"A perfect way to divert suspicion from himself. Berens was hit by one bullet, unlike Angleton. That implies that one member of the firing squad was deliberately aiming at him—aiming carefully, carefully enough to wound him but not kill him. That one person might have been an accomplice of Mike's, part of the plot, whatever it is."

"Don't be ridiculous," Snow said. "No one's gonna take a chance like that. The kid's been crippled, and he came real close to being killed. Even if he was willing to sacrifice his career, which I've been told is what's happened to him, he wouldn't trust some friend of his to aim that well. No one shoots that accurately."

Tom had worked with people who did indeed shoot that accurately. "You're probably right," he said. "I'm sure you know far more about such matters than I do. I've never fired a gun in my life." That part was close to the truth.

"Doesn't surprise me," Snow said with a sneer. "Nice try, anyway. You're still number one on my list."

When he left the building, Tom stood still for a moment, adjusting to the heat and bright sunshine. Strange, he thought, that so many men thought that knowing about guns and shooting was part of being a man, and that someone like Tom, who freely admitted lack of such knowledge, was thereby proving that he wasn't really a man. "I'm a medieval history buff," he could have told Snow. "I bet I know more about cross bows than you do." He knew that wouldn't have helped.

It would have helped matters if he'd told Snow about being out of the building searching for Mike Berens' lucky pen during the crucial few minutes while the blanks were replaced with live rounds. He wasn't sure why he'd said nothing about that. He'd save that for the right moment, he decided.

Thirteen

Records of real property transactions were kept in the County Assessor's office, which was located on the second floor of the county building. The county building was across the street from police headquarters.

Everything was close to everything else in Ransom. During his teens, that had made the place seem claustrophobic to Tom. It had made the town difficult to hide in, to lose himself in. Chicago, by contrast, had been a revelation and a wonder. The city's size and extent and diversity had been exhilarating. But by the time he had left Chicago, his face and name had been known everywhere, and the city had become threatening in its very anonymity. Death could be waiting for him around any corner, down any side street. Now, Ransom seemed safe, controllable, within his compass.

The records kept by the Assessor were all public record. At the long counter which separated visitors from the desks of the employees, Tom wrote his name and address on a short form, signed at the bottom where he promised that he had no criminal purpose in requesting information, and paid a ten-dollar fee. The clerk on duty, a thin older man with a grey face, a rattling smoker's cough, and the biggest bags under his eyes that Tom had ever seen on a human being, stepped through the opening in the counter and admitted Tom to a small room filled with metal shelves.

The clerk pointed to the leather binders stacked on the shelves. "Those are the records of property transfers, arranged by year and then alphabetically by street."

"You're kidding," Tom said. "It's all on paper? You haven't automated this stuff?"

The clerk scowled at him. "We've got computers. New records are on computer. Some of the older—" He paused for a long, frightening series of coughs that stirred an evil memory in Tom. After he had caught his breath, the clerk continued, "Some of the older ones are on microfiche. The time period you wanted is still on paper. We haven't got the money or manpower to put the old records on the machine. This isn't Denver, you know. They're all pansies up there."

Tom decided to let the matter drop. He would deal with the old paper records. And, as it turned out, the clouds of dust that rose from the relevant binder when he opened it.

He might as well have saved his time and his ten dollars. He gleaned nothing from the records for 133 North Elm that gave him any clues about his mother's fate.

There was a surprise in the records, though. At the time of Tom's birth, the house had been jointly owned by Donald and Angela Morisetti. Morisetti had been Tom's mother's maiden name. It was scarcely a common name in Ransom—or in this part of the country, for that matter. So the house had presumably been owned by Tom's mother's family. But after the disappearance of Tom's mother, the tax records showed Tom's father, Al Hamilton, as the owner.

Tom had not known that about the previous ownership of the house. Nor could he remember anything about the Morisettis. His mother had once said something vague about her parents being dead, but that was all she had said about them. That was during the same conversation in which she'd told her son that her maiden name was Morisetti. She had almost never spoken about her background, her childhood, her life before marriage. With a guilty shock, Tom realized that he'd never asked her about any of it. He hadn't even known that she too was a Ransom native, as this record indicated. He had been self–absorbed throughout childhood. Then she was gone, and it was too late.

When she disappeared, there had been no communication, no worried inquiries, from any family on her side.

Not from any on Tom's father's side, either. His father had had a brother and a sister, but Tom couldn't remember his father having any contact with them.

His father had died the year before Tom returned to Ransom. Tom had known about the death. He had known about his father's physical decline during the two years before that, too. Tom had not visited the old man during the two years when Al Hamilton was coughing and wheezing his way to the grave, and he had not come home for the funeral. Al had sold the house a year before his death and had used the profits to pay for medical care. His insurance from the school district had run out by then. Lung cancer is an expensive way to die.

And painful. Did you suffer enough, you old bastard? However much it was, it wasn't enough.

Tom closed his eyes and willed himself to calmness. He

prided himself on his self-control. He wasn't going to let the long-dead past rule him.

He opened his eyes again and concentrated on the official paperwork in front of him. This was his element. And this—calmness, detachment, emotionless intellectualizing—was how he had coped with the moral dilemma posed by his work in Chicago. The approach had served him well for years.

Follow the trail, he told himself.

Al Hamilton had sold the house to someone named Garrison. And then Al Hamilton had died. End of the trail.

He sat back and closed his eyes again. This time, he wasn't seeking calm. He was visualizing the interior of the house at 133 North Elm.

The front door opened into a small, cramped living room. He could see his father lounging in the armchair to the left. Al had a beer can in one hand and a cigarette in the other. He was wearing jeans and a T-shirt. The T-shirt fit tightly, showing his muscular arms and chest. The sort of father a boy should be able to admire and want to look like some day, Tom thought, instead of fearing.

A small black-and-white television was set against the far wall, opposite Al. His attention was glued to the screen. Even if Tom had been real, not a ghost of his own imagination, Al would have ignored him—except perhaps to yell at him not to block the screen as he passed by.

Tom might be there only in his imagination, yet he could smell the beer and the cigarette smoke, and the sickening sweetness of the stale beer spilled on the floor from previous cans and the stench of old cigarette butts in the ashtray on the floor beside the armchair.

Tom realized, suddenly, what the scene in Kathy Angleton's living room had reminded him of.

His memory carried him across the wooden floor with its scratches and gouges and burn marks from dropped cigarettes, and into the kitchen beyond. To his right, the stairway up to the bedrooms on the second floor. To the left, a small bathroom. Ahead, the kitchen.

It was the biggest room in the house. The table—white Formica on top, aluminum legs—filled up the center of the room. His mother's cookbooks were its centerpiece, held up by metal bookends from Sears. This room was as close to being Kay Hamilton's domain as it was possible for any part of this house of terror to be. He could see her standing in front of the stove, small and slender like him, frowning in concentration, escaping into cooking. When he was a boy, Tom had often resented her absorption in that task. It had taken her away from him, shut him out of her life. Now he understood that she had needed that escape. In his mind, she looked up from the pot she was stirring and smiled lovingly at him. *Welcome home, darling,* she said. *Did you have a good day?*

I've had so few good days, Mom. But it's a lot better than it used to be. I wish you were still alive to see how much better things are.

At the far end of the kitchen was the door to the basement. He imagined himself opening the door, switching on the light over the wooden stairs, and going down into the basement.

The space at the bottom of the stairs was cramped and shadowy. There was space for little more than the furnace and hot-water heater. Most of the extra space was taken up with piles of junk—stored down here against future need, supposedly, but all covered with dust and spider webs.

This was the important part. Tom concentrated, frowning in unconscious imitation of his mother, and visualized the basement floor.

He could probably buy the house. He could offer a purchase price well above its worth—surely enough to pry even the most attached homeowner loose. Then he could dig up the basement floor and make sure there was no body buried beneath it. But the longer he thought about it, the more convinced he was that the floor had always been the same. After his mother's disappearance, the floor had remained undisturbed. His mother was not buried down there.

Tom sighed, opened his eyes, and relaxed.

The offices of the *Roundup* were in the same block as the county building. Here, at least, all records were on microfiche.

Tom sat in a cool, quiet, well-lit, thoroughly anonymous room and skimmed each page of each edition of the newspaper published during the year of his mother's disappearance. Fortunately, the *Roundup* had been a small paper in those days. Its growth in size in an attempt to compete with the two dailies from the urban giant next door had happened during his years of absence. Unfortunately, he found no mention of his mother.

There was a section titled "Police Blotter" in most editions of the paper. The items in it ranged from traffic tickets for minor infractions to the very rare murder. There were even two missing-persons reports during the year he was looking at. But his mother's disappearance was not there. Had there been no one who noticed that she had vanished? No one who both noticed and cared? No one besides Tom?

No frantic, grief-stricken husband, certainly. And once again, no relatives of the missing woman.

It was more than a hunch but less than a full-blown theory that caused Tom to request the microfiches for the year of his birth and the two years thereafter. The article was on the second page of the Sunday edition, in the middle of July of the year in which Tom had turned one.

LOCAL MAN DIES IN MOUNTAIN ACCIDENT

Donald Morisetti, 67, a retired mining engineer, died in a tragic accident in the mountains this weekend. Morisetti was with his son-in-law, Alfred Hamilton, also of Ransom, when he fell down a steep hillside into South Tournant Creek.

Alfred Hamilton, who is employed as a janitor at Ransom High School, reported that the two men were fishing downstream earlier in the day and decided to try their luck higher up. "We had bad luck all day," Al Hamilton said. "I caught a couple of small Rainbows, and poor Don didn't catch anything. So we thought maybe it would be better higher up."

While they were climbing over a rock slide, the older man lost his footing and tumbled approximately twenty feet onto sharp boulders along the creek bank. Heedless of his own safety, Al Hamilton ran down the hillside to help, but his father-in-law was already dying from his injuries.

"I held him," an obviously grief-stricken Hamilton told the Roundup. "He died in my arms. The last thing he said was to tell me to take care of his daughter and wife and grandson."

Mr. Hamilton then drove into town to get help. Because it

was dark by then, nothing could be done that night. The body was brought out at first light the next day. An autopsy has confirmed that Mr. Morisetti died of a broken neck and severe head injuries.

There was more about Al Hamilton's grief. Tom gritted his teeth and forced himself through those paragraphs, just in case there was useful information in them. There wasn't.

Was he supposed to believe in Al's grief? It seemed transparently, intuitively obvious to Tom that his father had pushed his grandfather down the slope. Perhaps the fall hadn't really killed Donald Morisetti, and Al had hurried down the hill to finish the job. A competent autopsy would very likely have revealed the truth, but it didn't seem likely that the autopsy performed on Donald Morisetti had been competent and complete. In a town as small as Ransom in the days when Donald Morisetti had died, coroners were often untrained, not even MDs. The law might have required an autopsy in such a case, but that didn't mean that the man performing the autopsy knew what he was doing, or that he was likely to look very hard for signs of something unusual.

By now, Tom had convinced himself that Al Hamilton had murdered his father-in-law.

But why? What motive would he have had?

There was always the motive Tom knew so well: Al Hamilton's unprovoked, unpredictable rages. He had beaten his son and he had beaten his wife. Why not assume that he had been quick to strike his father-in-law as well? Donald Morisetti had been 67 at the time of his death. If, added to the physical weakness due to age, he had had a slight build like that of his daughter and grandson, then he would have been no match for the powerful and brutal Al Hamilton.

At the end, the article included a few paragraphs covering Donald Morisetti's career, the date of his marriage to Angela Patti of New York City, their move West, the birth of their daughter.

Tom stopped reading at that point and stared at the print. His mother's birth in a hospital in Denver. Another detail he had been ignorant of until now.

He started reading again—greedily, hungry for any details about his mother and grandparents. There was little enough. It was Donald Morisetti's death that fascinated the reporter, not his life. And his widow and surviving daughter seemed to be uninteresting compared to the colorful details supplied by Al Hamilton—how he had made his way down the loose hillside, how he had then climbed back up it, scraping his hands and knees ("He showed this reporter the large scabs encrusting both."), how he had run all the way down the trail to his father-in-law's pickup truck, how he had raced through the fading light down out of the mountains into town, how he had begged the police to go back up with him right away, despite the darkness, on the off chance that his father-in-law might still be alive.

This was not the father Tom Hamilton remembered. He wondered what his mother had made of the article.

It was enough. He took the sheet of microfiche from the machine, turned the viewer off, pushed his chair back, and stood up. It was all he could bear.

Fourteen

It was mid-afternoon when Tom came out of the *Roundup* building. He looked at his watch and suddenly felt hungry. He thought of going home and having leftovers. It wasn't an appealing thought. Then he remembered Janice Sheridan.

He hadn't spoken to her since their second lunch together. He felt guilty about that. They had seemed to be establishing a kind of friendship, and he knew that had she looked the way she did in high school, he would have been eager to pursue that friendship. Instead, he had let himself get wrapped up in the shootings of the two tenors and in research into his own past, and he had forgotten all about her.

He checked his watch again. It was 2:30. Surely she would have already eaten. He was sure that she couldn't just leave her office whenever she wanted to.

It was worth a try, though.

It turned out that the workers at the Department of Motor Vehicles were allowed two fifteen-minute coffee breaks, one in the morning and one in the afternoon. Tom arrived at the license bureau just as Janice was getting up from her desk.

"What a very civilized custom," Tom said approvingly.

Janice stared at him as though he were crazy. "They let the animals out for fifteen minutes twice a day, and you call it civilized?"

"Compared to being chained to the loom. But I take your point. Janice, I haven't eaten lunch yet, and I'm starving. If you'll come with me and promise not to tell me that I'm still weird, I'll buy your coffee."

"And a slice of cake."

"Whatever you like. I don't know about getting back here in fifteen minutes, though."

She shrugged. "Screw that part."

"Wonderful. I don't suppose any Indian restaurants have opened up here in the last twenty–two years."

"Indian? You mean like Chief Sitting Bull?"

"No, I mean like Mahatma Gandhi."

"Christ, Tom, you're not *still* weird, you're weird in a whole new way. There's a pretty decent Mexican place around the corner."

"Do they serve slices of cake?"

"I've changed my mind," Janice said. "I feel like a meal."

As they left, they passed the same two young women who had given him dismissive glances on his earlier visit to the office. This time, they seemed to be looking at him with open invitation. When they reached the sidewalk and the door had closed behind them, Janice said, "I told those two where you live now and what kind of car you drive. Told them you'd paid cash for both your house and your car."

"Money makes a man taller?"

"Absolutely. Money makes up for everything."

"Really? Would you have stayed married to Chuck

Hathaway if he'd had lots of money?"

They walked together in silence while Janice thought this over. Finally, she said, "Damn! I don't know the answer to that!" After another silence, she said, "Hell, no. I'd have left him even then. But I'd have gotten half the money in the divorce settlement."

"I remember that when you used to do those daredevil cheerleader tumbling routines, you always landed on your feet."

She chuckled. "I sure as hell wouldn't try to do those now, but I am still landing on my feet. So you used to watch me back then?"

"Religiously."

"In my little purple dress. I was really something, wasn't I?"

"You were the stuff that adolescent boys' dreams are made of."

Janice sighed loudly. "And now I'm the stuff that pastry chefs' dreams are made of. I'll tell you, Tom, I really don't care. I lost my need to be attractive to men around ten years ago. Here's the place."

Tom hadn't really been paying attention as Janice led the way down the block from the license bureau and then around the corner and down a side street. He had been much more interested in what she was saying. Now he found that they were in the middle of a seedy, run-down commercial block. Most of the businesses were closed and boarded up. They were in front of one of the few that were still in business. It was a restaurant, and the windows had thick bars protecting the glass. On the sidewalk beside the entrance was a broken bottle of cheap wine.

"A very young wine," Tom said. "Little body or bouquet, but a very satisfactory buzz." He read the name painted on the restaurant windows in bright green paint. "La Estrellita. Are you sure you want to go in here? Will I need a latex suit?"

"The food's great. Come on."

The tables filling the center of the large space were Formica and the chairs were covered with badly patched vinyl. Along the walls were booths, the seats of which were also covered with patched vinyl. They chose a booth.

The service was remarkably quick. Their waiter, a distracted young Hispanic man whose attention was on one of the waitresses, brought them their plates five minutes after they'd ordered. He thumped their plates down and muttered, "Hot plates. Watch it." Then he was off to take care of another table, but watching the waitress all the while. She was worth watching, Tom thought.

Hesitantly, Tom used his teaspoon to sample the sauce on his burrito. "Damn! This is *great*! This is gourmet green chili, compared to what I had in—where I've been."

Janice waited for him to say more but didn't prompt him for a place name. "Not Mexico, anyway," she said. "So you like it?"

"I certainly do." Tom looked around the large, dimly lit space. It looked much bigger on the inside than it had from outside. Most of the customers, he was interested to note, were Anglo. And there were a lot of them, even this late in the day.

The walls were painted dark green. Directly on the walls, someone had painted scenes of life in a village that had surely never existed in Mexico or anywhere else. The artist had signed each painting with a proud though illegible flourish. Tom chuckled.

"Don't do that," Janice said angrily. "Those drawings don't

have to be museum quality. They're there for the atmosphere, and the food is damned good. You said so yourself."

"Sorry. It's just..." Tom thought for a while. "Look, when I was still living here, I didn't know anything about art or opera. Or literature. Anything. In my house, music meant country and western. Pictures meant whatever was on that month's page of the calendar. I didn't learn anything about any of that until I left here. I educated myself—about music, art, literature, food, wine, politics, history. It wasn't easy. I transformed myself. I changed from being Al Hamilton's scared, stupid, ignorant, beaten kid to being a man who knew things, who understood things, who was respected." He stopped, surprised at his own passion, at his revelation of this much of himself.

Janice's anger softened. "Tom, those paintings on the wall don't threaten any of that. You can just look at them and enjoy them. That won't undo everything you've done and change you back into what you used to be." She forked some of her taco salad into her mouth and chewed it and swallowed it while she watched Tom absorb what she had said. Then she added, "Besides which, you aren't remembering yourself correctly. You knew too much even when you were a kid. I always thought you were a stuck-up snob back then. But you were scared. I guess I could see that a bit."

A stuck-up snob, Tom repeated to himself. Well, well. This has certainly been a day for revelations.

His food forgotten, he concentrated on the painting on the wall above their booth. It depicted a village square filled with grinning young men and women walking back and forth across the square, their arms about each other. An old man sat on a chair to one side, playing an accordion. Another old man next to him played a guitar. Old women watched the young people indulgently. It was an absurd fantasy, but a happy one.

It's a village without fear, Tom thought suddenly. That's what makes it seem so fantastic and unbelievable to me.

It was a scene from another world, one in which the Chicago and Ransom he had known could not have existed. He had lied to Janice. He had never managed to be respected. He had been feared.

Completely absorbed in the paintings, he examined the next one along the wall. This picture showed a group of women doing their laundry at a riverside. It was as impossibly happy and carefree a scene as the one in the first painting, and as far removed from reality as Tom understood it.

He couldn't make out the next painting because the angle was too acute. He switched his attention to the far wall. A group of men were shown in a bar, but they lacked the sense of depression and tension Tom associated with bars. Instead, those men were smiling, too. It was a friendly and relaxed place. Inviting, Tom admitted. If he were a frequenter of bars, that was the one he'd want to go to regularly.

And the next painting—

The next painting was of no interest compared to the couple who were in the booth below it. It was Jack Tourneau and Kathy Angleton, holding hands across the table and staring into each other's eyes.

Janice had followed his gaze. "The son of a bitch," she said quietly. "Ten years ago, he was a hell of a lot more discreet."

A fit of mean-spirited lunacy passed over Tom. "Let's take our plates over there and join them. For old times' sake."

Janice looked at him in astonishment. Then she grinned.

"Old times, huh? The old Tom Hamilton would never have done anything like that."

"The old Tom Hamilton was a dweeb. Or whatever we used to call kids like that back then. I've forgotten."

"We used to call you a nerd. Yeah, let's do it!"

Fortunately, their plates were no longer hot.

When he saw them standing up holding their plates and silverware, the waiter hurried over. "Is something wrong? Do you need something?"

"We're moving over there," Tom said, gesturing with his chin.

"To sit with some old friends," Janice added.

"We'll take care of this, if you can bring our other stuff," Tom said. Your tip will be very large. He tried to convey that thought with his smile, but he thought the waiter's expression betrayed annoyance nonetheless. He masked his annoyance well, though, which in Tom's view helped earn him a large tip.

Tom had intended to lead the way and sit next to Jack, but Janice was ahead of him. She stood in front the booth in which Jack Tourneau and Kathy Angleton were sitting and boomed, "Hey, Jack, fancy meeting you here! What a lucky accident! Mind if we join you guys? Come on, Tom, let's sit with them. Move over, Jack."

Jack and Kathy released each others' hands and shrank back from her in horror, squeezing themselves against the wall on the far side of the booth. Janice put her plate and silverware on the table beside Jack and sat down. Tom couldn't tell how she did it, but she seemed to spread out somehow, to become even fatter, so that Jack was forced to stay pressed against the wall.

Tom slid into the booth next to Kathy. "Good afternoon,

Mrs. Angleton," he said. "I hope we're not interrupting anything."

"Oh, you know her already," Janice said. I was just going to ask Jack to introduce us to his new friend. Angleton, you said?"

Since Jack seemed still unable to speak, and Kathy was looking from Tom to Janice and back as though she were a rabbit and they were foxes, Tom said, "This is Kathy Angleton, Janice. Mrs."

"She's a widow," Jack said defensively.

Janice had been raising a loaded fork to her mouth. She dropped it back on her plate. "You're so young! I'm really sorry."

Kathy looked at her gratefully. "Thanks. I'm starting to get used to it, I guess. A bit."

"With Jack's help?" Tom asked.

"He's good at that," Janice said. "When a girl hits a rough place in her life, Dr. Jack is there."

Kathy looked down at her hands, now safely in her lap, and said nothing.

Tom toyed with his food. "Have you ordered yet?"

"We've changed our minds," Jack said abruptly. "Move, Janice." He made getting–up motions. When Janice didn't move fast enough, he practically pushed her out of the way as he slid out of the booth.

Tom stood up and let Kathy get out. Jack took her hand and pulled her behind him as he stalked out of the restaurant.

Tom and Janice sat down again. They stared at each other for a moment. Janice said, "That *was* kind of like old times after all."

"Which old times are you referring to?"

The waiter spared her the need to answer. He approached

their booth holding two loaded plates. "These are hot," he said mechanically. Then he noticed that the original two customers had left. "Are they coming back?" he asked.

"Not in this century," Janice said. "Leave the food. We'll take care of it."

As he watched her devouring one of the newly arrived burritos, Tom said, "Back in the good old days, when I used to watch you tumbling in that little purple dress, I never realized you had such a large appetite."

Janice chuckled. "I would have swallowed you in one bite back then." She picked up a floured taco, rolled it tightly, and bit off a third of it.

Tom toyed with his own food, watched her, and mulled over a variety of strange and tangled images.

Fifteen

It was a bit of shock to Tom to realize that this was Friday—not even a week since the performance during which Mike Berens had been shot. It seemed more like a month. Oddly enough, the pace of events in Ransom had proved to be faster than that in Chicago.

And his answering machine was busier here than his voice mail there had been. When he got back from his extended late lunch with Janice—extended by Janice's wish to order a margarita and dawdle, and then a second margarita, and then a third—he found three messages waiting for him.

One was from Andy Snow, asking him to drop by again at his earliest convenience, but no later than noon the following day. Tom shook his head and wondered what the man was up to with this petty harassment.

The second was from Jack Tourneau. It was a speech—long, slurred, rambling, and angry. The gist of it was that if Tom ever did again anything like what he had done that afternoon in La Estrellita, Jack would beat the crap out of him. "And that goes for your fat friend, too," Jack concluded. Tom heard a female laugh in the background, and then Jack hung up. Tom was interested to note that Jack's bluster had no effect on him at all, but that he felt offended and angry on Janice's behalf.

The third message was from Ellen Tourneau.

"Tosca lives," she said. "We open again in two weeks. Third time's the charm. Call me, Tom. I'm going to need your help a lot this time around."

He called her. As he listened to the sound of the ring, waiting for Ellen to answer, Tom wondered how many tenors with a death wish there could be in a town the size of Ransom.

"Hello?" Her voice was so dull and subdued, that for a moment Tom wasn't sure it was Ellen.

"Hi, this is Tom Hamilton."

"Tom!" Now it certainly was Ellen, cheerful and warm, glad to hear from him, her attention focused on him and him alone.

"I got your message."

"Yes, that one. The one I left on your machine. Well, we're going to do it again. Nothing can kill opera. Jack's become more unreliable than ever, so I'd like you to be my main helper this time around."

"Are you going to use a recording for the Mario role this time?"

Ellen laughed. Given what had happened to her first two Cavaradossis, it was a remarkably cheerful laugh. "No, of course not! I've scrounged someone up. Name's Ken Hillerman. He's inexperienced, but he's a natural talent. I think he'll do."

"You're going to train someone without any background, and you'll have him ready to perform in two weeks? Ellen, that's ridiculous."

"It won't be easy. We should discuss this further. And talk about what I want you to do. We have a lot to discuss. We left things hanging when you were at the house. Why don't you come over now, and we'll settle a lot of things?"

Or I could just go up to the zoo in Denver and jump into the cage with their Bengal tigress. "Is Jack there? He left me a message today, too, and I'd like to discuss that with him."

"Of course he's not here. Don't be a fool. Do you think I'd be asking you to come over if he were here? I haven't seen Jack since this morning. He probably called you from his office."

"I suppose so." But Tom didn't think so. There had been something about the call, and something about the female laugh he had heard, that made him think otherwise.

"So how long will it take you to get here?" Ellen prompted. "Fifteen minutes?"

"It's still not a good idea, Ellen."

"Tom, damn it, I've waited for you for over twenty years!"

He couldn't keep himself from laughing at that. "Really? Pining every day? Worshipping my picture in the high school yearbook?"

Ellen laughed, too. "Oh, all right, so I exaggerated a bit. But as soon as I saw you that night at the first Tosca, I realized that I should have been waiting for you. We're not old yet, Tom. We can still undo our mistakes."

Not all of them, he thought. "I'll call you tomorrow," he said finally. "For tonight, I want a quiet evening at home. Alone."

"I've missed our lunches," Ellen said. "We kind of stopped doing that. How about tomorrow?"

Tom patted his stomach. Still hard and firm, but that wouldn't last. This was another difference with the old days. After his mother's disappearance, he had spent much of his remaining time in Ransom underfed and hungry. Now he was spending his days here overfed and stuffed. The girls he had been hopelessly in love with had grown into women who kept wanting him to eat. "Do you like Mexican food?"

"Pretty much, yes."

"I'll take you to a place downtown. Quite good. I just found out about it today."

"Is it one of those grungy hole-in-the-wall places where the food is surprisingly good?"

"It is indeed a grungy hole-in-the-wall that holds surprises."

"Sounds great." To his relief, Ellen hung up without urging him again to come to her house.

Tom looked at his inviting living room and its view of the lights in the town below, and he sighed in regret. He really had been anticipating with pleasure a quiet evening at home alone, with beautiful music on the CD player, a small glass of bourbon on the table beside his armchair, and a good book. "I have lived for art and bourbon," he muttered. "Retired for it, at any rate."

He left the lights on in the living room so that the house would look occupied. Then he left and drove down the hillside into town.

In the late twilight, Lincoln seemed not just run down but alien and threatening. There were few parking spaces available. People had returned from work, and the curbsides were occupied by a range of old cars—the sort of cars whose drivers breathed a prayer of thanksgiving at the end of each commute, thanking God that their vehicles had made it all the way.

Kathy's house was in the middle of the block. The closest parking space Tom could find was at the end of the block. Much better this way, of course. He'd prefer that no one in the house know he was there. Not yet. He felt uneasy, though, getting out of his new, expensive, dramatically out-of-place car and walking down the dim sidewalk.

It'll be dark soon, he told himself, and no on will be able to see my car properly. But he didn't really believe his own reassurances. As a boy, he'd always had the feeling that hostile eyes were forever watching him, and the years in Chicago had reinforced that feeling.

And in fact, he could still see the cars along the curb well enough to note the other one that looked out of place. He had missed it somehow when he had driven past the Angleton house, looking for a parking space. This car was also new, a pale gold Accura Legend. It was parked in front of Kathy's house. Tom stared at it, wondering if it represented insurance money. Had Jerry Angleton's golden tenor turned into this?

It was surprisingly quiet. This was the sort of neighborhood, Tom judged, in which people not only owned dogs but let them run loose. Fortunately, none seemed to be running loose at the moment. He half expected a pack of them to show up any moment—barking loudly at best, menacing him at worst. He stepped off the sidewalk and onto the patchy grass between Kathy's house and the one next to it. This wall of the Angleton house was windowless, just an expanse of vertical wooden boards with the paint peeling off.

Tom walked along the wall, listening, hearing nothing. There was no alarm of any kind from the house next door, either.

There was a fence ahead of him. There was a gate, unlocked. It squeaked very faintly when he opened it. He stood still for endless moments, but there was no reaction, no raising of an alarm, and he moved on. The back yard had a lawn as patchy as the one in front. In the middle of the yard was the trunk of a long-dead tree, still in the ground, still vertical. Tom wondered how secure it was. He could imagine it falling over on someone some day.

The Angleton house had only one story. The rear wall of the house had two windows and a door. Both windows were dark. The bedrooms must be on the other side of the house, he guessed, facing the next house down.

Now that he had come this far, Tom wondered what he ought to do next. This is not my way of gathering information, he reminded himself.

He stood unmoving and listened. He could hear a faint murmur of voices, perhaps those of a man and a woman, but he couldn't be sure. And he couldn't be sure where the voices were coming from. He might be hearing the next-door neighbors, or even someone's television.

There seemed to be no alternative. Tom stepped up to the back door of Kathy Angleton's house and tried the handle.

The door was unlocked. Was the girl crazy? Living alone in a neighborhood like this, why did she leave her back door unlocked after sunset? Tom felt a kind of avuncular annoyance that made him forget for a moment that he was the one breaking into Kathy's house.

He stood in the doorway with the door still open, trying to make out details in what little light there was from outside. This seemed to be the kitchen, unsurprisingly. During his previous visit, he had not gone beyond the living room. That must be beyond that archway to the right, he guessed. He would have to go that way and then look for the bedrooms.

He felt faintly ridiculous doing this, especially considering that he wasn't entirely sure what he was looking for. Imagine if he were caught in the house, and Andy Snow were called!

Tom took a step forward, and the lights came on.

Jack Tourneau stepped into the kitchen from the archway, stark naked. He was holding a pistol that looked amazingly big. He was yelling incoherently. The gun wavered in his shaking hand.

Sixteen

Tom leaned against the kitchen counter for support. "Jack, for God's sake, point that somewhere else."

Jack stopped yelling. "Christ Almighty, what the hell are *you* doing here?" He lowered the gun until it was pointing at the floor.

"That's what I was going to ask you. And why are you naked?" The second question was, of course, the answer to the first. Tom now knew the truth of what he had come here to verify—a suspicion he had hoped, for some vague sense of old times' sake, would prove false.

Jack looked down at himself as though surprised to see his own uncovered skin. He grinned. "Guess I forgot myself. Does it bother you?" He had already recovered his customary cockiness.

"That's one of the biggest ones I've ever seen," Tom said. "Potbellies, I mean."

Jack glared at him. "I could shoot you, you know. We call it the Make My Day Law. Passed a few years ago, while you were away." He raised the gun and pointed it at Tom again. "You broke in, I could shoot you, no one would ask questions."

"I thought that law applied to the homeowner, not to the

homeowner's tenant's widow's married lover."

Tom shifted his gaze to Kathy Angleton, who was peeking around the archway, looking confused. "Good evening, Mrs. Angleton. How is the recovery going?"

She stepped into the kitchen, hastily tying the belt of her robe. She pressed herself against Jack Tourneau's side as though for protection.

"That's my gun hand," Jack said importantly. "Move around behind me, honey. Slowly. No sudden movements. To my other side."

Tom laughed. The laugh sounded natural and unforced to him, and he hoped it sounded that way to Jack. "Do you really want to shoot me after all, Jack? And then go through all the explaining?" Tom had had a pistol pointed at him only once before. That time, the man holding the gun had been a professional killer. Tom realized that he had felt less worried then than he did now. He had talked to the killer and explained why it would be better to let him go than to kill him. The killer had weighed various factors and then decided against shooting Tom—all quite cold blooded and unemotional. Jack was unpredictable.

"If I let you go," Jack said, "I'll have to do a lot of explaining anyway, won't I?"

That was more cold blooded than Tom had given him credit for. "And what about your witness?" Tom asked.

Kathy had followed Jack's instructions and now stood on his other side, holding onto his free arm. "You did break into the house," she pointed out. "Jack could shoot you, then put his clothes back on, and we'd say he was visiting me to see how I'm holding up, when we heard you coming in through the back."

Tom let the counter bear his weight again. His knees felt weak. "Is that your gun, Jack? Do you have a permit to carry it?"

"No, but that's just a minor fine. No biggie. Be worth it not to have to listen to Ellen talking about you any more, praising everything about you, going on and on."

Tom saw the expression that passed across Kathy's face, and he relaxed. As was his wont, Jack had said too much.

Kathy let go of Jack's arm and moved away from him. "That's why you want to shoot him?" she asked. "Because your wife has the hots for him? Well, fuck you, you just lost your witness." She stalked out of the kitchen. A moment later, they heard a door slam.

"Well, hell," Jack muttered. He put the gun on the counter beside him.

"The course of true love," Tom said. "Are your clothes locked in the bedroom now?"

Jack waved his hand. "Fuck off, okay? Just go away."

That seemed to be a good idea. As he made his way back toward his car in the now almost-full dark, Tom realized that he had discovered something else on this trip, in addition to the suspicion he had set out to verify. He had come here to see if Jack Tourneau was indeed sleeping with Kathy Angleton, but he had also discovered just how ready Jack was to commit cold-blooded murder.

Tom sat in his car, thinking. When he had visited Kathy Angleton the first time and Jack had been there, pawing the young woman, Tom had dismissed Jack's heavy-handed behavior as typical of Jack, a Jack made incautious by alcohol. And he had thought that Kathy's grief was that of a young wife who had adored her husband. Now he realized that he had misjudged the entire situation.

Jack had been made incautious by drink, certainly, but that had caused him to let Tom see his normal private behavior with Kathy. They had already been sleeping together by then. Kathy's grief had surely been real. But perhaps she had still loved her husband enough to be shocked into grief by the suddenness and violence of his death. For all Tom knew, her grief had vanished minutes after Tom left the house.

Or it might even have been an act. Her husband had been a pretty good stage actor. Perhaps she was skilled at acting, too. Tom found it hard to reconcile the way she had seemed to be feeling that night with the face she had shown him tonight.

And then there was the matter of the pregnancy, and Jack's eagerness to see Kathy abort. Who was the father? Was that complication behind her emotional behavior during his first visit? Or had her emotions been unsettled because of the physiological effects of pregnancy?

Did her calmness and self-control tonight mean that the pregnancy had been ended?

And then his thoughts veered to Ellen. Apparently, Jack did think of Tom as a rival for his wife. And Ellen's attraction to Tom wasn't entirely an act.

He started his car and came agonizingly close to driving to the Tourneau house. But in the end, he went home and to bed.

"Lieutenant."

"Hamilton."

"Why am I here this time?"

"I wanted to know what you're looking for."

"I beg your pardon?"

"You've been looking through property records and old newspapers," Snow said. "I want to know why."

"I don't know that that's any of your business," Tom said. "How did you find out what I've been looking at?"

"This is a small town. I'm much more a part of it than you are."

"Those were all public records. I have the right to look at any of them."

"Of course," Snow agreed. "And no one's trying to stop you from doing just that. But I'm interested in what you're looking for and why. You attracted my attention when you showed up here with no history for twenty-plus years and paid cash for a new Lexus and that enormous house on a prime lot."

"Check, not cash."

Snow grinned. "Yeah, check. I wish you had paid by cash. I'd have liked that even more. Anyway, I really want to find out where you were for all those years and what you were doing there."

"Assuming you do find out," Tom said, "will you then order me out of town by sundown and let me pick up my six-guns at the town boundary?"

"What six-guns? You've already told me you've never fired a gun. You know what I think? I think you're the kind of a guy who hires other people when guns become necessary. And I think that may be a clue to what you've been doing since you left the old hometown."

"I think you have an overactive imagination."

"What were you looking for?"

"My past, Lieutenant. My mother disappeared when I was a

boy. I think my father murdered her. I'm trying to find out for sure." Was that sympathy on Snow's face, fleetingly, or had Tom imagined it?

"I've read those records," Snow said. "Nowadays, if a guy's wife disappears, especially if there's a record of domestic violence, we just assume the husband murdered her and proceed on that basis. The Ransom cops back then really fucked up. Anyway, you know you aren't going to find anything after this long, Hamilton. Twenty–four hours, remember? You quoted that number at me. So how likely is it that you'll figure out what happened after more than thirty years?"

Yes, there was sympathy in his voice. What good that would do, though, Tom couldn't imagine. "There's nothing else I can do," Tom said. "Are you satisfied?"

"If you're telling the truth, then that takes care of the problem. *This* problem. Makes me wonder, though, what you were so busy doing for twenty–two years that you couldn't take the time to go after your father while he was still alive and maybe the evidence wasn't quite so cold."

"Good–bye, Lieutenant. I have a lunch date."

Before Tom could leave, Snow said, "I just verified one thing. You get tense whenever I talk about investigating what you've been doing while you were away from Ransom. That shows me that it's something worth looking into."

Tom walked the eight blocks to La Estrellita, leaving his car parked in the police station lot. He needed to work off his anger. Every time he encountered Snow, it seemed, the policeman came out on top. Snow succeeded in manipulating him, in pushing his buttons. Tom had begun by underestimating Snow's intelligence and professional competence, and that had been a mistake. But then he had underestimated the man's competence at manipulation and control, at applied psychology.

Not that Snow had succeeded in making Tom reveal anything about himself or his past. He had proven his ability to make Tom angry, to knock Tom off balance so that Tom never learned anything useful from him. But Snow had yet to learn anything useful about Tom. There was that, anyway.

Thinking that, Tom slowed down. He had been walking at full speed, head down, ignoring those he passed. Now he stopped at a corner and looked around.

He had passed the license bureau and walked down the block and around the corner without being fully aware of it. He found that he was in a curious transition zone. He was at the beginning of the block that held the restaurant. Behind him, the street looked busy, prosperous, and well maintained. Ahead of him, the rot began. Which way was the boundary moving? Was prosperity advancing in this direction, so that those boarded-up storefronts would one day be open again and bustling? Or was the border between wealth and decay moving the other way, so that some day the entire town would be consumed, would decline into a lingering death?

He realized with great surprise that it mattered to him. He cared what happened to Ransom.

The town had symbolized pain and rejection to him for so long, and he had come back for reasons he couldn't pin down but which were not positive, were not love for his old home. Now he found himself worried about the town's future. He had never really belonged here, and he certainly didn't now, but he wanted to. Snow had said that he was more a part of Ransom than Tom was. It was depressing to think that he might be right.

Walking more slowly, Tom continued to the middle of the block, to where La Estrellita, at least, was still packing them in.

Ellen was waiting for him. She was sitting at the same booth at which, the day before, he had seen—and from which he had driven—Jack Tourneau and Kathy Angleton. It was a coincidence, but an unsettling one.

Tom slid in across from her. "Hi. You found it without any trouble."

Ellen gestured vaguely. "I've driven past it, but I never thought of going inside before. Looks better than I anticipated."

"Wait till you taste the food."

Their conversation continued on a shallow level. They avoided serious topics, which to both of them meant Ellen's two previous sexual invitations. They talked about the decor, the paintings, the menu, and then, when their food had been delivered, about the excellence of the food.

Tom was content to let matters stay at a trivial level. It felt much safer. Sooner or later, he supposed, Ellen would get around to the matter of the next opera performance, and then they'd be able to talk about entirely non-emotional, non-threatening matters for as long as they wished.

Tom realized that he was eating the way Janice Sheridan did, so that he could keep his mouth full and thus not have to say much.

Ellen looked at the paintings lining the walls, at their waiter, and at the clientele, and said, "You know, Tom, all of these beautiful, dark-haired people and their passionate music and their hot, spicy food makes me think of..." She took a delicate bite and chewed thoughtfully.

Tom stopped chewing and breathing.

Ellen swallowed and said, "Of all those passionate Italians in Tosca." She smiled at him. "Men are so foolish. Did you think I was going to talk about something else? I told you I wanted to talk about you helping me on the next production."

Tom breathed again, chewed, swallowed, and said, "I'm not as easy to fool as I used to be. Where are you going to rehearse and perform this time? The school auditorium's still locked up, I suppose."

"It's still locked, but I spoke to some friends on the school board, and they put pressure on the police chief and he talked to Snow. So now it'll be open for rehearsals, but there'll be a policeman watching the door until we leave, and he'll lock the place behind us. I don't know yet what we'll do about the performance. I'll deal with that when the time comes."

Tom couldn't imagine Snow bowing to such pressure. So he isn't worried about protecting the crime scene and any evidence his people haven't yet found, Tom thought. Which in turn implies that he thinks he already knows all he needs to know. "I'll be happy to help you if I can," he said. "But you know I'm more a watcher than a doer. I prefer to be sitting in the audience."

Ellen nodded. "Evaluating and critiquing. I know. But I'm not going to ask much of you. I want you to be in charge of the rifles."

"Props, I hope."

She shook her head. "Nope. I still want that look of authenticity. Yes, yes, I know what you said about the rifles being from the wrong era, but I think that real rifles still have a lot more emotional impact on the audience than silly little toys do, even if they do come from the wrong century."

"Where did Jack find six more people willing to lend him their rifles? At this rate, Ransom will have no tenors left, and the police department will have all the 22-caliber bolt-action hunting rifles locked up. I wouldn't mind the last part, actually."

"Andy Snow finally agreed to release the rifles from the first opening night. We'll be reusing those."

"Well, skip the blanks this time. Do without the shock effect of the rifles firing."

"And do what? Have the firing squad pull their triggers and shout 'Bang!'? And have the audience burst out laughing during Mario's death scene?"

"Well, that's a point. So have your new tenor wear a bullet-proof vest, and make sure he signs a very detailed waiver before he goes on."

"You're being silly. Nothing's going to happen this time. We're not dealing with a crime here, Tom." She seemed about to say more but changed her mind.

"Drop the other shoe."

Ellen sighed. "It's basically what I said to you before. Jack was in charge of the prop rifles during the first performance. You know how unreliable Jack is, and how alcohol affects him, and what his attitude toward this whole enterprise of mine has been. I think he was careless and not paying attention, and he put in real bullets instead of the blanks. It may have been automatic. It's something he's done often enough when he goes hunting, and maybe he happened to have live rounds with him and did it automatically. Or maybe he did it just by accident. You know how careless he is about where he puts things."

Such as his dick, Tom thought. "What about the second performance? The same kind of accident or automatic motion, the same just happening to have live rounds on him?"

"I haven't figured that one out yet," Ellen admitted. "But you remember how drunk Jack was that night. He probably didn't know what he was doing. I don't know. Maybe his drunkenness that night makes it even more likely that he'd go through the motions of loading the rifles automatically."

Her theory had sounded absurd to Tom the first time he'd heard it. The theory still sounded absurd, but there was an additional element that Ellen didn't know about, and that element suggested something else to Tom.

The additional element was the fact that Jack was sleeping with Kathy Angleton and had already been doing so at the time of Jerry Angleton's murder. Was it possible that Jack had deliberately set up a seeming accident in order to get Jerry Angleton out of his way? Jack was an oaf, but until recently, Tom would have said that he wasn't capable of such cold-blooded murder. After the confrontation in Kathy Angleton's house last night, Tom could no longer say that.

"All of this is between you and me, of course," Ellen said. "I know I can trust you. I certainly don't want that jerk Snow getting this idea in his head. Who knows what he'd do."

"I'm surprised you've stayed with Jack for so long," Tom said. He immediately regretted saying it.

"I'm a pragmatist," Ellen said. She paused, then continued in a bitter tone. "I don't have any marketable skills, you know. I never thought I'd need them. My marriage was good for the first few years. Maybe as long as the first ten years. I should say that I *thought* it was good. By the time I began to see things more clearly, I was almost thirty. By the time I started thinking seriously of leaving him, I was past thirty."

"Not too old to change your life," Tom pointed out.

"It was for me. I'm not the kind of woman who does well living alone. I need someone." She glared at Tom. "There was no one else."

"This isn't the only town in the world. You could have moved."

Ellen shook her head. "This is my home. Both my parents were ill around that time. I felt I had to stay and help them. My brothers moved away years ago. They were no help at all. It was all up to me."

"Your parents are both dead now."

"And I'm middle-aged. And I still don't have any skills. All I can do is put on small-time operas with small-time would-be professionals. I'm not kidding myself about that. It's not something I can take with me somewhere else and make a living with. It's pretty funny," she added. "You were the kid no one thought would amount to anything, and I was one of the golden ones. Look at us now."

You're still one of the golden ones, Tom thought. And I still don't know what I've amounted to. "I'm surprised about your brothers," he said. "I don't remember them all that well, but I had the impression that you got along with them."

"Oh, sure, when we were all kids. They had a lot of problems with Mom and Dad. I suppose they were jealous of me. Classic stuff, you know—the older kids who feel left out when the baby of the family comes along and gets all the attention and love. So they used to spend as much time away from home as they could. They used to go on long camping and hunting and fishing trips. They were nice to me, though. They treated me like a kid brother. When I was small, they used to take me to a rifle range. They taught me to shoot there. And then when I was a teenager, they even took me hunting with them a few times."

"Gee, you went out in the woods with jealous siblings with loaded rifles?"

Ellen laughed. "No, I'm telling you it wasn't like that. They didn't seem to blame me for anything. They blamed our parents. I really enjoyed those trips," she said wistfully. "Took a deer, one of those times. But then my brothers got old enough to leave home for good, and that was that. They went as far away from Ransom as they could. Petey's living in Florida. Paul went all the way to Europe. He lives in London. I don't have any contact with them. They didn't even come back for either of my parents' funerals. They didn't care about Mom and Dad, and they don't care about me."

After a pause, Ellen continued. "Well, anyway, there's one thing I've learned: Never give in to self–pity. I made my own bed, and I'm going to manage to sleep comfortably in it until the end."

As though she had flicked a switch, she changed back to cheerfulness and efficiency. If it was an act, it was an admirable one, Tom thought. She maintained it perfectly for the rest of the meal.

On the sidewalk outside the restaurant, Ellen said goodbye in a voice that was still cheerful and gave Tom a sisterly kiss on the cheek. Then she climbed into an old Honda Accord with dead paint that had once been blue and drove away.

Strange to think, Tom told himself, that Jack Tourneau had gained for himself the girl Tom had so longed for, and then Jack had set about pursuing other women and alienating Ellen. Equally strange, though, that Tom had turned down Ellen's offer of herself.

Not so strange, really, he argued with himself. The two things are closely connected. Ellen's offer to you didn't come from her heart but from her hurt feelings and her fear for her future. You couldn't accept an offer made on that basis. If she came to you, how long would she be happy with you? How long before she realized she'd made a mistake?

But I'd be happy! he cried silently. I wouldn't be lonely for a change! Don't I deserve that?

He remembered one of the very few useful things his father had ever said to him: No one deserves anything. You get what you take, and that's it.

Seventeen

Considering how much his boyhood house obsessed him, how large it loomed in his memory, Tom realized that it was odd he had visited it only once since his return to Ransom. Even that had been only to look at the outside. Perhaps that was because it offered him nothing other than terrible memories—no information, no solution to the central corrupting mystery of his life, no sense of finality or conclusion.

It was also odd, it suddenly occurred to him, that he had not yet made any attempt to track down Nick Jaruzelski. If Nick were still alive, he might be a source of information.

Would he still be alive? Tom tried to call up an image of the man from the past and guess at his age back then. But all he could summon up was an aura of kindliness and concern.

And power: He remembered Nick as a powerfully built man, not quite as tall as Tom's father but much broader and more solid. Back then, Tom had not understood most of the currents between the adults around him, but a couple of times he had sensed that Nick Jaruzelski was close to attacking Al Hamilton.

He remembered coming home from grocery shopping with

his mother one day, happy to be alone with her.

As they approached the front door, Al erupted from the house yelling at Kay because of some infraction of his rules. He hit her. Without a sound, she collapsed onto the concrete sidewalk. Tom stood watching, bewildered. Then he looked up at the house next door and saw Nick Jaruzelski standing on his front porch, hands balled into fists. Al followed Tom's gaze. He laughed at Nick, but he went back into the house quickly.

Nick came over then and raised Tom's mother to her feet. "Are you all right, Kay?" he kept saying.

"Go home, Nick," she mumbled. "Please."

Nick looked at the Hamilton house for a long time, and Tom knew that Nick was battling with himself, wanting to do what Kay told him, but also wanting to storm into the Hamilton house and kill Al. In the end, he squeezed Kay's shoulder and went back into his own house.

The second time was after Kay Hamilton's disappearance. Tom was about ten. It was late afternoon. Al was drinking. After the third beer, Al started muttering curses and insults aimed at his absent wife. Then he began beating his son.

Tom was able to pull away and run from the house. Al caught up with him on the sidewalk outside. He slapped Tom. It was a blow that would have been a heavy one, given Al's size and strength, even if the victim had been another grown man. It lifted Tom off his feet and threw him back and to one side. He fell half on the sidewalk, half on the dirt patch in front of the house.

Dizzy, Tom looked up at the looming silhouette of his father standing over him. The shadow was bending toward him. Tom curled into a ball to protect himself from the next blow.

He heard a shout, a deep-voiced bellow, and the shadow vanished. Tom opened his eyes to see his father sprawled on his back on the sidewalk, his face covered with blood. Nick Jaruzelski stood over him, his right hand balled into a huge fist. Nick was shouting almost incomprehensibly. "You bastard! You bastard!" he seemed to be saying, over and over, as though he couldn't think of anything else to say, or didn't need to.

Al struggled and finally managed to sit up. He held his head in both hands. He moaned—a pleasant sound to Tom's ears.

Nick finally calmed down enough to say, "Don't touch that boy again! I'll kill you if you hit him again."

Al got himself onto his hands and knees and crawled away. When he reached his own front steps, he grabbed the railing and pulled himself to his feet and climbed the stairs, shaking visibly. He staggered to the front door of his house, turned around, leaned against the doorway for support, and shouted, "Why don't you mind your own business, you shithead? I'm the boy's father! I got the right!"

Nick took a step toward the house, and Al disappeared inside it, slamming the front door behind himself.

Nick took Tom into his house and sat with him while he cried. Harriet, Nick's daughter, came home from work and fixed supper for all of them. Tom spent the night sleeping on their couch. He slept soundly for the first time in years. He felt safe for the first time in years.

A week later, when Tom was back at home, the scenario repeated itself, but this time with a different ending. This time, Al locked the front and rear doors.

Tom escaped after the first blow, but the only retreat was his bedroom. He managed to get inside it and lock the door while his father was still stumbling up the stairs. His father pounded on the door a few times, then gave up and went back to the living room to resume his evening's drinking.

That was when Tom understood how little protection Nick Jaruzelski could really offer. No one could protect Tom except Tom himself. And Tom could do little for himself physically. His brain was his only weapon.

He had honed and strengthened that weapon over the years. It had given him power for some years and enough money to last him for the rest of his life. It had brought him back to Ransom.

Was Nick Jaruzelski still alive? If he was, did he still live in Ransom? At the very least, did his daughter still live in town?

Tom decided that he should start by going to what had been Nick's house. It was Sunday afternoon. Despite the season, it was cloudy and cool with on-and-off drizzle—the kind of weather Coloradans tend to consider unsuitable for doing things outside. So he thought he had a good chance of catching the current residents at home. It was possible that the people who lived there now—or one of the neighbors—might be able to give him some information about Nick and Harriet. People in Ransom kept track of each other.

There was a parking space in front of 135 Elm. Tom maneuvered his Lexus in carefully. He wondered if the same two young toughs were around, and if they were, if they'd menace him again. His brain wouldn't suffice as a weapon against them. Perhaps he should try to overcome his aversion to guns and look into buying one. Under his real name, he was clean. Background checks would reveal nothing. It would be a simple enough matter to buy a pistol that he could carry with him in the car or in his pocket.

And risk killing someone, he told himself. Doing it yourself. Directly. Not by issuing an order. There'd be no distance.

His knock was answered by a tired middle-aged woman. She looked him up and down and turned hostile. "Yes?"

Tom smiled pleasantly. "I'm not selling anything."

She started to close the door at that line. Tom said quickly, "I used to live next door, and I wanted to find out—"

The woman opened the door fully and stepped out onto the porch. "Tommy Hamilton!"

"Yes, Tom Hamilton. That's right. I'm sorry, I don't—"

She grabbed him in a sudden fierce embrace, then stepped away from him just as suddenly, looking embarrassed. "I'm Harriet. Nick's daughter. Don't you remember me?"

"Harriet Jaruzelski? Good God, I didn't think you guys would still be living here!"

Harriet shook her head. "Harriet Fischer. I got married a couple of years after you left town. My husband Joe and I live here now. My dad's up in Denver."

"The house got too big for him? He's in an apartment?"

"I wish that was it," Harriet said sadly. "He's in an assisted living complex. He's not doing good, Tom. Come inside. I'll give you the address. I know he'd like to see you. He still talks about you. He always wondered what became of you. We used to worry that your dad—Well, never mind that. I want to hear all about your life. Joe just went out to get some plumbing supplies. He should be home soon. I've told him about you and your dad and...and your mom. He'll be happy to finally meet you. God, is that your car?" She laughed. "You've done okay, then! Listen to me. I can't stop babbling!"

Tom's eyes were filled with tears. He turned away to look at his car, an excuse to wipe his hands across his eyes and clear them. "Oh, yeah, that's my car." He turned back to Harriet. "My life has been pretty boring. Nothing worth telling about, really. I came back home to start a whole new life."

She grabbed his arm and pulled him into the house. "It won't be boring to me! Oh, I wish the kids were still at home! I've told them about you, too. They were fascinated by your story."

Tom let himself be led into the kitchen and seated at the table. It was an aluminum table with a white Formica top—just like the one in his own house during his childhood. He remembered this one from his one night of safety at the Jaruzelski house.

Tom experienced a sudden jolt, a mental dislocation. He realized that he wasn't sure if he was remembering his mother's kitchen table correctly. He had confused the two kitchens and the two tables—the Hamiltons' and the Jaruzelskis'. He tried to call up again the picture of his mother concentrating at the kitchen counter and the table behind her, and it all seemed indistinct and uncertain. How could such an important memory be unreliable?

Harriet was saying, "When your mom..."

"Disappeared," Tom said.

Harriet nodded. "When she disappeared, that's when my dad's health starting deteriorating." She stared at him, as if wondering if she should tell him the next part. "He was crazy about her, you know."

"I didn't know. I was too young to see that. Thinking back

about it now, though...Yes, I think I can see it now. Damn! He would have been so much better for her!"

Harriet smiled. "That's not saying much, is it? But yes, he would have been good to her. He was good to my mom. They really loved each other. I was twelve when she died, and I remember how depressed he was for a long time after that. Then we moved into this house and he started getting to know your mom a bit, and that's when he really started recovering. And then—Well, you know what happened."

Tom shook his head. "I don't know. I've never known. Now that I'm back in Ransom, I'm trying to find out. Harriet, I don't even know if my mom's still alive somewhere! Maybe that bastard murdered her and buried her in the mountains, or maybe she ran away because she couldn't endure any more." His voice had risen. The control he had worked for for so many years, and had achieved, had broken.

Harriet took both his hands and held them across the table. Just as he had while sitting next to Nick in this house thirty years before, Tom wept. This time, it was Harriet who comforted him.

He stopped, shocked at himself. He withdrew his hands and smiled at her. "I'm all right." He pulled his handkerchief from his pocket and dried his eyes and blew his nose. "I'm all right," he repeated. "As I told you at the door, I didn't know you were still here. I was just hoping that whoever was living here could give me some sort of lead to help me track you or Nick down. I wanted to talk to Nick and see what he could tell me. Can you give me the address where he is now?"

"Of course." Harriet got a small message pad and a pen from the counter underneath the wall-mounted telephone and scribbled on it. "Here. It's in Denver, like I said. Out on the east side, near where the old airport used to be. You can visit any time before five o'clock. That's when their dinner time starts. You have to be a relative to get in after five."

Tom looked at his watch. It was almost two. "I could be there by three if I left now. It's Sunday. Traffic is light."

"He'll be so happy to see you." She hesitated. "But...Well, I really wanted you to meet Joe. You could have supper with us tonight, and then you could go and see Dad tomorrow morning. He's always perkier in the morning, anyway. He gets pretty tired after lunch."

How could he reward Harriet's warmth now and her concern thirty years ago by telling her that a family dinner with her and her husband was exactly what he wanted to avoid? He feared her questions about his activities during the last twenty years. But even more, he feared the effect she had on him, the ease with which her presence, the associations she had with his past, dissolved the shield he had erected between himself and the outside world. He seemed unable to maintain his valued emotional distance in this house.

"I can't stay for dinner in any case. Let me give you my phone number." He used a sheet from the same message pad and wrote his number on it. "How about if you and Jack come over to my place next Saturday evening? I'll provide dinner. I'll invite some other people, and we'll have a nice party."

The animation in Harriet's face faded away. She stared at Tom for a long moment. Then she forced a smile. "You cook, Tom?"

"No, but that's why God invented takeout."

"Well, I'll discuss it with Joe and let you know if we can

make it."

As he drove away, Harriet was standing in the doorway watching him. Even from a distance, Tom could see the expression of sadness and disappointment on her face. He waved at her and managed a cheerful, friendly smile. He felt awful about what he had just done. But he also felt safe.

Eighteen

Tom didn't drive to Denver that afternoon after all. He decided that he, too, would be a lot fresher in the morning. He was afraid that seeing Nick again would be as emotionally stressful as seeing Harriet had proved to be, and he wanted to be as well prepared for that stress as possible.

He did, though, call Harriet and repeat his invitation to dinner the following week. He told her he had decided against a party and wanted to have dinner with just her and her husband. He could tell from her voice how pleased she was, and it lessened his guilt considerably. He'd deal with her questions about his past somehow. He had almost a week to think up convincing lies.

It would probably be good for him to have a collection of consistent lies ready for other people, too. He couldn't continue being vague and evasive.

Tom left his house at ten on Monday morning. Late enough to miss the worst of the traffic on I–25, early enough so that he could spend as long with Nick as both he and Nick wanted.

Golden Days was south of the wasteland that had once

been one of the world's busiest airports. The assisted-living complex consisted of three one-story buildings in the form of spokes radiating from a central hub. The hub contained the main entrance and the receptionist's desk.

The parking lot was cracked and buckled from the roots of the maples and cottonwoods that had grown up through it. The old trees were large by Colorado standards, and uncared for. The building also looked old and unkempt, and so did cars already parked in the lot. Yet another jolt of guilt for Tom. Why hadn't he offered to help pay for Nick's care? He could be moved to some place better than this. Didn't Tom owe Nick that much? Tom had so much money now, and yet so far he had used it only to indulge himself in luxuries.

The lobby gave Tom a somewhat better impression of Golden Days. The inside of the building was as worn and old as the outside, but it was much better cared for. The young woman behind the receptionist's desk smiled at him in a friendly way, told him Nick was in Room 15 in the Evans Wing, and assured him that he could go to the room.

"The Evans Wing?" he asked.

"That one." She pointed to one of the three hallways leading off the reception area. "The others"—she pointed—"are the Long's Wing and the Gray's Wing."

Named after the three 14,000-foot mountains visible from Denver, Tom realized. "I'm surprised any of your patients are willing to live in the Gray's Wing," he said. "Maybe you should rename it Silver."

"Our *residents*," she said, emphasizing the word, "seem to like it as it is."

Tom was pleased by the protectiveness and defensiveness

in her voice. He hoped that attitude was typical of the Golden Days staff.

He didn't recognize the voice that told him to come in when he knocked at the door with the number 15 on it. Nor did he recognize the man sitting in the wicker armchair inside the room, facing the door and smiling at him. A wheeled stand with an oxygen tank stood beside the chair. A clear plastic tube led from it and passed across the man's face, under his nose. This was an old man, a thin man, a weak, shrunken, grey–faced, pitiful man. Nick must be elsewhere. Tom wanted there to be some mistake. "Hi," Tom said, "I'm—" Looking for Nick Jaruzelski, he was going to say.

"Tommy! Think I wouldn't." Pause for breath. "Recognize you? You haven't changed. Harriet called. Last night. Haven't slept. Waiting for you."

Tom closed the door behind him and walked forward until he was standing in front of Nick. All that protective strength, shriveled into this! Tom sank to his knees so that he was looking up at Nick, instead of down. Nick held out his hands and Tom took them. They were slender and frail. "I'm sorry," Tom said. "I'm sorry that it took me so long to come back."

Nick's smile grew wider. "Doesn't matter now, Tommy. Glad I got to see you. Always wondered what happened." His speech was punctuated with long pauses while he recovered from the effort of speaking. He took a few breaths each time before continuing.

In one way, it helped that Nick had deteriorated so much. It made Tom feel strong and protective—and kept him from dissolving in weak tears as he had with Harriet. "I got away," Tom said. "I waited until I finished high school, and then I left town. I don't know why I waited that long to leave."

"You had friends here. Could have let them help you."

"I had to help myself. I had to go to another place where no one knew me and..." He thought for a while. "I had to create a whole new Tom Hamilton—the way I should have been instead of the way I was."

Nick squeezed his hands. "Looks like you did it."

Tom got to his feet again. "I think so. I couldn't come back until I was ready to. Now I want to find out what happened to my mother."

Nick's smile disappeared. He put his hands over his face and rubbed his eyes. "Oh, God, Tommy." His voice was muffled. "Poor Kay! I keep thinking about her. I want to know, too."

Tom looked around the room. It was furnished like a motel room, with a large bed, a small desk, another wicker chair like the one Nick sat in, and a bathroom. The bed had railings, and the bathroom doorway was unusually wide.

Tom pulled the other chair over to face Nick's and sat in it. "Help me, Nick. Tell me everything you know. I was a child. I didn't know what was going on."

Nick's hands dropped to his lap. There were tears on his cheeks. "Didn't know much either, Tommy. Most of it was behind closed doors. Your dad was pretty careful. Pretty sure he was beating both of you. What could I do about it? Once, I asked your mom to leave him. Told her she could come and live with me and Harriet. Told her there wouldn't have to..." He looked away, embarrassed. "You know, *be* anything between us. Up to her. Whatever she wanted."

"What did she say?"

"She couldn't do that. Would be wrong. Said she was

grateful, though." He smiled again at the memory. "She was kind."

"Yes," Tom said. Kind. That was how he remembered her most of all. "You were in love with her, weren't you?"

Nick nodded. "Oh yes. I never said anything. She was married. I was an old man compared to her. Twenty years older! That one time—only time I managed to say how I felt."

"I'm glad you had Harriet with you after your wife died, Nick. And your other children."

Nick smiled again. "The older kids all left, but Harriet stayed. You met her husband?"

Tom shook his head.

"Hope you will. He's a good boy. She moved out when she got married. Joe had a little place. But she came over every day, almost, to check on me. I got sick, couldn't keep the place up. Too much work. Real good early retirement package. Moved up here." He gestured around him. "It's okay. I signed the place over to Harriet and Joe. They had a couple of kids by then. Needed more room."

A couple of years earlier, when Tom had ferreted out the information that his father had sold the family house to pay for his own terminal medical care, Tom had thought nothing of it. Except for the possibility of evidence about his mother's fate being hidden somewhere in the place, there was no reason for Tom to want to hold onto that house. He hadn't questioned his father's right to sell it. He certainly had had no intention of contacting Al to complain about the sale. Now, though, Nick's words made him wonder.

At the County Assessor's office, Tom had determined that the title to the house was indeed in Al's name, so there had been no legal question about his right to sell the house. But how had the house passed from the Morisettis to Al Hamilton? There had been nothing in the records Tom had seen showing that transaction. Nick said he had signed his house over to his daughter and son–in–law, but that meant that legally he had sold it to them for a nominal sum, and if Tom had been looking for the record of that transfer, he would have found it at the County Assessor's office, too. So where was the record of the transfer of the house at 133 North Elm Street from Donald and Angela Morisetti to Al Hamilton?

"Nick, did you know my grandparents? The Morisettis?"

"Nope. Sorry, Tom. They died three, four years before I moved to Elm Street. Neighbors told me about it. How your granddad died in the mountains. Then your grandma."

"Another accident?"

"Broken heart. What the neighbors said. Poor woman. Nice folks. That's what everyone said. Must've been, with a daughter like Kay." Nick looked embarrassed. "Sorry, Tom. Didn't mean it that way. You're not like your father. Not at all."

Tom smiled. "Don't worry, Nick. I didn't think you meant it that way." I'm more like my father than you know. It's probably a good thing I'm not as large and strong as he was.

What does it mean to say someone died of a broken heart? Would there be an autopsy in such a case? And what would it show? What would it have shown in my grandmother's case?

A black man came into the room carrying a tray. At first, Tom thought he too lived at Golden Days and was one of Nick's friends. He turned out to be a worker, there to deliver Nick's lunch. Nick introduced him as Stanley.

Tom examined him while he exchanged friendly banter

with Nick. Tom decided he might be as old as Nick, but the contrast was startling. Stanley was slender and moved quickly and easily. His energy and vitality highlighted how little of both Nick had left.

Nick looked at the skimpy portion on the tray on his lap and sighed. "Used to eat steaks. Big potatoes. Hell, pizzas!"

"Yeah," Stanley said, "and I hear you used to smoke three packs a day and drink whisky, too. Old fool." He laughed to take the sting out of the words.

Nick nodded slowly. "Young fool. Middle–aged fool. Smart now."

Now that it's too late. The unspoken words were understood by all three of them.

Stanley patted Nick on the shoulder. "You eat all that up, this time. You hear me, my man? It's good for you."

"Do my best," Nick said. "Steak would be nice, though."

"So would an eighteen–year–old girl," Stanley said. "We've both got as much use for either one. I'll be back for the tray in an hour. Got other deliveries to make." He nodded goodbye to both of them and left the room.

Nick smiled at Tom. "Got some friends here."

Nineteen

When he had driven into Denver that morning, just after he left Interstate 25 to head toward Golden Days, Tom had passed a store called The Gun Man. A silhouette of a six gun took up most of one plate-glass window, and a drawing of what was apparently intended to be John Wayne in a Hollywood cowboy outfit took up the other.

Tom passed the store again on his way back from Golden Days. He slowed down, speeded up, passed the store, then slowed down again and used the parking lot of a supermarket a block away to turn around. Judging by the name and the window decorations, The Gun Man might be a place that specialized in Old West memorabilia, or even movie posters. But at least it was convenient.

The inside turned out to be much more serious than the outside. And bigger. The building extended further back from the road than was apparent from the street. Not even in Trager's headquarters in his sprawling home in the suburbs north of Chicago had Tom seen so many handguns and rifles.

In Trager's home, the storage had been arranged for efficiency. Here, the emphasis was on display.

The place was empty of customers, though. Lunchtime on Monday must not be a prime time for buying guns, Tom decided. That in turn made him wonder what the prime time was.

It was an old building with wooden floors and high ceilings. The floors were well polished, and the lighting was modern and bright. Along with the rifles and handguns on the walls—all the way up to the ceiling—and the display cases along the walls and in the center of the store, this gave the place a curious look of Victorian comfort and calm. Tom wandered around, looking, and wondering what he was looking at. And for.

He also wondered what the owner looked like. Tom imagined he would be either an aging ex-Marine with a Semper Fi tattoo on one muscular arm, or a nervous psychotic like some of the men who had followed his orders when he worked for Trager.

Neither of these, as it turned out.

Tom was approached by a serious-looking young man with a goatee and a braided ponytail who introduced himself as Gerald Gun. "That's my real name," he added quickly. "Call me Gerald. How can we help you today?"

"You're the owner?"

Gun nodded. "Lock, stock, barrel, and trigger." It sounded like a rehearsed line.

"I'm not really here to buy anything," Tom said. "I'm looking for some information. I don't know anything about guns."

"Understood. You're worried about the rising crime rate, and you want something to protect yourself and your home and your loved ones."

"Well, no. Actually, I live in a pretty low-crime area. In

Ransom. It's the country, compared to this."

"Ah, then you want something for hunting! Great! Let me show you something I think would be perfect for you." He lifted a rifle from the wall and held it out to Tom.

Tom looked at it with distaste.

"Take it," Gun ordered.

Tom took it. He held it with one hand under the stock and one under the barrel, as though he were a wall bracket.

"Put it to your shoulder. Pretend you're aiming at a grizzly headed right toward you."

Tom obeyed. "I thought there weren't any grizzlies in Colorado."

"Don't you believe it. Beautiful machine, isn't it? Laurona Express. Just beautiful."

"It's as big as I am."

"You'll get used to that."

"And as heavy." Tom's arms were already growing tired.

"Has to be." Gun took it from Tom at last and held it in front of him, looking at it admiringly. "Just barely over eight pounds. So it's not that heavy. You'll get used to that, too. Chambers a 375 H&H Magnum. 2700 feet per second muzzle velocity if you use soft–point ammo, which is what you'd want for that grizzly." He stared at the rifle for a moment longer, absorbed in its lines. "What do you think?"

"How much does it cost?"

"Well, with the Magnum option, I could get it down to just a bit over $3,000."

You saw my car when I drove up, didn't you? "You carry the ammunition for it here?"

"You bet. Everything you need." Gun placed the rifle

carefully on a nearby counter, then went to another counter which contained stacks of small, brightly colored cardboard boxes. He held up a box with the word *Remington* on it. "Here's what you want."

"What if I wanted to fire blanks? Just for practice, I mean. To get used to the feel of the weapon."

"The rifle," Gun corrected him. "I don't carry any blanks in 375 caliber. You can probably find them somewhere. Or you can load your own. Some people prefer that. I carry a full range of reloading equipment and supplies." He must have seen the distaste on Tom's face, for he said, "Tell you what, though." He reached under the counter again and brought out another box. "These are 22 caliber blanks from Winchester. You can keep the Laurona for the real thing, and then you might want something else in 22 caliber for fooling around with blanks. Or even just for, you know, plinking."

"Plinking?"

"Yeah. Shooting at beer cans or bottles or prairie dogs. That sort of thing. That's fun on a quiet Sunday afternoon." He moved toward the wall again. "Let me show you what I'd recommend for that purpose. It's cheaper than the Laurona. Lighter, too. I think you'll really like it."

"No, actually, I think I'm an indoor sort of guy. A couch potato." Tom felt guilty about using the man as an information source and encouraging him when there was no chance of a sale. He thought he shouldn't just say thank you and goodbye and leave the store. "You said something about protection against crime?"

"You bet! Come this way." Whatever disappointment Gun might have felt was lost in his new enthusiasm. He walked rapidly down the length of the store to yet another counter. "Now, what I say is, for home protection you need something small. Forget the Dirty Harry gun. If you're going to buy something like that, you might as well just stick with the Laurona rifle instead." He laughed. Tom laughed. Gun turned serious again. "You want something you can keep in your bedside table or slip into the pocket of your robe. You want something reliable for close–up work." He drew a revolver from under the counter and put it on the glass for Tom to admire.

"New England Firearms. A nice little gun. Pick it up. Only weighs about three and a half pounds. Holds nine shots. 22 caliber. Only 135 bucks."

A 22–caliber revolver. One of Trager's killers had once told Tom with great enthusiasm that he favored such a weapon himself. "Easy to conceal," he had said. "Simple, reliable, easy–to–clean mechanism. And best of all, Jimmy, it *doesn't* have a lot of penetrating power. See, you always shoot the guy in the head. Only makes sense, right? Anywhere else, he may survive. But some of these guys, they use the biggest gun they can find. They shoot the man in the head. Blows away half his skull and brain. But maybe not the important part! He may be able to talk after that! I've seen it happen. You just never know. The brain's an amazing thing, Jimmy. So what you do instead, you put a little 22 up against the back of the man's head and you pull the trigger. You make sure you're dealing with low muzzle velocity. Close up like that, the bullet's got enough velocity to penetrate the skull once, but then it can't get out again, so it bounces around inside the guy's head, banging off the inside of the skull. Turns the whole brain to mush. No squealing. That's the real secret: low penetrating power. You remember that, Jimmy."

"Low penetrating power," Tom muttered.

"Oh, no, don't worry about that," Gun said. "This gun can throw a 22 Short, or a 22 Long, or even a 22 Long Rifle."

"You can fire a rifle bullet from this?"

"Oh, sure. I can show you a lot of others in this case that'll do the same thing. They're versatile. I tell you, sir, you'd be really happy with this gun. Anyone breaks into your house, he's dead. Just make sure he falls down and dies inside your house. Makes it easier."

"You're talking about the Make My Day law?"

"That's right. No questions asked if you drop the guy inside your house. If he's outside, it can get a bit sticky."

"Whereas inside, it's just the floor that gets sticky."

Gun laughed. "That's a good one."

"There are background checks nowadays, aren't there? Before I can buy this, I mean."

"That's right." Gun waved his hand dismissively. "Doesn't mean anything. Just papers to fill out. Man like you," he looked Tom up and down quickly, "I bet you'd have no problem. I can tell just by looking. I've been in this business long enough. I can fill the forms out for you now and fax them in. Then I'll give you a call when it all clears. What do you think?"

"I think...I think I need to think about this." Tom turned and walked quickly from the store. He got in his car, started it, and drove for a block before he turned into the same supermarket parking lot as before. He stopped, turned the engine off, and sat, shaking.

He had wanted to buy it. He had wanted to use it. Not just on a target. On a human being.

At first, his attitude had been the old one of aversion, even hatred, for the deadly machines and for those who made them and those who used them. And then Gerald Gun's enthusiasm had seemed funny—a kind of pitiful gun porn. And then, finally, it had become fascinating.

Fascinating. Fascination. No, Tom told himself, that implies something from the outside, some kind of charm or spell. This came from inside you. It's your father. You're not just your mother's child. You're half your father's, too. It's that half that was able to do the work you did in Chicago. Trager gave the orders, and you passed them on, but you put the word in his ear first, you told him who threatened him or had betrayed him, who needed to be destroyed.

No, not "destroyed"!

They weren't rabid animals. They were human beings, and they were murdered. Use that word! Anything else is a euphemism. You're just as capable of murder as your father was. Maybe more so. You don't know that your father murdered anyone, but you do know that you caused people to be murdered. You're a murderer at heart.

Twenty

When Tom got home from Denver, it was about 2:30. He tried to drive away the corrosive thoughts that had been eating at him during the drive home by doing some work with the telephone and the white pages.

After a series of calls to various state government offices, he knew this much: Wills were probated in the district court covering the county in which the deceased was resident and were filed in the office of the clerk of the district court. Phillipot County, of which Ransom was the county seat, was part of Judicial District 29, along with two other counties, Julian and Westbury. The offices of District Court 29 were unfortunately not in Ransom but in Kenner, the county seat of Westbury County. That was on the eastern plains, about a two-hour drive from Ransom.

Tomorrow, Tom thought. He was exhausted. It had been a day of revelations, one of which he could have done without.

He went to bed early and dreamed of death.

Toward morning, he dreamed that he was holding the 22 revolver he had been shown in the gun shop, holding it against the back of Jack Tourneau's head. He was firing it. He was watching, with the magical vision of dreams, the bullet tumbling about inside Jack's head, destroying his brain.

Jack changed into Ellen. Tom forced himself to wake up and lay staring into the grey light of predawn.

The clerk of District Court 29 was impatient.

Kenner was a small, tired, dusty town out on the plains. There was nothing to distinguish it from dozens of other similar towns in eastern Colorado. It made Ransom look lush, green, and vital. Other than the court offices, everything in town seemed to be oriented toward agriculture, and from what Tom had read, agriculture had not done well in eastern Colorado this year. The few people on the sidewalks were dispirited, and the pickup trucks had seen better days. The place looked the way Tom felt. It made him want to hurry with his business and get back to Ransom as quickly as possible.

One of the dispirited locals pointed out the office building housing the district court offices. Inside it, Tom found the impatient clerk, a tall, overweight man in blue jeans and Western shirt who stood behind a counter facing the door, drumming his fingers.

Tom said, "Hello, is the district court—"

"Yes. What do you need?"

"Probated wills. I need to look up—"

"Fill this out." The clerk pulled a sheet of paper from beneath the counter and held it out to Tom.

Tom stood at the counter to fill out the form, a short one that requested his name, address, telephone number, and Social Security number. The clerk drummed his fingers throughout.

Tom handed him the completed form. "You must get lots of

business in here. Busy schedule."

The clerk scowled at him. He examined the form and made a notation on it. He pulled out another form and put it on the counter. "Now this one."

The second form requested the names, Social Security numbers, and addresses at the time of death of the people whose wills Tom wanted to examine. "I'm afraid I don't know any of the Social Security numbers."

"Of course you don't," the clerk said with open contempt. "Fortunately for people like you, the documents are cross-filed by last and first name in our computer system. If the names and addresses match, I'll find them for you."

"You're very efficient and competent."

"Yes."

"I'm glad your records are automated."

"Of course they are. This isn't some backward town like Ransom."

Tom wrote his grandparents' and mother's names, and 133 North Elm Street, Ransom, Colorado on the form and handed it back. The clerk pointed toward one wall where a microfiche reader was set up on a small table. "Wait there. I'll bring you the ones you need if I find them."

He did find them. He brought three microfiche sheets to Tom and then returned to the counter and his finger-drumming.

Tom tried to shut out the background noise and concentrate.

The house had been the joint property of Donald and Angela Morisetti, so presumably it would have passed to Angela without complication after Donald's death in the mountains. When Angela died, complications might have arisen unless she also had a will. Given Kay Hamilton's youth and poverty at the time of her disappearance, Tom thought it unlikely that she had had a will. He had written his mother's name on the form just in case. The large white letters on the top of one sheet of microfiche, however, said HAMILTON, KATHERINE.

He put that one aside carefully and started with the one labeled MORISETTI, DONALD.

It was short and uncomplicated. Donald Morisetti had left everything he owned to his wife. If she died before he did, everything was to go to his only child, Katherine.

Angela Morisetti's will was a mirror image of her husband's. Everything she owned went to her husband. If he died before she did, then it all went to Katherine.

The dates on both wills predated Tom's birth by a year. That would put the date a month or two before his parents' marriage, he thought. He couldn't be entirely sure. His knowledge of the details of his parents' lives was maddeningly incomplete.

It was surprisingly hard to put his mother's will into the viewer.

The date on Kay Hamilton's will was one week after Tom's birth. It might have been copied from those of her parents. Anything she owned at the time of her death was to go to her husband, Alfred Hamilton. If he were to die before her, then Thomas Hamilton, her only child, was to inherit everything.

On some level, Tom had thought this will would be one last contact with his mother, something with the stamp of her personality on it. Instead, it was dry and impersonal. There was nothing of his mother in it, no feeling, no hint of the loving presence he treasured in his memory.

His father had stolen everything from him—even his maternal grandparents, as Tom now suspected. These impersonal sheets of plastic were the total of his emotional inheritance.

"When you're finished," the clerk said loudly, "please return those to the front counter. As the sign on the wall in front of you says."

Tom pushed himself to his feet and brought the microfiche back to the counter. He half expected to see indentations in the heavy wood where the clerk was doing his drumming, but there were none. "You must have calluses by now," Tom said.

"This job does that to you, all right."

Driving down the main street of Kenner on his way to the state highway that would take him back to Ransom, Tom thought that people must have been less suspicious when he was a child. It was probably television that had changed things, he decided. All those dramas with characters with complex, evil plans. The two deaths and one disappearance that had given Al Hamilton possession of the house on Elm Street would have aroused the suspicions of a modern district attorney. As Snow had pointed out, the disappearance of Al Hamilton's wife by itself would have been cause for an investigation. But apparently in Ransom thirty years ago, no one had done anything.

Perhaps even a sleepy, dying little town like Kenner hid secrets, murders, disappearances, mysteries that no one would ever solve. Human passions and crimes were the same everywhere, Tom thought. They just seemed closer and more threatening in the city than in a small town, but that was an illusion. Small-town people were no better than their city brethren. Thinking of Trager and his mob, Tom decided that the best one could say in defense of people in small towns was that their evil was less well organized.

Which seemed quite naturally to bring him back to the murder of Jerry Angleton and the crippling of Mike Berens.

He was out of Kenner by now and driving through rolling hills covered patchily with brown, dry grass. A few cows munched away at it placidly, ignored by a huge black bull. Normal instincts must be blunted in such a setting, Tom thought. A city bull, if there were such a thing, would be much more alert.

It seemed wrong to be thinking about murders and guns in this bucolic paradise, but Tom felt guilty that he had put it all aside for so long in favor of investigating his own life.

He started by reviewing his list of suspects. His original list was now down to these people:

Jack Tourneau
Karen Franks

Karen was there because he couldn't think of a good reason to remove her. Jack was there because of Tom's boyhood resentments. All of which seemed to make his list not very useful. What a shame, he thought. Lists of suspects always seemed to work so well for Hercule Poirot. No doubt that resulted from the tidy nature of the crimes Christie set up for her creation to solve. Real life—real crime—was so much messier and less orderly.

What about the murder method? After his experience at The Gun Man the day before, Tom found himself thinking in terms of guns and bullets instead of people and their emotions.

Andy Snow had told him that the live bullets that had been substituted for the blanks were a common variety available in gun shops all over the area. But was it possible to narrow the search a bit? Could a forensics lab determine which batch the bullets came from, assuming they had all been manufactured together? If so, then the shipping records from the manufacturer might be sufficient to determine which gun shop those particular bullets had been sent to. The shop's records would then show who had purchased those bullets. If the shop didn't keep records of who bought which kind of ammunition, the salesclerk might happen to remember the particular sale.

If I were still in Chicago, Tom thought in annoyance, I'd have called up one of the police detectives who were on Trager's payroll and asked those questions. Andy Snow is hardly likely to tell me anything.

Then he realized that the answer must be no, anyway. No, the police didn't know which manufacturer's batch the bullets came from, or to which gun shop they had been shipped, or to whom the shop had sold them. If the police had known that much, they'd have made an arrest by now.

Wait a minute, he thought. I'm asking the wrong question.

What counts isn't whether the police can determine all of that. The important question is whether the murderer thinks the police can determine all that!

If I were the murderer and I thought the police could do that, what would I do?

I wouldn't buy the bullets in Ransom, where I'm known. Or any other small town around here. I might not be known in Kenner, say, but I'd be memorable there because I was a stranger. One of the bigger cities, then. Denver or Colorado

Springs. In either one, I could count on just being another stranger buying a box of bullets.

Which means, Tom realized, that I need to visit every gun shop in both Denver and Colorado Springs and describe both Jack Tourneau and Karen Franks and ask if either one has bought bullets there. Karen they'd probably remember. If Jack was his usual boorish, talkative self, the might remember him, too.

Assuming they'd answer my questions. Can I convince anyone that I'm a police detective? Not likely.

He was just passing under Interstate 25. Soon he would come to a side road on the left. If he took that, he would head south for about a mile and then reach County Line Road. He could take that back east to the interstate, get on it, and go north to Denver and begin his investigation immediately. While he drove north, he would try to think up some convincing story that would make the people who waited on him in the gun shops tell him everything he wanted to know.

Or he could go home and do nothing for the rest of the day.

After the emotions he had felt on handling the microfiche with his mother's will on it, going home and doing nothing appealed to him far more. Tomorrow morning would be time enough to get started on his gun shop quest.

Twenty-One

On Wednesday morning, Tom went to the Ransom Public Library and looked at the listings for gun shops in the Denver and Colorado Springs yellow pages.

The library didn't open until ten a.m., which meant that, after copying down addresses from the telephone directory, Tom couldn't hope to be in either of the two cities to start his research until noon at the earliest. He thought that that should be enough time. There couldn't be more than a dozen gun shops in either place, he was sure.

He was wrong.

According to the directories, there were more like a hundred gun shops in Denver and about half that number in Colorado Springs. And they were scattered all over both cities and the surrounding suburbs.

This could take me months! he thought in despair.

He closed the directory and leaned back. The directory was bound in a sturdy library hard cover and closed with a loud slap. Tom's chair creaked. The college student sharing the table with him looked up, startled, from the term paper she was slaving over and glared at him.

"Sorry." She was lovely, Tom thought. What would she say if a man twice her age asked her to go have a drink with him?

Well, well, he said to himself. A few lunch dates with Janice Sheridan and Ellen Chernikov, and you just get all puffed up and overconfident. She's probably too young to drink legally anyway.

Might as well copy down the first few Denver addresses and give them a try, he thought. He needed to feel that he was doing something, working on solving one mystery.

He leaned forward and reopened the directory. The chair creaked and the directory cover slapped against the table. The girl glared at him again. She had a charming glare. "Sorry," he repeated. He smiled at her, hoping she'd consider his smile a charming one.

"Shithead," the girl said. "Go fuck yourself."

That was one of my shortest-lived fantasies yet, Tom thought.

He copied down the first ten gun shop addresses, closed the directory with a satisfyingly loud slap, and got up. His chair creaked one last time. "Knees," he told the girl. "Happens to everyone after thirty."

He was halfway to Denver before inspiration struck.

He tried his story out at the first store on his list. "Hi. I'm trying to buy a present for a couple I know, but I want it to be a surprise. I know they're hunters, so I'm thinking of a nice rifle of some sort, but I don't know what kind of ammunition they favor. 22, I'm pretty sure. I wonder if either of them came in here in the last month or two to buy ammunition." He described Karen Franks and Jack Tourneau.

The clerk he was speaking to said, "This is the weirdest question I've ever been asked, and that's saying something." He looked at Tom suspiciously, but then he thought for a while and said, "Don't remember anyone looking like that. Either one. Let me ask the other guys." He went through a doorway labeled EMPLOYEES ONLY and left Tom standing alone. After a while, he returned and said that no one else remembered dealing with a customer like either of those Tom had described.

Tom thanked him and left. That had gone much better than he had feared.

At the next store, the conversation was almost identical, except that at the end, the middle-aged woman who owned the place said, "Why don't you just surprise them with a really nice piece of home protection like this—" she pulled a silver and grey automatic pistol from some hidden place in her clothing "—lovely machine. Walther PPK. They'll love it. Only $1200, and I'll throw in the ammunition."

She, too, must have seen Tom's car. "It's something to keep in mind. I may be back for it."

He managed to hit all of the shops on his list, but it took all day. No one he spoke to remembered anyone who looked like either Karen Franks or Jack Tourneau. Few of them acted suspicious. Half of them tried to sell him something else as a gift for the gun-loving couple. The last group included two who tried to persuade him to buy a handgun that the couple could use to defend their home against the army of human predators they all seemed convinced, despite all crime statistics to the contrary, were infesting the city. One man urged Tom to buy a pair of handguns for his friends, a his-and-hers set.

He was middle-aged and heavy set, with a shirt that was

unbuttoned all the way to his belt, exposing both his luxuriant chest hair and his impressive belly. "Look! Just look!" he cried. "Aren't they sweet? I ordered the case special."

It was a handsome case—cherry wood, with gold hinges and a dark blue velvet lining. The two guns resting in it were silver colored with black grips. "I like the contrast between the silver and the lining of the case," Tom said.

The other man looked at him curiously. "Nickel."

"Of course. I meant the color. No trigger guards?"

"Blow away the intruder that much faster. If you're sleepy and the guy's coming into your bedroom, you don't want to fumble around and put your finger in the wrong place. And with this beautiful pair, both you and the Mrs. can aerate him at the same time. The one on your right, that's the man's one, that's a 22 Mag. Puts a very nice hole in your target. The other one, that's for the lady of the house. It's called the Black Widow, that model. Chambers a 22 Short. You can also buy a version that's set up for 22 Long Rifle, but I prefer to steer the ladies toward this model. It's a matter of hand and wrist strength." He looked Tom up and down. "You said this was for a friend, right? And he's bigger than you?"

"Oh yes. Quite a bit."

The man nodded. "Then this would be just up his alley. What do you think?"

"Black Widow," Tom repeated. "Do your female customers like that name?"

The man laughed. "You bet they do! Tickles them."

"And they take your advice about what model to buy?"

"Hell, yes." He pulled his shoulders back. It made his belly project all the more. "I'm the kind of man, women take my advice. Women like that firm hand anyway. You know that. I can see you're the kind of man understands that. Oh, okay, so not every damned one of them follows my advice. I had a woman in here a few weeks back, pretty big, pretty strong. I steered her towards this model I'm showing you right now, but she insisted on the Black Widow with the conversion chamber for the 22 Long Rifle. I had her try a few shots with one in my basement. I'm set up down there. She convinced me she could handle it. She went home real happy." His attention wandered and he smiled. "She had...really nice wrists." He caught himself and said, "See, that's one of the things I really love about this business—the way you get to interact with people."

As you advise them how to kill each other, Tom thought. "Well, I'll certainly keep that lovely pair of guns in mind. Thanks for helping me."

By the time Tom had finished with all ten shops, the sun was already setting, and he felt exhausted. Just as well, he thought, that there were no more gun shops on his list.

And what had he learned in exchange for one day of his life? Very little. Neither Karen Franks nor Jack Tourneau had bought ammunition at any of the ten shops he had visited.

Assuming no one was lying to me, he thought. And if any of them were? Well, there's nothing I can do about it. I just have to assume they're all telling the truth.

He had learned a little more about the nature of gun porn and the delusions some people labored under about the level of violence in the world around them. And he still had something like ninety gun shops to check in Denver alone.

Thursday was much like Wednesday, but spent in a different

city.

Once again, Tom went to the library in the morning. This time, he copied down the first ten addresses of gun shops from the yellow pages for Colorado Springs. This time, the college student he had annoyed the day before wasn't there. Off screwing with some beardless youth, no doubt, Tom thought. Those supple young things tend to do that.

He then drove down to Colorado Springs and repeated his story at ten gun shops there. The reactions fell into the same categories as before, he again learned nothing useful, and once more it was sunset by the time he finished.

As he drove slowly north on the interstate, caught in a sluggish flow of traffic that wasn't quite a jam, he calculated that at his current rate of investigation, he would only be halfway through the gun shops in the telephone directory by the planned date for the third opening night of Ellen's opera. So if the third tenor was also in danger of being shot, the young man would have to take his chances. Tom wouldn't be able to solve everything brilliantly in time to save him.

Too damned bad, he thought. I'm not going to work on this any more tonight. If anyone has earned an evening off, I have.

As the distance from Colorado Springs increased, the number of cars on the highway diminished. Thirty minutes, Tom estimated. Thirty minutes to a nice quiet evening at home.

Twenty-Two

The phone was ringing as he opened his front door. Tom sighed and considered letting the answering machine handle the call. Answering machines and voice mail had handled so many important calls for him over the years. Now that he was supposed to be peacefully retired, letting the machine continue to answer for him seemed like a fine idea.

But instead he hurried into the living room and snatched the receiver up before the machine could intercept. "Tom Hamilton here."

"Tom, this is Ellen. I'm at the school. We're rehearsing, and I need you to do me a favor."

Tom groaned. Tonight was the first rehearsal for this attempt at staging Tosca, and he'd promised Ellen he'd be there to help with the props or in any other way he could. "Christ, Ellen, I'm sorry. I'll be right there."

"Oh, don't bother. Obviously you have more important things to do. Maybe you have a date. I'll get Jack to help."

Jesus, Tom thought, I'm getting the nasty part of marriage to Ellen without benefit of the good parts. "Ellen, please calm down. I'll be there in a few minutes, okay?" He hung up before she could say anything else.

As he drove down the hillside toward the lights of the town, Tom wondered why Ellen needed him there at all. Since it was the first rehearsal, what would they be doing? Sitting down and reading their parts aloud to each other? Stumbling around on the stage and trying to figure out who stood where? In either case, they hardly needed his help.

But when he reached the auditorium and hurried in by the stage entrance at the rear, he discovered that his real role tonight was to keep Ellen from exploding with frustration.

"*Ogni pennello è sozzo*!" she yelled at the young man playing the sacristan. "Don't say *ahg nee*! It's not English, it's Italian!"

Tom reflected that Jack would have said that it didn't make any difference, since no one in the audience knew Italian. Jack would have had a point.

"Italian?" Tom asked.

"Oh, God, I'm glad to see you! Yes, Italian. I decided that would have more impact than the English translation we were using."

An untrained singer, a new role, and a new language. Tom wondered what would be the most diplomatic way to tell Ellen that she had gone completely over the edge. Instead, he turned coward and said, "It's only the first rehearsal. Don't concentrate on the details at this point."

"It's only the first rehearsal for Ken," she snarled, gesturing toward the recently recruited tenor. Ken Hillerman tried to disappear into his chair. "Everyone else has gone through this over and over already, up to and including two opening nights!"

She stopped at that point as everyone looked at Ken and

thought about those two opening nights and the fates of Ken's two predecessors.

"Take a break," Ellen said, her voice suddenly weak. "Tom, come outside with me. I need some air."

It was still light outside. The sun had just set, and the air was already cooling. The temperature always dropped rapidly in Ransom after sunset because of the altitude and the dryness. At this time of year, the difference between the high temperature during the day and the low during the night often exceeded forty degrees. A huge moon was rising, almost full.

As they walked across the empty parking lot, Tom said, "At least go back to English. That way, only Hillerman will have to learn new lines. In a language he speaks, which will help a bit."

"Hmph. The world is full of weaklings."

He changed the subject. "You're going to be cold. Would you like me to go inside and get your coat?"

"No." She smiled. "Jack would never even have thought about my getting cold. That's just like you, Tom. You were always thoughtful. That was always one of the nice things about you."

"I thought it was one of the reasons I never had any dates."

"No, your sarcasm was one of the reasons you never had any dates. Let's not talk about that, please. And don't worry about me getting cold. I'm used to this climate, remember. I've lived here all my life. And *I'm* not a weakling."

She was wearing a long-sleeved dress with pockets. She put her hands into the pockets and said, "There. Now I'm fine." After a pause, she said, "Listen, I came out here because I needed a break from those kids and they needed a break from me. But I also wanted to think about something. Now I've thought about it, and I've figured it out."

She took her hands out of her pockets again. Putting them in the pockets, Tom realized, had been a touch of drama, a way of inflating Tom's concern for her comfort. The kids in the Tosca cast could learn a lot from Ellen.

They had reached the grass at the edge of the parking lot. They turned around and headed back toward the building. Ellen put her hand on Tom's shoulder and stopped him. She gestured with her chin toward the auditorium. The cast members were standing outside, near the small stage door, indistinct in the dim light. Tom caught a few words, snatches of conversation. A couple of them puffed on cigarettes, the glow of the burning tips standing out in the gathering gloom.

"They'll ruin their voices," Tom said. "Destroy their careers."

"Hell, they have no careers to destroy. Except for Karen, and she didn't bother showing up tonight."

"I noticed."

"You would."

"Are you going to discipline her? Drop her from the cast?"

Ellen sighed. "She knows I'm not going to do that. Where would I find another Tosca like her in this town? She knows her lines and moves. She was never a problem."

"Still, she should be here to go through her scenes with Ken. There's a lot for them to do together. Especially if you stick to the Italian plan."

Ellen waved her hand impatiently. "You're right, of course—about Karen and about the Italian. But never mind that. That's not what I wanted to tell you. I think the real problem right now is the effect of what happened to Jerry Angleton and

Mike Berens. You saw how everyone reacted just now when I stupidly made them think about it."

"I saw."

"It's like being thrown from a horse."

"I think it was a lot more like being shot," Tom said. "In both cases."

Ellen snapped, "Oh, Tom, for Heaven's sake! That's not what I meant. I mean that the whole cast is like someone who's learning to ride a horse and gets thrown. You know what they say: The best thing to do is to get right back on the horse. Don't wait, don't let your fear grow."

Tom had always considered that piece of advice to be one of the silliest in the repertoire of those given to repeating platitudes. He felt that the fact that horses occasionally threw their riders was a message from the Universe that human beings were not supposed to climb onto horses in the first place.

"Perhaps I'm not quite understanding the analogy," he said. "The cast is here rehearsing again, so what more do you want them to do?" And neither Jerry nor Mike is in a position to do any horse riding, he thought.

"I want them to shoot at each other."

"What?"

"I want to jump ahead to the final scene. I want to rehearse the firing squad and the execution of Mario. We don't even need Karen. We'll skip all the music, all the singing. I just want them to go through the motions of standing Mario against the wall and shooting him."

"And this will make them all able to ride horses again?"

"It will if the rifles are loaded with blanks and there's noise and flame. And this time, the tenor playing Mario doesn't really get hurt."

"Did you get a lot of tickets for reckless driving when you were a teenager?"

Ellen smiled. "I got stopped a few times, but I used to smile sweetly and make sure my skirt was hiked up pretty far, and I never got a single ticket. What do you think?"

"I think it's actually a pretty good idea. The horse riding thing, I mean."

"Great! Now all I need is to get the rifles and the blanks again."

Tom hadn't had a chance to look at the props he was supposed to oversee. As soon as he had arrived at the auditorium, he had become involved in Ellen's temper tantrums. "You don't have everything here already?"

"No. That bastard Snow is playing games with me. He's found some reason to delay. I'm sure he'll release the rifles in time for opening night. I'll talk to his wife, and that should guarantee it. But at this point, I still don't have them. We're using toy rifles for rehearsals."

"Well, that kills your idea, doesn't it?" He wondered why Ellen had wanted him present during rehearsals. Not to supervise the borrowed rifles, obviously. She was still following some secret emotional agenda, he realized. Behind the scenes of Tosca, she was directing some other opera, and he had been cast in it without his permission. He hoped it wasn't Carmen.

"Not entirely. It would be better if we could do the full-blown thing—all of them carrying rifles firing blanks. But I'm hoping that one real rifle will do the trick. Jack has quite a collection of his own, you know. Most of them aren't bolt-action 22s, but that doesn't matter tonight. He keeps them in a locked cabinet in his study, and I don't have the key. However, he doesn't have any more room in the cabinet, so while he shops for a new one, he's leaving one of his rifles out. He says that one isn't much good, anyway, and he prefers the others, so he doesn't really care if someone breaks in and steals it. The bastard paid two thousand dollars for it, and now he says it isn't good enough for him. He keeps it in the basement. There's an old bookcase down there, and the rifle's up on top of that. The door to the basement is just off the kitchen."

"I remember."

"That's right, I guess you would. The rifle is a 30–06. I know he keeps blanks of that caliber in one of the drawers of his desk in the study. The house key's up on the top of the brick ledge to the right of the front door. You can be back here with the rifle in a quarter of an hour or less. Should work out perfectly."

"I was wondering why you were giving me so much detail," Tom said.

"That's actually why I called you. I was going to ask you to go to the house and get the rifle and the blanks for me. You hung up and dashed over here before I could tell you."

"Wouldn't it make a lot more sense for you to cancel the rehearsal for tonight and then bring Jack's rifle with you the next time?"

"No. The sooner you get back up on the horse, the better it is. Not to mention that I can't afford to delay this rehearsal in any way, not with such a short time left before we reopen. You can see that, surely. And it's obvious that I can't leave these kids alone while *I* go and get the damned thing." She gestured toward the crowd around the stage door. An argument had broken out.

"You could just call the house and ask Jack to bring it down here," Tom suggested. "Quickest of all."

Ellen sneered. "You really think Jack's there? Nowadays, he's often not even around when I'm at home in the evening, and you can bet he won't be there when I'm not. Jack's being a young boy these days. He's out playing boy games. And even if he were there, I wouldn't trust him to remember what I asked him to do. He'd just put it out of his mind. Oh, hell, Tom, he'd probably do that deliberately, given his feelings about my opera production."

"Why don't you send him?" Tom pointed at the police car parked nearby. The man behind the wheel was barely visible. He had the seat tilted back as far as it could go, and he appeared to be asleep.

"He's supposed to be watching us with an eagle eye," Ellen said. "If I wake him up and try to send him on an errand, he'll get suspicious."

"Let sleeping dogs lie. That's probably wise. All right. Do you have an alarm system in the house?"

Ellen laughed. "You have been away for a long time, haven't you? No one bothers with that sort of thing in Ransom. Maybe up in Denver, but not here. You've been in the big city for too long, Tom."

"Not long enough to learn how not to be manipulated by small-town girls, apparently."

Ellen smiled but didn't answer. She turned and strode toward the stage door.

Twenty-Three

Driving from the high school toward Applewood, Tom let himself drift into a fantasy in which he sold his new house for only a moderate loss and then moved to some place he had never been before, where no one knew him under any name. Southern Arizona, perhaps. Or northern Washington.

But even in those places, he wouldn't be far from the tentacles of the mob. He knew that as well as anyone. All in all, he was surely safest here, where Tom Hamilton was known as a local boy. Word would not get back to Chicago that Tom Hamilton had shown up after living elsewhere for twenty years, whereas a stranger in some rural area might draw dangerous attention.

He parked on the street in front of the Tourneau house. No point in subterfuge, such as parking a block or two away, when he was going to walk through the front door.

The moon was almost full and well above the eastern horizon, partly obscured by clouds. Despite the clouds, the moonlight was sufficient for Tom to make his way up the long, curving driveway. Once again, he was struck by the omnipresent odor of pine needles. The Rockies smelled clean and dry.

Chicago had smelled rotten.

The driveway curved past the front door. He climbed the curving, red–brick steps to the wide front door. This is as close to living in a mansion as Jack is ever likely to get, Tom thought. Or Ellen, for that matter.

The key was where Ellen had said it would be. It unlocked both the regular bolt and the deadbolt. Tom thought that the presence of the deadbolt contradicted Ellen's dismissal of the need for alarm systems in Ransom. Wherever you lived, he thought, peace of mind and the feeling of safety were important. He had deadbolts in the front and back doors of his new house but he too had no alarm system. On the other hand, he didn't leave the door key outside in an obvious place.

He felt for a switch on the wall beside the front door and found it. He hesitated for a moment, wishing he had brought a flashlight.

Yeah, right, he told himself. What if a police car passed by and the police saw the flashlight beam through the window? Wouldn't Andy Snow love to have you brought in on a breaking and entering charge?

Despite that, when he flicked the switch and the lights came on, Tom felt uncomfortably exposed. He was an intruder in this house. He couldn't imagine ever feeling like anything else in the Tourneau house nowadays.

He tried to put that out of his mind and concentrate on his task.

First the basement and the rifle, Tom thought. Then the blanks in the study. He'd get those on the way out.

He remembered the way to the kitchen. He remembered much about this house and the kindness of the elder Tourneaus.

Having turned on the light in the entranceway somehow made it easier to keep turning on lights as he went, on the principle of in for a penny, in for a pound. And bright lights they were, too—floor lamps, track lighting, lamps on end tables, all with high-wattage bulbs. That was a change from the old days. It was too much, too bright, too harsh. It gave everything a washed-out, characterless look and made the furniture look cheap. Odd, he thought, that he hadn't noticed this effect on his previous visit.

He took a moment to admire the kitchen. This too was changed from the old days. Had the Tourneaus hired a professional to redesign it for them? He'd have to remember to ask Ellen for the name. If he had a kitchen like this one, he'd probably feel more like learning to cook the kind of food he liked to eat.

Gourmet cooking for one, he thought. Seems kind of pointless.

Stop procrastinating, he told himself.

There were two doors at the far end of the kitchen, set into adjacent walls. Tom remembered that one of them led down to the basement and the other one into the garage, but he couldn't remember which one was which.

He chose the one on the left at random and pulled it open. In the light from the kitchen, he could see the hood and headlights of a pale-gold Accura Legend.

He froze for a moment. Then he forced himself to close the door quietly and open the other one. A flight of wooden stairs led downward. Tom felt on the wall beside the door and found the switch. Below him, fluorescent lights flickered for a moment, then came on, revealing the basement.

Up to this point, he had acted almost mechanically. The car in the garage meant that Ellen was wrong and Frank was still in the house. Maybe he was on the telephone to the police right now, reporting an intruder.

I'm here on legitimate business, Tom reminded himself. Ellen will back me up.

He realized he had bent over furtively. Now he straightened and walked calmly down the steps into the basement.

The basement, at least, was mostly as he remembered it. On the whole, it was a standard middle-American party room. Paneled walls, wet bar, couch, television set, built-in shelves holding a few sports trophies. The television set was much bigger than the one he remembered. There was also an upright piano and a small bookcase filled with old college English textbooks—possibly a small bow to Jack's profession, although those might also be left over from Jack's father. None of the books was new. Jack, Tom thought, was just the type not to have read anything in his field since getting his Ph.D.

On the top of the bookcase, about at chest height for Tom, was a rifle.

You wouldn't leave a rifle in a basement in Chicago, Tom thought irrelevantly. It's the dryness that makes it okay here.

There were people he'd known in Chicago who would have taken one glance at this weapon and told him all about it—make, model, and advantages and disadvantages. To Tom, it was nothing more than a machine designed to kill. Some of these machines were designed to kill animals, some to kill men, but "kill" was the significant part. He wondered if this rifle had fired one of the fatal bullets into Kathy Angleton's husband.

No, he realized. The firing squad used 22s. Ellen said this one was...He tried to remember. A 30–something. He laughed aloud. You have to have a 20–something to kill a twenty–something. You're overtired, he told himself.

He picked up the rifle and tucked it under his arm, so that he looked like a figure from an illustration he remembered in an Edwardian novel.

He went upstairs, clicked off the light, closed the basement door, and headed for the study.

Of all the rooms in the house, this was the one Tom associated most strongly in his memories with Jack's father. A gun cabinet was mounted on one wall, but other than that, the furniture was completely unchanged. But the ever–present smell of pipe tobacco was gone, and so was the neatness. Jack's father had often quoted the old maxim, "A place for everything and everything in its place," and he had followed that rule scrupulously. Now the room was as paper littered and disorganized as Andy Snow's office.

The desk was the massive apple wood one Tom had admired as a boy. He wondered if there was any chance Jack would sell it to him.

The desk had four drawers on either side. Seven of the eight were unlocked. They contained a jumble of old letters, coins, small office supplies, dirty facial tissues, old banana peels and apple cores, and much other evidence of the inferiority of Jack Tourneau's character to that of his father. They did not, however, contain bullets of any kind, blank or otherwise.

The final drawer, the top one on the right, was locked. Tom tugged at the handle a few times, hoping it was actually stuck, but it was the only drawer with a keyhole, and he was sure it was locked and that it was the one with the blanks. Tom found that he wasn't looking forward to Ellen's reaction when he returned to the school auditorium and told her of his failure.

He smelled cologne and alcohol.

"Oh, it's you. At least you broke into *my* house, this time, instead of Kathy's. What the hell are you doing here?"

Tom turned slowly, remembering the confrontation in Kathy Angleton's house and not wanting to alarm Jack.

This time, he discovered, Jack was fully dressed and not armed. Jack was wearing slacks and a sweater that looked as though they'd been slept in. He was standing in the doorway of the study, blinking at the light.

Tom relaxed. "I came to get this." He held the rifle up.

Jack paled and stepped back. "What're you—Is this some kind of revenge?"

"Jack, it's not even loaded! Unless you leave loaded rifles lying around your house."

Jack recovered his poise. "No, no, of course I don't. For a moment, I thought—Never mind. Hey, that's my KDF! Give that to me!" He came forward and snatched it from Tom's hands. "This cost me two thousand bucks! You trying to steal it?"

"It cost you that much, and you leave it on top of a bookcase in the basement?"

"That's none of your business. I want to know what you're doing here."

Tom explained the mission Ellen had sent him on.

"I don't know if I should believe you," Jack said. His face began to grow red. "You're screwing my wife, and now you're breaking into my house and trying to steal one of my rifles." His voice rose. "I didn't kill you before, in Kathy's house, when I had the chance. I should do it now."

Tom saw movement behind Jack. "No more killing, Dr. Tourneau." Andy Snow stepped into the study. He held a pistol pointed at Jack's chest. Three uniformed policemen pushed into the room behind him.

Snow came forward—too close. Jack whipped the butt of the rifle stock outward and knocked the gun from Snow's hand. Snow gasped in pain and staggered back.

The three uniformed men leaped on Jack and bore him to the ground.

"It's not loaded!" Tom yelled. He realized suddenly that he didn't really know if that was true. It didn't matter, though. No one was paying attention to him. By now, the three policemen had Jack fully subdued. The rifle was lying a few feet away. Jack was down on his stomach, his hands being pulled behind him to the small of his back, while one of the men put handcuffs on him. Another one had his foot on Jack's head. The third man rose to his feet and gave Jack a couple of leisurely kicks in the side of the knee.

Jack shouted—a gurgled, muffled sound.

"That's enough," Snow said. "Get him to his feet." He moved his right hand as thought testing his wrist. Then he picked up the rifle and looked at it with interest. "Nice," he said.

Jack's clothes looked even more rumpled than before. There was now a rip in the side of his sweater. His face had acquired some red splotches, and a bump was swelling on his forehead. He looked subdued in a way Tom had never seen him before—which gave Tom so much pleasure that he felt ashamed for a very brief moment.

"What is all this?" Jack said. He was trying to conjure up his usual bluster and domineering manner, but it was a weak and unimpressive attempt.

"You have the right to remain silent," Snow began, smiling happily.

Twenty-Four

By the time Snow finished, Frank was whimpering and tears were rolling down his cheeks. "I didn't do anything!" he kept saying.

Snow laughed. "You assaulted a police officer. But maybe you're too drunk to know what you're doing." He gestured to the uniformed policemen to take Jack away. They did so with great enthusiasm and considerable roughness. Tom and Snow stood listening to the rumble of their feet as they tramped to the front door with Jack.

When the house was silent again, Snow said, "I love to see a grown man cry. In fact, I expected to see you crying, Hamilton." He sniffed the air. "Or shitting your pants, but I guess you didn't."

"Lieutenant, what the hell are you talking about?"

"Tourneau was about to kill you with this rifle, that's what I'm talking about. It's a good thing for you that I showed up, or he'd be burying you somewhere in the mountains about now."

Tom shook his head. "I still don't know what you're talking about. I came here to get that rifle for Mrs. Tourneau. Dr. Tourneau and I were having a conversation, that's all."

"That's not what I heard when I came in. It was pretty damned clear that he was gearing himself up to attack. Like I said, it's a good thing for you I showed up—a good thing Mrs. Tourneau called me up and told me about you being on your way to confront her husband."

"Confront her husband?"

"With your suspicions that he engineered the shootings of Jerry Angleton and Mike Berens. She told me you were coming here to force him to confess. Which, considering your size compared to his, was pretty damned stupid of you. I'm wondering if there's something else going on. *Are* you screwing his wife? You gotta be careful about stuff like that, Hamilton. It's almost as dangerous as detective work."

"This is too strange to believe," Tom said. "Lieutenant, you're fantasizing. Nothing happened here other than what I told you. The rifle isn't even loaded."

"Bullshit." Snow examined the weapon quickly. "Well, crap." Before Tom could say anything, Snow said, "All right, forget the fucking rifle. He was still talking about killing you. If you'll cooperate with me, I'll bet I can come up with something serious to charge him with."

"Is this what you call 'serving and protecting'? I'm not going to help you charge a man with something he didn't do."

"Sooner or later, that man's going to take a shot at you, Hamilton. I can tell." He stared at Tom for a while, then shrugged. "Okay, if you won't do your part, then I can't protect you. There's always assaulting an officer, of course."

"That was almost an involuntary movement on Jack's part," Tom said. "Jack heard a voice behind him, turned, saw a man with a gun coming toward him, and struck out in self–

protection. I'll testify to that."

"Why the hell are you protecting him?" Snow asked indignantly. "It won't do that guy any harm to spend a few hours behind bars. You think you'll score points with his wife by keeping him out of prison? Ah, to hell with it." He turned and stalked away toward the front door.

Tom followed. He stood in the doorway and watched Snow get into a police car parked in the driveway. The interior light came on when Snow opened the door, and Tom could see one of the uniformed men in the driver's seat and the other in the back with Jack. The door closed, the light went off, the car sat there for a long time with no evidence of life.

At last the back door of the police car opened, and Jack climbed out. He was not handcuffed, and none of the policemen got out with him. Jack stood uncertainly in his driveway next to the car. The engine started, and the car drove away. Jack stood watching it go.

My good deed for the decade, Tom thought. Snow was probably right and this will come back to haunt me.

But his good deeds weren't over. He spent a half hour getting Jack back inside the house and calmed down. Jack was babbling incoherently at first. When his speech cleared up, he demanded a large drink, and he guzzled it down. The alcohol seemed to calm him a bit, but not so much that Tom couldn't see how terrified he was. Jack had always been one of the town's golden boys. Being treated this way by the police must be a new experience for him. It was certainly a frightening experience for him.

Jack asked for a second drink.

"I don't think that's a good idea," Tom said.

"Please!" Jack whined. "I really need it. This has been a terrible evening!"

Anything to make you shut up, Tom thought. He waited till Jack had almost finished the second big glass of Scotch with one cube of ice and very little water. Then he said, "Can you unlock that desk drawer for me and give me a blank cartridge for that rifle I came here to get? The one you grabbed from me?"

Jack didn't answer.

"Jack?"

Too late. Jack was unconscious.

"Shit," Tom muttered. Ellen's idea was a silly one, anyway, he told himself. It was past time to go back to the school auditorium and tell her so.

Tom had once heard singing referred to as "controlled shouting." The shouting he heard as he entered the high-school auditorium wasn't controlled at all. Ken Hillerman had snapped at last. He was no longer seated, no longer trying to disappear into his chair. He was standing in the middle of the stage, his face was red, and he was bellowing at the top of his lungs at Ellen.

Ellen was standing, too. She was close to Ken and seemed to be enduring his tirade calmly, but as he walked down the aisle and came closer to the stage, Tom recognized on her face an expression he had seen there a couple of times in high school. Both times, she had just been insulted and was preparing her response.

This time, her response was surprisingly mild. She waited until Ken ran out of breath—which happened much sooner than it should have for someone who hoped to sing a lead role in a

Puccini opera—and then said, "You have been utterly inadequate in every respect from the very beginning. Your voice is inadequate, your sense of pitch is inadequate, your memory is inadequate, your self-control is inadequate, and I strongly suspect that you are inadequate in other ways. You're fired. Get off my stage."

Ken looked more relieved than insulted. He ran down the steps into the auditorium and up the aisle, pushing past Tom.

The rest of the cast had remained seated, watching the exchange with fascination. Ellen turned to them and said, "You might as well all go home now. I'll have to unearth one more Mario. I'll call you when I'm ready to start rehearsing again."

There was a general scraping of chairs against the wooden stage and a murmur of conversation as the other cast members stood. They folded their chairs with a loud clatter and began to move backstage, jostling each other, getting in each other's way. They reminded Tom of students released from an assembly in this auditorium twenty years earlier.

Tom waited until Ellen was alone on the stage before climbing the steps to join her. "I don't have the rifle," he said.

Ellen turned toward him and gasped. "Oh, Tom!" She pressed her hand to her chest. There was one chair remaining on the stage, the one Ken Hillerman had been using. She sank into it. "Thank God you're okay! After you left, I remembered that Jack was at home after all. He had intended to go out, but then he started drinking and fell asleep. You know how he is. Anyway, as soon as I remembered that he was there, I began to worry about how he'd react if you walked into the house. He's paranoid sometimes. Especially when he's been drinking. I didn't know what to do! Finally, I thought of Andy Snow. I called him up at home and made up some story about you going to the house to confront Jack because you suspected him of being behind the shootings."

"He was that concerned for my safety? I'm surprised. Why didn't you just call up the main police station downtown?"

"I was afraid they wouldn't take me very seriously. 'Officer, I'm afraid my husband is going to get angry.' They'd have laughed at that. But I had the feeling that Snow would welcome the chance to act like one of the cops on those real-life cop shows. I had his home number from his wife, so I called him there."

"Well, thank you for making that call. I suppose it's possible that Jack might have turned violent if Snow hadn't shown up. Snow had a couple of policemen with him and they...they roughed Jack up a bit. Don't worry, though. He's unharmed. And asleep." It seemed a good time to change the subject. "You were remarkably easy on that kid. Back in high school, that one time I dared to ask you for a date, you did a much better job of destroying me."

Ellen shrugged. "He snapped. He couldn't take it. Better to find out at this stage instead of later. I didn't want to destroy him, I just wanted him to go away without arguing or causing a problem with the rest of the cast. I don't remember you ever asking me for a date."

Which shouldn't surprise me, Tom thought. It was an incident he would never forget. He would never forget her words or her expression while she spoke them.

A year after that incident, a mathematics teacher named Jerry Cobb had made the mistake of ridiculing Ellen's homework in front of the entire class. She hadn't dismantled the man verbally as she had Tom, but she had worn that same expression for the rest of the day. Two months later, Cobb had resigned and left town. Tom had wondered for years if Ellen had been behind that, and if so, how she had done it.

"Well," Ellen said. "I suppose I might as well go home now and see how bad the damage is."

"Nothing got broken."

"Don't be silly, Tom. It all got broken a long time ago."

"Where's your coat? I'll get it for you."

Ellen sprang to her feet with surprising energy. "Don't bother. I'll get it. I'm determined to do everything for myself from now on. No more depending on men."

"All that because of an unsatisfactory tenor?"

"And baritones and basses and all the rest of them. Men of all types." She walked quickly off stage. A folding chair remained in the wings, and her coat was folded over its back. She picked it up and struggled into it.

"It's not cold outside," Tom told her.

"I'm wearing it for psychological comfort," Ellen said. She led the way out of the auditorium.

Outside, Ellen stopped beneath one of the parking lot lights and waited for Tom to catch up. The combination of artificial light and bright moonlight washed out details, but despite that Tom could see a sheen of sweat on her face. "You see, it *is* hot," he said. "Better take your coat off." He reached out to help.

"My, but you're eager to undress me. You had your chance at that, kid, and you turned me down. The truth is, I don't feel well. I think I may be coming down with something. Or maybe it's just anger and tension after dealing with those idiots this evening. I'm going to go home and go to bed."

"What about Jack? The mood he was in when I left him—"

"Don't worry about Jack," Ellen said firmly. "I can handle him. I understood what you meant when you said he was sleeping. He might have slept it off already and be gone for the evening. Or the night. With Jack, you never know. It's gotten to the point where we just share the house and not much else."

Tom shook his head, not knowing what to say, and hoping the gesture would save him from having to say anything.

"But since you're so eager to see more of me," Ellen said, "how about lunch tomorrow?"

"If you'll be okay by then."

"A good night's sleep always takes care of whatever I have. And I always sleep well, no matter what's going on around me. I'll be okay. If I'm not, I'll call you."

They arranged to meet at noon at La Estrellita.

Tom walked her to her car. "Reliable, aren't they?" Tom said, putting his hand lightly on the Accord's faded paint.

"Wanna trade?"

"Not really."

"Didn't think so. This one better be reliable." She climbed in, closed the door, and rolled down the driver's window. "I'll probably have to keep it for another 100,000 miles or so. This is all Jack feels we can afford for me at the moment. Especially given the payments on his."

Tom said, "Call me when you get home if there's any problem with Jack."

"Will you come to my rescue and beat him to a pulp?"

"No, I'll call Andy Snow."

Ellen laughed and started her car. "Noon," she said, and accelerated away from him.

Tom stood for a long time, lost in a memory of Ellen driving past him twenty years earlier, looking much the same. Her hair had been longer in those days, and it had streamed out the window. She had seemed to him, then, to embody liberty and escape. Tom the boy had thought that if only he were driving away with Ellen, away from Ransom and into the world of freedom and all delights, then he would want nothing else forever, and all his childhood agonies would vanish at last.

Tom the man shivered as if shaking off a spell and walked to his own car and drove home.

Twenty-Five

Friday dawned dry, clear, and crisp. It was now mid-September, and Colorado was displaying itself at its best. Tom had always liked autumn more than any other season in Ransom. Colorado summers were too hot, the winters too cold, and spring too short—or, in some years, non-existent. But Colorado autumns were incomparable. While in Chicago, he had dreamed of their dry, breezy coolness. He had been astonished by the colors of the trees in Chicago in autumn, and in contrast the uniform yellow leaves of autumn in Colorado seemed pale and boring, but the air made up for that. Even at their best, Chicago autumns never filled him with optimism and energy as Colorado autumns did. It was an optimism that had always been betrayed by events during his boyhood, and yet it had persisted nonetheless. His mother had loved those days, too.

Tom ate a light breakfast, put on his lined windbreaker, and spent a couple of hours walking along the hiking trail that began across the road from his house. The lot to the south of his was still empty, and the house to the north—even larger than Tom's—was complete but still unoccupied, with a raw, fresh look to it that Tom's house was already beginning to lose. The land across the road was still forest. Most of the lots near Tom's house were still empty.

Just beyond the newly completed house to the north of Tom's was a long stretch of open space—acreage bought years earlier by the city and exempted permanently from development. The hiking trail ran through the open space. Except for the trail itself, the area looked the way it must have before the town existed. A hundred yards down the trail, and Tom could believe he was in the mountains, far from any town.

He had come up here once as a kid and had seen deer and what he thought was a mountain lion—a shape almost as much canine as feline, sliding out of sight behind a low bush. Foolishly, he had run to the spot, but there was nothing there. He had never been sure if he had really seen anything or if he had imagined it. Now that houses were being built up here, he thought it unlikely he'd see any deer in the area, let alone a mountain lion. The steady push of the town into the foothills had just as steadily pushed back the wilderness and the creatures that lived in it.

In one place, the trail turned east and emerged from the trees to skirt the edge of the cliff overlooking the town. The view was much the same as that from his living room. Tom paused for a while and imagined that he was a boy again. He had stopped here, back then, and looked down at the town he lived in, amazed that it looked so small and far away and unimportant, amazed that the pain of his life, which so dominated everything when he was down in Ransom, seemed to belong to someone else, to a kid stuck down there in the valley.

He remembered now that he had wanted to stay up here forever. He supposed that the seed had been planted then that would later grow into the decision to buy a house up in these hills. He had not made the connection before. When he came back to Ransom, buying one of the new, luxurious houses dotted along the hillside overlooking the town had seemed a natural thing to do. He had forgotten all about that boyhood hike. Now he found himself remembering it intensely.

When he was here as a boy, the steep cliff and the rocky ground far below had frightened and exhilarated him. Now he wondered if he should have the area in front of his house fenced off for safety. No, not fenced. A stone wall built of native rocks would blend in nicely. That way, he wouldn't have to worry about drunken party guests falling over the edge. If he ever gave a party.

Children, then.

If he ever had children.

No, he'd leave the property as it was. The cliff edge was still both frightening and exhilarating to him, just as it had been twenty–five or thirty years before. He'd hate to lose that.

He walked a bit further before turning back. There were a few aspens along the trail, which surprised him, given the seeming lack of water. Some of their leaves were already turning yellow. That also seemed surprising. Didn't that usually start later in the year? Was it determined by the weather during the summer, or by the weather during the preceding winter? For all he knew about the local plants and soil, he thought, he might as well have grown up in Chicago.

Ransom was a small town, and yet it was possible to live a life circumscribed by its perimeter. He had gone away and had educated himself about wines and literature and music and art, and about men even more evil than his father, and about secrets and manipulation and the inducing of terror. Now it was time to purge himself of some of that and learn about his home instead. If he ever did have children, he wanted to be able to pass on to them only good knowledge.

The air had warmed up considerably by the time he left the house to meet Ellen for lunch. He wore jeans, running shoes, and a short–sleeved shirt. The breeze was cool but not cold, and the autumn sun felt pleasant on his bare arms.

By the time he found a parking space downtown and walked to the restaurant it was almost 12:15. Ellen was waiting for him. She was drumming her fingers on the table and frowning, but when she saw him walking toward her, she relaxed and smiled at him. "I thought you were going to stand me up," she said.

"How likely is it that I'd miss a lunch date with Ellen Chernikov?" Tom asked as he slid into the booth opposite her. Ellen Tourneau is a different matter, he thought, and I probably should have stayed home.

Ellen laughed. "You say the nicest things. Using my maiden name is one of them."

It seemed to Tom that every time they spoke, he found himself needing a verbal distraction, something to divert the conversation from its disturbing path. "Jesus, what happened to your wrists?" He had been looking at her face and had just noticed how red her wrists were. It wasn't immediately obvious in the restaurant's dim light, but the more he looked at her arms, the redder the skin just above her hands looked. "Did you burn yourself?"

Ellen looked embarrassed and put her hands in her lap

quickly. "It's nothing. It's just something that happened—that I did last night." She looked at him quickly, then glanced away and down.

"Does it hurt? How did you do it?"

"Don't press me, Tom. It's not easy to talk about."

"Jack's responsible, isn't he?" It was a guess, but once he put it into words, Tom was sure he must be right.

Ellen forced a laugh. "He always is, isn't he?" Her shoulders and face relaxed and she put her hands back on the table for Tom to see. "Yes, it was Jack. When I got home last night, he was still there, and he was feeling aggressive. Needed to convince himself of something, I guess. He wanted to play one of his old games. It involves...It involves tying me to the bed. I didn't want to play, and I tried to get loose. Finally, I decided I'd better just go along with it and let him do what he wanted and get it over with. That's what I usually decide," she added bitterly. "By then, I'd hurt my wrists pretty badly."

"That bastard!"

"Ssh!" Ellen looked around quickly. "Calmly, Tom. It's not something new. I made my bed—" She stopped as if realizing how unfortunate the saying was in her case. Then she shrugged. "Yes, that's what I did." She glanced down at her wrists. "It looked worse this morning. It's already getting better. It's not all that bad, really. See?" She held her arms out over the table for Tom to examine. Automatically, foolishly, he took her hands in his.

"It's not worth getting angry about," Ellen said. "Not any more, anyway. I supposed you get used to anything. Actually, I'm angrier about his jacket."

"His what?"

"His jacket. His suit jacket. You remember when he lost his jacket at the opera? He was too drunk to remember what he had done with it? Well, I found it this morning. I was looking for something else, and I decided to check the trunk of Jack's car, just on the off chance that what I was looking for was in there. Instead I found his jacket. I think what happened was that during the opera performance, he felt hot because of all that alcohol, and he went outside—stumbled and staggered outside, probably—and dumped the jacket in the trunk of the car, and then he didn't even remember doing it. It was crumpled up and dirty. Oil stained, even." She shook her head. "It probably cost more than any item of clothing in my closet, but that doesn't matter to Jack. Anyway, I took it in to the drycleaners on my way here. They said they'd try to get it clean again, but they weren't sure if they could."

Still trying to control his anger, Tom said, "Jack was careless with his clothes and schoolbooks when he was a kid, I remember. He was always thoughtless about the things...About his belongings. He hasn't improved at all, has he?"

She smiled a slight, ironic smile. "Old problems don't go away, Tom. Usually, they just get worse with the years." She squeezed his hands.

Her hands were larger than his. That didn't surprise him. She was taller than he, and larger boned. What did surprise him was the strength he felt in her hands. What surprised him even more was the sexual arousal that surged through him. Images of Ellen making aggressive love to him filled his imagination.

As though her thoughts were paralleling his, Ellen said, "You know, I've wondered what it would be like to be with a man who wasn't bigger and stronger than me. Someone smaller, someone I didn't have to be afraid of. Someone who would enjoy having me be the powerful one." She smiled slightly. "Someone who would be a bit afraid of me."

"Have you folks decided what you want yet?"

Their waitress was standing beside the booth, order pad in hand, discreetly expressionless expression on her face. It was the same young woman at whom Tom's waiter had been staring longingly on his first visit to the restaurant. Close up, she seemed even more worth staring at, but it was her value as a distraction that made her most welcome to Tom. He found himself staring at her name tag, which read "Tomasina."

"Tomasina," Tom repeated. "That's an interesting coincidence. I assume Tomasina is the Spanish feminine form of Thomas, and that's my name."

The waitress stared through him.

"I'd like the wet burrito," Tom said. "With pork and green chili."

The waitress nodded and turned to Ellen and took her order.

After the waitress had left, Ellen began to giggle. "See, Tom," she managed to say, "*your* old problems are still with you, too."

"I wasn't trying to hit on her," Tom said defensively. "I really thought it was an interesting coincidence, and I wanted to make sure that I understood correctly about her name."

Ellen fought off her fit of giggling. "That's my point, Tom."

Despite her flirtatiousness the night before, despite the emotional revelations and the handholding and the sexual suggestion, Ellen's behavior during the rest of their lunch didn't go beyond friendship. No more handholding, no more revealing of painful secrets, no more leading remarks. They talked about neutral subjects, even managing to touch on the weather. Once, Tom asked her how she felt about rehearsals and the cast and finding a new Mario, and Ellen waved a hand and said she didn't want to talk about any of that. She wanted to get away from it for a few hours.

"And I want to go the drug store after lunch and get some kind of skin cream for my wrists," she added.

He thought she wanted to turn the conversation back to Jack and her unhappiness. He was almost ready to say, "Leave him. Don't worry about money. That part will be okay."

Instead, she said, "Speaking of drugstores, did you know that Maxwell's is going to close down at the end of the month? I've been going there since I was a kid, and now they're being forced out of business by that big new discount place in the mall. Isn't that a shame?"

Tom agreed that it was, and they went on to talk about the future of Ransom and the current spurt of growth.

Oddly, by the time they had finished eating, Tom felt that on the whole the lunch had turned out to be relaxing. The food seemed even better than it had the previous two times. The light conversation was all he felt ready for.

And yet he said goodbye to Ellen outside the restaurant with a strong feeling of regret and unfinished business.

She gave him a quick, shy hug and kissed his cheek and said, "Thank you for listening and for being such a good friend." He was aware again of her height and strength. That awareness made her long, troubled marriage seem like something titanic, something awesome from which Tom Hamilton had best keep his distance.

She did make her own bed and must lie in it, Tom told himself repeatedly as he drove home. Stay out of it. It's none of your business. You can't correct the world's mistakes. You can't even undo the mistakes you've made yourself.

Go home, he told himself, and listen to some good music, drink a good cocktail, read a good book, and then go for another walk along the hiking trail. Altogether, a civilized and pleasant day. Everyone should live that way.

His attempt at detachment from the rest of the world, and especially from Ellen and Jack Tourneau, lasted until four o'clock, In the middle of the good music, cocktail, and book, Ellen called him, near hysteria, to say that Jack had just been arrested and charged with murder.

Twenty-Six

Tom drove over to the Tourneau house first. Ellen had been almost incoherent when she called, and Tom hadn't been able to understand much beyond the fact that Jack had been charged with murder. After saying that and pleading with Tom to come to her immediately, Ellen had hung up.

It wasn't even clear to Tom whom Jack was supposed to have murdered. Jerry Angleton was the most publicized victim at the moment, but for all Tom knew, there had been another murder in Ransom in the last few days in which Jack was implicated. Maybe a cuckolded husband, Tom thought, and Jack shot first. Too bad, if that's the case.

Tom drove carefully. The cocktail had been a strong one—he had felt the need for some mental numbing—and even though he had drunk only a little more than half of it, he was aware that he was having trouble concentrating and reacting.

Rush hour, such as it was in Ransom, was beginning. As Tom drove down the hillside, he encountered a few cars on the other side of the road, heading up toward home. Those were the lucky Ransomites who were wealthy enough to live where Tom did. Even so, the faces he glimpsed through the windshields looked grumpy and tired and ready for an argument. When he reached the bottom, the true beginning of the town itself, the traffic increased abruptly. Tom gripped the wheel more tightly and willed himself to concentrate on all the cars around him, on the traffic lights, on street names, on the pedestrians.

He pulled into the driveway of the Tourneau house. As soon as he stopped in front of the house, Ellen opened the front door and ran down the steps toward him. She tried to pull his door open, but it was locked. He unlocked it and got out, and she threw herself against him, flinging her arms around his neck. Tom staggered back. Only the car kept him from falling over. The door handle dug painfully into the base of his spine. Ellen clung to him, her face pressed against his cheek, weeping.

Tom put his arms around her and held her tightly, feeling her need for protection and support. He had never held her before. It felt surprisingly awkward, given her greater size. He felt almost like a child trying to hold and comfort an adult.

He couldn't tell what his own feelings were—physical desire, the wish to protect, a combination of the two? He hated himself for mentally standing aside and analyzing his own feelings at a time like this. He wanted just to feel, not to observe, and he couldn't make himself do that.

He stroked her hair, trying to calm her down. "Ellen, Ellen," he said softly, "I'm sorry, I can't understand you. What are you trying to tell me?"

She pushed herself back from him. She seemed to be asserting control over herself. She put one hand out and wiped his cheek. "Your face is a mess," she said, trying to smile. "From me. I'm sorry."

He hadn't noticed. "It doesn't matter. Let's go inside."

Inside the house, Ellen led the way into the living room and collapsed onto the couch. The last time Tom had been in this room, Jack had been on the couch, semi–comatose from drink. Or possibly pretending to be semi–comatose.

"Can I get you something?" Tom asked. A drink, he meant, the idea of alcohol suggested by the remembered image of Jack on the couch and by the fuzziness that persisted in his own thoughts. Or a drug of some kind. Anything that would dull Ellen's senses and reactions and make the situation seem less emotionally dangerous to him.

"Coffee. Instant is fine. The kettle's on the stove, and the coffee—Never mind. It's silly to try to tell you where everything is. I'll take care of it."

She pushed herself up from the couch and stood, a bit unsteady and pale, but determined. Tom stepped toward her to support her, and she waved him away. "I've got to stand on my own, Tom. I can't keep depending on you or anyone else. That's been my mistake all along."

She pushed past him and went into the kitchen. She filled the kettle and put it back on the stove, turned on the burner, took out two mugs and teaspoon, got out the jar of instant coffee from one of the cabinets. She seemed to find the mechanical process soothing, or at the least distracting. Tom was reluctant to bring her back to the reality of what had happened, but he had to ask her the question.

"Why was Jack arrested? And whom is he accused of murdering?"

Ellen stopped with the spoon dug into the crystals of coffee in the jar. "His jacket. It was my fault. You remember I told you I found his suit jacket in his car? And I took the coat to the drycleaners? Well, they started to process it this morning, and apparently they found a bunch of blank rifle cartridges in one of the pockets."

"22–caliber Long Rifle bullets," Tom guessed. "With Jack's fingerprints all over them." Tom felt sick at the news. He despised Jack, both from the old days and because of the way Jack behaved now, but he didn't want to see the man convicted of murder. That would be...Tom thought about it. It would be disproportionate.

"No," Ellen said. "No fingerprints at all. Except for the ones from the clerk at the drycleaner's who found them. Snow says that's even more incriminating. If the presence of the bullets had been innocent, he says, Jack would have handled them normally, with his bare hands. This means he wiped them off and was planning to dump them somewhere, so that if they were found, no one could connect them to him. He wiped them off and dropped them in his coat pocket, and then he got drunk and forgot about them. That's Snow's version."

"So he's charging Jack with Jerry Angleton's murder?"

Ellen nodded. "Oh, and the attempted murder of Mike Berens, as well. Snow's being thorough."

"This thing about the bullets isn't sufficient. He can't convict based on this."

"Snow seems to think he can. You know, he was very kind when he told me. I was surprised. He tried to tell me in a gentle way. Trying not to upset me. He even told me to feel free to call him at home."

"He did this by telephone?"

"Oh, no. He came to the house. I called you after he left."

"That's what I assumed in the first place." Tom felt slightly annoyed at Ellen's uncharacteristic mental disorganization. "He came here to arrest Jack, of course."

Ellen shook her head. "No, he called here first, asking to speak to Jack. I told him Jack was at a faculty meeting on campus. Then Snow asked me what building that was in. I told him, he thanked me and hung up, and then about an hour later, Jack called me, hysterical, to say he was in the police station downtown, charged with murder. I couldn't get any sense out of him, so I asked him to put Snow on the line, and he explained it to me. Then a little while later, Snow showed up at the door. After Snow left, I called you."

Tom looked at his watch. Almost five o' clock. "Did Snow say whether he was going back to his office? I might still be able to catch him there."

"I think he said he was going home. He had just finished his shift, and his wife was waiting for him with, he said, a big dinner and a stiff drink. Why?"

Tom shrugged. "Maybe I can do some good. Find out if there's any more to the case against Jack than just the bullets. You have a lawyer?"

"Mark Pressler. You remember him? He was in our class in the old days. You met him and his wife, Julie, at the opera, at the opening night. The first one."

The night of Jerry Angleton's death. Or perhaps his murder by Jack. "Oh, yes, I remember him," Tom said. "From the good old days. He was a real prick in high school."

That elicited a laugh from Ellen, which seemed to cheer her up a bit. "Yes, he was. And now he's a really good lawyer."

"I knew his wife already", Tom said. "She's the real-estate agent I bought my house through. I remembered the name of the company from when I was a kid. So I got the number from Information and called. Julie Pressler answered the phone. Fine's Fine Properties. Hard to forget a name like that. And I especially remembered that sign over the office on Main."

"That big ugly yellow sign," Ellen said. "I'd forgotten about that! Julie moved to town about ten years ago and went to work for Mr. Fine. By the time he retired, she was running the place, and he sold it to her for next to nothing. That's the story I've heard, anyway. As soon as he died, she had that sign taken down. But she kept the name."

The inconsequential talk seemed to have helped Ellen a lot. She looked much steadier on her feet, and there was color in her cheeks again.

"I bet you're right," she said suddenly. "I bet there isn't a real case against Jack. I bet Snow will have to let him go. The worst that could happen is that they'll convict Jack of accidentally putting those bullets in the rifles because he was too drunk to know what he was doing, and he'll have to spend a few months in prison. Maybe a year. They don't execute anyone in this state, anyway."

Tom knew better. Colorado had followed the national trends—hanging first, then the electric chair, then the gas chamber, then no executions at all for a time, then finally the switch to lethal injection. Combined with the ugly mood that had swept the state along with the rest of the nation, a combination of unjustified paranoia about crime and panicky viciousness toward those convicted of violent crimes, this meant that Jack was in real danger of being convicted and then put to death.

"I'm going to Andy Snow's house," Tom told her, happy that he could avoid answering her implied question about Jack's fate.

"Maybe he's had his big dinner and stiff drink and he's in a mellow mood. You haven't called Pressler yet?"

Ellen shook her head. "I'll do that as soon as you leave."

"You're sure he's a good lawyer?"

Ellen smiled a twisted little smile. "A couple of years ago, he defended Jack against a sexual-harassment charge from one of his students. Oh, yes, he's good. You should have seen how competently he took that girl and her story apart."

Tom almost said, "Sounds like the perfect lawyer for Jack," but he thought better of it. "If Pressler doesn't need you to do something right away, you should probably go to bed early." Belatedly, Tom realized he had stepped back into the center of a minefield. "And get some sleep," he added lamely. "You look like you need it."

"I don't think I'll be able to sleep," Ellen said with a sigh. "Not that it'll be the first time I've lost a night's sleep because of my husband, but at least this time, I know where he is. That's okay." She held up her hand, even though Tom had not moved. "I'm just feeling self-pitying. I'll get over it."

He couldn't suggest that she call her family after what she had told him about her brothers. Nor did he want to suggest that she ask a friend to stay with her. He knew intuitively that she would say that she had no friends close enough for her to want to ask that favor, and then he'd be back in the minefield. Instead, feeling foolish at uttering such a cliché, he said, "You'll be okay. You've always been strong."

She brightened. "You're right! Always have been strong and always will be. Call me after you speak to Snow and let me know if he says anything encouraging."

Twenty-Seven

Before he left Ellen, Tom looked up Andy Snow in the telephone directory. Given Snow's apparent big-city background, Tom half expected the number to be unlisted, but there was a listing for Andrew Snow, and the number was the same as the one Ellen had for him.

The address was on Corona Drive, a street name Tom didn't recognize. Back in his car, he pored over the street map of Ransom and finally found Corona. It was on the eastern edge of town, in what had been farmland in Tom's youth. Ransom wasn't growing very rapidly, but it was growing, and most of the growth was eastward, onto the plains and toward Interstate 25.

Fortunately, the last traces of Tom's cocktail had faded away while he was in the Tourneau house. He could drive to Snow's place without worrying about the police and without, he hoped, smelling of alcohol when he arrived.

Tom drove north until he hit County Line Road, which ran along the north edge of town, and turned east onto it. The sun was setting behind him, deep yellow and blinding in his rear-view mirror, and the edge of the full moon was just pushing above the horizon ahead of him. The air temperature was dropping rapidly. Tom had rolled down all the windows when he started, because his car had grown hot and stuffy while he was in the house with Ellen. Now he rolled them up again. He turned on the radio and pushed the button for one of the two classical stations in Denver. Reception was less than perfect, but it was good enough for him. He wanted something that would calm him and put him in a contemplative and rational mood by the time he reached Snow's house.

Traffic was surprisingly light considering the time of day. By the time Tom reached the suburban cul de sac in which Snow's house was located, little more than fifteen minutes had passed.

The house was two stories high with a two-car attached garage and a postage-stamp size lawn, distinguishable from its neighbors on either side by having two saplings sticking up from its lawn, whereas each of its neighbors had only one sapling apiece. All the houses in the neighborhood seemed to have the same white vinyl siding, and they glowed in the twilight. A strange uniformity, Tom thought. Didn't the people living here want to be different from their neighbors, to stand out?

The sidewalk was white, too, and flat—quite a contrast to the stained one, buckled by tree roots, in front of the house Tom had grown up in. There were children's toys in some of the yards, but not in Snow's. It was a far newer neighborhood than the one in which Tom had spent his boyhood, and surely a much safer and quieter one. But our lawn was larger, Tom thought. Then he laughed at himself.

The door opened as Tom approached it. Andy Snow stood unwelcomingly in the opening. This was a different Andy Snow.

He wore jeans, running shoes, and a t-shirt and looked less authoritative. But he looked more muscular and dangerous in these clothes, and his hostility was even more open than usual. "Knew that was your damned car," he said. "I'm off duty now. Go away. Call me on Monday morning."

"I was just about to say that I'm sorry to bother you at home, but—"

"Fuck off, Agatha."

From somewhere inside the house, Diane Snow called out, "Andy."

Snow hesitated, then sighed and said over his shoulder, "All right, all right." He turned back to Tom. "What do you want?"

"I was just speaking to Ellen Tourneau. I told her I'd see you right away and see what I could do to help Jack."

"Oh, so you've switched from Agatha Christie to Perry Mason?"

"I'm neither a detective nor a lawyer, as you know. I'm here as a friend of the Tourneaus, that's all."

Snow shrugged. "Well, hell. Come inside, then." He motioned Tom in, closed the door behind him, and led the way down the main hallway. "We'll talk in my office."

Tom was interested to see that the house was as neat as Snow's office at the downtown police station was messy. He was also interested to see fairly good prints of nineteenth-century English landscapes on the wall of the hallway, including some quite non-traditional ones. He stopped in front of one, moonlight over water, shining on a bridge in the foreground, so magically real that Tom could feel the cool, damp air and imagine the texture of the bridge railing. "Grimshaw!" he said in delight. "You see his stuff so rarely."

"Not rarely enough," Snow said. He had stopped when Tom did and was now standing waiting, with obvious impatience. "My wife bought those."

"Oh, I see. These belong to your wife, the woman with such good taste in music." And such lousy taste in husbands. Must try to keep this friendly, Tom reminded himself. "I like her taste in paintings, too."

Snow muttered something unintelligible and led the way to a small room at the end of the hallway. It must have been intended as a storage room. Snow had managed to squeeze a small desk into it, and an old wooden swivel armchair. There were wooden shelves attached to the walls, covered with a confusion of papers and books lying on their sides. The desk was covered in much the same way. A computer was at one end of the desk, up against the wall. Overhead, a fluorescent light shed a cold and sterile light. Snow motioned Tom into the room and shut the door. The two men were almost face to face, jammed into the tiny remaining floor space. The air was motionless and hot.

"What a delightful little *pied-à-terre*," Tom said.

"Jesus, you're a pompous ass."

"You're right, and I apologize," Tom said, trying to sound sincere. "I really didn't want to get off on the wrong foot with you again, the way I keep doing. I came here to ask if there was any chance of Jack Tourneau being released while your investigation is under way. He's known in the community. He has a stake here. He has no reason to run away."

"He's a murderer and he attempted a second murder. The guy's a danger to the community, and we're all safer with him locked up. Hell, Agatha, he threatened you. I heard it, remember? I'm surprised you don't want him locked up permanently. Clears the field for you with his wife, too."

Tom ignored the bait. "Lieutenant, Jack has a very good lawyer, who will state his case much more effectively than I just did. It seems to me there's a good chance the lawyer will persuade a judge to set Jack free for now. Why embarrass yourself? You know your case against him is weak. All you have is the blank cartridges in his jacket. Anyone could have put them there. You're not going to convict him with that kind of evidence."

"That man," Snow said slowly and deliberately, "is staying behind bars if I have anything to say about it. And considering how well I get along with the D.A., I think I do. He'll never get free. With any luck, he'll get the death penalty. Hell, what am I saying? There's no luck involved! It's going to happen. And as for his great lawyer, Mark Pressler is a dickhead."

"I have to agree with you there," Tom said. "But from what I hear, he's still a very good lawyer. You know, I don't understand your hostility. What do you have against Jack? You act as though he's your personal enemy."

Snow turned away and leaned over his desk. He fiddled with the papers there as though searching for something. It was self-control he was searching for, Tom realized. Snow stopped fiddling, and there was silence in the room. Tom became aware again of the heat and the stifling closeness. Finally, Snow said, "We moved here seven years ago, Diane and me. Diane got friendly with Ellen Tourneau pretty soon after that. She met Jack Tourneau. Almost right away, he came on to her." He stopped talking and stood unmoving.

"Oh, Jack makes passes at just about every woman he

meets. He was like that as a boy, I remember. You mustn't let it get to you. Jack's one of those men who operate on the theory that even if ninety-nine percent of the women say no, you're still ahead because of the one percent who say yes."

"You don't understand," Snow said bitterly. "Diane...Diane didn't say no."

Tom stared at Snow's back in amazement. He was trying to imagine sweet-faced and sweet-natured Diane Snow being attracted to a boor like Jack Tourneau, and failing.

"We've both aged a lot since then," Snow said.

What in God's name was Jack's secret, Tom wondered. He had always been a lout, a self-centered clod, and he had always been successful with women. What could they possibly see in him?

Snow turned around again. His face was rigid, tense. "Satisfied now? You've uncovered my big secret."

"Why did you tell me? Why did you trust me with this?"

"You can be trusted with secrets. I can tell that about you. I think you have a lot of interesting secrets locked up in your head. I told you so that you'd understand just how I feel about Tourneau, the shithead, and why I'm going to do everything I can to make sure he stays behind bars and never gets out of prison alive."

"Lieutenant, you're saying this is just a personal vendetta. You're pursuing revenge because of the injury Jack did you. You're not pursuing justice."

"I'm pursuing both," Snow said. "It doesn't make any difference what's behind it. I could be driven by revenge, like you said, or I could be driven by my sense of duty. It doesn't matter. In the end, in both cases, justice gets done. A killer gets punished. It doesn't matter why the cop goes after the killer. All that matters is that he gets him."

"You have my sympathies for what happened. Please believe me, Lieutenant. It's obvious that it still hurts."

"Still hurts!" Snow shouted. The sound was deafening in the small room. Snow's face grew red, and he seemed to swell with his anger, growing even wider and more powerful looking, more menacing. Tom wanted to back up, but his back was already against the door, and there was nowhere to go.

Snow brought himself under control. "You don't know anything about me, Hamilton. And I don't know enough about you, although I'm working on that. But I do know about your childhood visits to the downtown police station and how the cops used to take care of you when they could. You had a bad time as a kid, and they tried to help you. So you think of cops as your buddies, and you think a cop has to give you special help. Well, not this cop. You're going to have to do some relearning. I'm not your buddy, and you can quit trying to pretend that you're mine. You're wasting your time here. Wasting mine, too."

Tom sighed and nodded. "It does look that way. But whether you want it or not, you have my sympathy." He managed to step away from the door enough to open it, and he headed toward the front door.

On the way, he passed what must have been the family room. He glimpsed a comfortable couch and a television set facing it. Diane Snow sat on the couch, eyes glued to the television screen. She noticed Tom passing by, though, and jumped to her feet and came to the door of the room. "Tom," she said, "I'm sorry you have to leave already. Are you going to be seeing Ellen any time soon? If you are, please tell her she has my support and she should feel free to call me for help at any time. Will you do that for me?"

Tom looked at her smiling, warm face and could imagine why Andy Snow had fallen in love with her. What he could not imagine was why she had fallen in love with Andy Snow. Snow and Jack Tourneau—it was impossible to accept that either man was her type. "I'll certainly do that, Mrs. Snow. Goodnight, now." Tom continued toward the front door, feeling as though he'd stepped into an alternate universe, one that made even less sense than the universe he was familiar with.

It was a feeling made even stronger when he stepped outside. The full moon was completely above the horizon now, flooding the lawn and pathway with its light, changing the cul-de-sac into something painted by Grimshaw.

As Tom was walking down the pathway toward his car, Snow called out his name from the house. Tom turned. Snow was standing in the front doorway, hands in his pockets. In the moonlight, Tom could see a smile on Snow's face.

"Forgot to tell you something," Snow said. "Right before that dry-cleaning store called me about the blank bullets in the pocket of Jack Tourneau's coat, I got another call from Mickey Fredericksson, the *Roundup* reporter. He was working on a human-interest story about the aftereffects of crime, and he was interviewing someone connected with this case, and he got something really interesting. But I don't want to spoil the suspense for you by telling you about it now. You'll hear about it soon enough. You'll probably see it on the news tonight. Or in tomorrow's paper, for sure. Have a nice evening."

Chuckling, he closed the door, leaving Tom standing on the pathway.

Twenty-Eight

Tom did not have a nice evening.

The first thing he did when he got home was call Ellen. He needed to tell her that the visit to Snow had gone badly. He supposed he had to pass on Diane Snow's message, too.

There was no answer at the Tourneau house. Instead, he was answered by an answering machine. He left a brief message saying he would try again later that evening. Surprising, Tom thought as he hung up. Ellen wouldn't have gone out, surely. Not at a time like this. She might have gone to bed early and turned the ring off.

He had an uneasy feeling and wondered if he should go back to Ellen's house to check on her.

He hesitated for a while. Then he looked up the number for Mark Pressler. Before he did anything else, Tom thought, he should make sure that Ellen had indeed called Mark. She would not have neglected something so important, surely. But Tom also wanted to make sure that the lawyer's fees would be covered. Jack's parents would be able to take care of that, even if Jack and Ellen themselves couldn't, judging from what both Tourneaus had said about the elder Tourneaus' money.

However, Jack's parents seemed still to be away on their cruise and out of touch, and Tom's opinion of Mark Pressler was such that he wasn't sure how long the lawyer would be willing to wait for a first payment.

Julie Pressler answered the telephone. Tom recognized her voice instantly from having dealt with her by telephone while arranging the purchase of his house. He remembered that she had asked him repeatedly for a number where she could reach him, just in case something came on the market that would be perfect for him but was likely to be snapped up by some other wealthy client. He had persistently refused and had told her that he would call her regularly to check on the situation. He hadn't wanted her to know what city he was calling from. How many people in Ransom now knew of his odd behavior? He judged Julie to be a discreet woman who kept her clients' peculiarities to herself, but he had been mistaken in such judgments before, sometimes with frightening consequences.

"Hi, Julie. Tom Hamilton. Is Mark available?"

"Hi, Tom." Her voice lacked its customary excessive sparkle. She spoke as though she had tragic news to tell him. "No, I'm afraid not. He's in conference with a client. Did you want to leave a message?"

Tom hesitated. He didn't think he ought to tell anyone other than Mark Pressler himself that he was willing to pay the legal bills for the Tourneaus for a while, until they were able to arrange everything. "It's about Ellen Tourneau," Tom said at last. "If you could have Mark call me when he's free."

"Oh, Ellen! She's the client he's with now. She came over to talk to him about Jack. Um, you know about Jack, don't you?"

"I know that he's under arrest." And I know that there's

something else that's making Andy Snow very smug, but I don't know what it is. "That is what you meant, right?"

"Oh, yes, that's what I meant. Ellen came over to discuss that and to get Mark's advice and to see what he could do for Jack. Tom, you're an old friend of both Ellen's and Jack's, aren't you?"

"I've known them practically since the cradle." But to answer your question, no, not really.

"Good. That's what I thought. I've been calling some of their friends and asking them to come over tonight so that we could have a sort of...Oh, I don't know. Not a party, of course, because there's nothing to celebrate. More like a comfort gathering, if you see what I mean. To support Ellen and let her see that she's got friends and people who love her here in town. That she's not alone. Could you come, too?"

Tom glanced over at his cocktail, still half full but with the ice completely melted now, and at the book lying open on the couch, and he wondered if he could be included among those who loved Ellen in the sense Julie meant. "Sure. When?"

"Some people should be arriving in a few minutes. Why don't you come over right away?" Before hanging up, she gave him directions to her house. They were very precise and clear directions, as had been those she had given him for finding his own house.

For a moment, Tom considered swallowing the now-diluted remnants of his drink to fortify himself for the evening ahead. Prudence prevailed and he poured it down the drain in the kitchen sink.

He took his brown windbreaker out of the closet by the front door. Then he decided that something a bit dressier would be more appropriate, so he went to his bedroom and got the charcoal grey woolen blazer he had bought just before leaving Chicago. It had appealed to him in the store, but he had found the wool surprisingly scratchy and annoying where it touched him, both at the cuffs and the top of the collar, and so he never wore it. It seemed right tonight, though—both sufficiently formal and rather somber.

Julie Pressler answered the door. She wore the same uniform as she had at the opera. She also wore a serious expression. Tom asked how Ellen was holding up.

"Oh, she's doing remarkably well. Come in, Tom. This way. We're all in the living room."

A fairly large group was already gathered in the living room. They had obviously been invited somewhat earlier than Tom had, and it occurred to him that his own invitation had been an afterthought, probably prompted by his telephone call.

They were by and large the same people he had been introduced to in the lobby of the school auditorium while waiting for the first performance of Tosca to begin. "Our crowd," Ellen had called them that evening. They were obviously still "our crowd," despite everything that had happened, and Tom still felt the subtle message from them that he wasn't one of them.

Except from Fred Pernowski, who bounced up to Tom radiating his usual energy and said loudly, "Hey! Another human being, at last! Man, am I glad to see you. I'm so tired of stuffed shirts."

Arlene Pernowski hurried to his side. This time, there was none of the amused tolerance of the last time. "Fred, for God's sake! Show some sense."

"Okay, okay." But he did lower his voice a bit. "But look at all those faces, would you? This is a wake."

Tom looked. Fred had a point. Everyone else was trying to match Julie Pressler's expression. They were also trying to ignore Fred.

"It's a sad occasion," Arlene said.

"Hell it is," said her husband. "A murderer's behind bars, and Ellen's free again to...um, do whatever she wants."

"So you're going to be representing Ransom this year in the Mr. Tact competition, are you?" Tom asked.

Fred's shout of laughter echoed off the walls.

Arlene said, "If he doesn't get lynched first."

Someone in the crowd had caught Fred's eye. "Oh, look," he said, "it's the fashionable preacher. I think I feel a theological dispute coming on. 'Bye, Tom." He turned away and cut into the crowd in search of his quarry, who turned out to be a tall, slender man with wispy blond hair.

Arlene muttered, "Better keep this under control," and hurried after her husband.

Tom heard the blond man groan and say, "Not tonight, Fred, I have a headache," and then came Fred's unmistakable shout of laughter.

It felt hot suddenly. Tom shifted inside the coat that had seemed such a good choice in his cool house. He could feel sweat running down his back.

He checked his watch. Just after nine p.m. How much longer would this go on?

The group of Ellen's dear and intimate friends had been growing steadily since Tom's arrival. There were now perhaps two dozen people in the room, although the room was so large that there was no sense of crowding. He had the feeling, listening to the mingled voices, that the mood was growing lighter and this was turning into an impromptu party.

Tom struck up a conversation with a woman whose name he couldn't remember. He had been introduced to her on the second opening night and remembered only that she had something to do with the business school at CCC. She was around sixty, he judged. Grey and plump. Safely unattractive and exceedingly unlikely to be attracted to him. He felt a desperate need for a neutral conversation with no tension of any kind.

Like him, she was observing the crowd from the outside. Tom stepped up to her and said, "Hi. We met at the opera. You probably don't remember—"

"Tom Hamilton, prodigal son," she said, holding out her hand. "Of course I remember."

"I wasn't clear on how you know Ellen. Through the college, somehow? I'm sure I was told that, but I must have missed it." What was this woman's name?

She looked surprised and then laughed. "You don't remember who I am, do you? Beth Morrigan." At Tom's blank expression, she laughed again. "I know Ellen from a long time ago. I was her ninth-grade algebra teacher. Yours, too."

"Miss Osborne!" Tom said. "Jesus Christ!" He felt a shock much like that when he realized that the woman in the Motor Vehicle office had once been the girl he had known as Janice Sheridan. How could this be the elegant, beautiful teacher he had fantasized about for one school year? "But that's impossible," he said. "You look like you're my age. You must be Miss Osborne's daughter."

Beth chuckled. "For that, I'd go back and change your grade to an A if I could. On second thought, no, I wouldn't. You always were the sharpest boy in the class, but you were completely honest back then."

"Did you think so?" Were you so blind to what I was trying to hide from the rest of the world?

"I'm sure you had your little secrets. Every child does. They always seem so terribly important to the child, even though an adult realizes how unimportant they are."

"I used to think you were amazingly perceptive and understanding and sympathetic."

"Oh, I was," Beth said placidly. She turned her head suddenly. "Oh, look. Here's Ellen at last."

Twenty-Nine

Ellen and Mark Pressler had emerged from wherever his office was hidden. Ellen stopped in surprise at the sight of the crowd, and then, as she realized that they were all her friends and were all there as a gesture of support and comfort, she smiled. It was a sweet smile with no affectation or complexity, the smile of a happy child. It transformed her into a younger Ellen—not the self-confident young woman of their high-school years, overly aware of both her new sexual powers and her social status, but a still younger Ellen, perhaps the Ellen Tom had shared Beth Osborne's algebra class with, a girl who had just begun to develop physically, who had not yet become unapproachable and unattainable, who had still been direct and honest.

"Thank you," Ellen said to the crowd. "Thank you." She turned to Julie, who had stepped up to give her husband a peck on the cheek. "Julie, thank you so much for doing this for me."

The crowd thronged around her, everyone talking loudly with just a touch too much cheerfulness. Tom, as usual, stood on the outside watching.

Ellen caught sight of him. She pushed her way free and hugged him, forcing a grunt from him. "Tom, thank you especially." She kissed his cheek, then released him but grabbed his hand and held it tightly. He felt uncomfortably that, in the eyes of everyone else there, he had been placed into some sort of special relationship with her, a specially intimate friendship, that he had no wish to claim. "I don't know how I could hold up under all of this if not for my friends," Ellen said.

Mark took the floor. He did it without moving or speaking. Somehow, he took over the crowd. They all fell silent and turned toward him simultaneously.

Tom wondered if that was a learned skill. And if it was, how did one learn it?

"I just wanted everyone to know," he said, his voice that of an experienced public speaker, "that I expect to have Jack back home again in next to no time. And I'm confident we can get the charges against him dropped."

The crowd applauded. Ellen let go of Tom's hand so that she could join in enthusiastically. Tom kept his hands clasped in front of him. When the applause had died down, Ellen grabbed his hand again.

"What does Mark mean by 'no time'?" It was Fred Pernowski. He had moved close to Ellen while the rest were applauding. "Tonight? Tomorrow? Monday morning?"

Ellen shook her head. "I don't really know. Mark was making some phone calls to try to arrange for Jack's immediate release, but there's apparently some sort of hang-up."

"Probably Monday morning," Fred said. His breath smelled of alcohol. Tom wondered how he had found time to drink in the midst of puncturing stuffed shirts. He also wondered where Fred had found the booze. Tom wouldn't have minded a drink himself.

"You know," Fred said, "I wonder if all the stories they tell about the men in prison are true. It's pretty funny to think of Jack being on the receiving end for a change." His laugh boomed out.

Arlene had been talking to someone else, but Tom could tell that she was keeping one eye on her husband. Apparently, she had been keeping an ear cocked, too. She turned away from the other person and stepped to Fred's side, frowning angrily. "Jesus, Fred," she said in a low voice, "will you shut up?"

"That's all right, Arlene," Ellen said. She was pale, and her grip on Tom's hand had tightened. "Fred can't help it. Fred, Jack can defend himself. He's a big man, as you know. Quite tall."

Fred laughed again. "Touché!" He clearly wanted to say more, but Arlene dragged him away.

"So nice of your friends to show up to offer you love and support," Tom murmured.

Ellen squeezed his hand still tighter. "Thank God you're here, Tom." Her grip was beginning to hurt him.

Someone else approached her. Ellen introduced him to Tom as Archer Terrell, also a member of the English faculty at CCC. Terrell, a tall, beefy young man with an excess of hair, looked down his nose at Tom and dismissed him visibly, then turned his attention to Ellen. "I was in the meeting with Jack and the department chair when the police showed up and arrested him," Terrell said. "Very distressing. We were all upset. The chair most of all, I think. So realistically, what does Pressler think his chances are of getting Jack off? I mean, I know that Mark's a very high-powered lawyer, and if there are loopholes in the law, he's sure to find them, but I understand that the case against Jack is pretty clear cut."

"Don't be ridiculous," Ellen said angrily. "Jack has his faults, but you know perfectly well he's not a murderer. Jack could never kill anyone. And Mark's not looking for 'loopholes.' He's going to get Jack out of prison and get the charges dropped because Jack's innocent."

"My, what touching faith!" Terrell sneered.

"I believe in the system," Ellen said.

"No, I meant in your husband."

"Go away," Tom said mildly.

Terrell pretended to finally notice him. "I beg your pardon? Are you threatening me," he chuckled, "physically?"

"Of course not," Tom said. "I'm much too small to do that. But I know where to hire some very large, ill-mannered young men with no scruples at all."

"Hmph," Terrell said. He left quickly.

"I'm sorry I said that about size before," Ellen said. "I was aiming it at Fred, you know."

"It's nothing," Tom said. He wished she would finally let go of his hand. What must they look like to the rest of the crowd? "I'm beginning to wonder if this gathering is such a good idea. So far, these people aren't doing you much good."

"Oh, Fred's just being Fred. And as for Archer, he's just hoping he'll move up the academic ladder if Jack is forced to resign. The rest of them are much nicer."

For a while, he thought she was right. The other people who approached Ellen to speak to her—and they all approached her, rather than the reverse, as though she were a patient in bed, unable to move, or perhaps a queen receiving her subjects—expressed sympathy and offered whatever help she needed. At times, Tom thought he detected an undercurrent of *schadenfreude*, but he couldn't be sure and thought he might be imagining it.

Fred Pernowski's voice blasted through the babble filling the room. "Hey, Mark, it's ten o'clock. How about turning on that great projection system of yours so that we can look for Jack on the news?" Without waiting for Mark Pressler to reply, Fred shouted for everyone to follow him into the family room.

Ellen hesitated, then made up her mind and followed the crowd. She pulled Tom along with her.

The family room was almost as large as the room they had just left. One wall was taken up by the projection screen. Colors flickered across it as the system warmed up. Most of the floor space was empty. The only furniture was a long, white leather couch against the far wall.

"Wow!" Fred Pernowski yelled. "You could have a threesome on this couch while you're watching a wall full of porno flicks!"

Someone else yelled, "Maybe even a foursome! Who's for it?"

There was more laughter than embarrassment as far as Tom could see. Where *is* the alcohol? he wondered. He looked around in hopes of seeing a bottle somewhere. And was there any left?

The picture took shape.

The set was tuned to one of the Denver stations. The logo of its news program appeared. That gave way to a desk behind which sat one of the standard-issue pairs of evening news anchors—a pretty woman in a pretty dress and a handsome man in a handsome suit, indistinguishable from their competitors on other local stations.

First came a garbled rehash of the major national stories, interrupted by frequent commercials, then some inane chatter between the pretty pair, then some more commercials. Finally, the woman said, "There has been an important break in a major local story. It has to do with murder, opera, and the small central Colorado town of Ransom."

The crowd applauded as though the CCC football team had just scored a touchdown.

After a quick summary of the shootings of the two tenors singing Mario Cavaradossi, a name which the male news anchor tried twice to pronounce before giving up, the broadcast moved on to the big item, the breaking story: the arrest of Jack Tourneau for the murder of Jerry Angleton and the attempted murder of Mike Berens.

There was film of Jack being escorted into the police station in downtown Ransom. This elicited a few cheers and whistles from the crowd gathered in the Presslers' family room. The story was over at last, Tom thought. The worst was over. Whatever Snow had been talking about, it wouldn't be on tonight's news.

He glanced sideways at Ellen. Her face was surprisingly placid. Jack's arrest might be a hot, breaking story to the television news people, but it was of course old news to this crowd. Tom relaxed. Perhaps now this painful evening could end and he could go home.

The female anchor said, "And now for the latest development in this shocking story. This afternoon, in an interview with Mickey Fredericksson of the *Ransom Roundup*, the widow of one of the two victims dropped a bombshell."

The crowd watching the big screen fell silent. Tom held his

breath. Irrationally, he cursed Snow.

Mickey Fredericksson had been brought into the news studio. He sat at a smaller desk than that of the two anchors, facing them. He was an aging small-town newspaper hack who had long ago given up any hopes of rising above writing a saccharine column about local life, and now, suddenly, he had come face to face with what could be his big break. He shifted constantly in his seat, probably giving the cameraman fits. The movement made his face move from side to side and up and down on the television screen, giving the viewer the illusion that Fredericksson's head had become detached from his body.

"Thanks for coming here to talk to us, Mickey," the female anchor said.

"Thanks for asking me, Billie."

"Mickey, I understand you've interviewed Kathy Angleton, the young woman whose husband, Jerry, was the opera singer who was shot in Ransom a couple of months ago."

Mickey interrupted her. "One month ago. August sixteenth."

"Yes, of course. And while you were interviewing her, she told you something that seems to blow this case wide open, is that right?"

"I think so, Billie. As you know, I've been pursuing leads in this alleged murder case, doing some very quiet behind-the-scenes investigative reporting, in the process of which I interviewed Kathy Angleton, the widow of the alleged victim, Jerry Angleton."

The male anchor tried to hurry him along. "And what exactly did she tell you?"

"Bill, as you know, I was interviewing Mrs. Angleton, and

she told me that she was romantically involved with Professor Jack Tourneau, a teacher here at Colorado Central College, and the alleged murderer of Mr. Jerry Angleton, Kathy Angleton's late husband."

The two anchors exchanged exasperated glances. The woman said, "I understand you taped the interview and we have that clip ready right now."

"Not exactly," Mickey said quickly. "Actually, I interviewed her in her home first, at which time she told me of her alleged romantic involvement with Professor Tourneau. I was then able to persuade her to let me repeat the interview with a camera present. As you know. But," he added, "I have her sworn affidavit that everything she said in the second interview, she had already said in the first interview."

"Alleged interview," Fred Pernowski called out, but this time, his audience shushed him and he subsided.

The studio scene gave way to the living room of the Tourneau home. Tom saw the scratched floor and worn rug he remembered, and the old couch and two armchairs. On the huge screen, they looked even more pitiful, more worn, and the room looked even more cramped than in reality. Kathy Angleton sat on the couch looking much as she had when Tom saw her there. Her belly had swelled more, but at the same time, she looked much more rested, less drawn.

Mickey Fredericksson spoke from off camera. "Mrs. Angleton, you say that you and Professor Jack Tourneau, who was your teacher in college, have been romantically involved?"

"We were," Kathy said. She was also, Tom noted, far calmer and more self-controlled than when he had spoken to her. She looked directly into the camera as she replied. "I ended it a while ago."

"You were sleeping together while your husband was still alive?"

"Yes. Before he was murdered."

Tom felt Ellen's hand slip away. She folded her arms beneath her breasts and stood leaning forward slightly, staring intently at the screen, her lips compressed.

"While you and Professor Tourneau were still having your affair, I understand he said something to you that you think might have relevance to your husband's death?"

"Yes, that's right. A couple of times, Jack talked about how convenient it would be if his wife and Jerry would just go away somehow. He used to talk about them both dying in accidents or something. He said that that way we'd be able to marry each other and be together and his career would still be safe."

"How did you feel when he said things like that?"

"I felt..." She looked away from the camera and down at the shabby carpet. "I think I was a fool. I realized that after Jerry died."

"Was that why you ended your affair with Professor Tourneau?"

"I guess. Mostly."

"And why did you decide to tell me this today? You must realize that this will have an impact on Professor Tourneau."

She looked back at the camera, glaring. "Because this is the only way I can make him leave me alone. The son of a bitch keeps calling me up and whining. He wants us to get back together. I think he murdered my husband. I hate him."

The tape ended and the studio reappeared. The vapid interchanges between the two anchors were lost in the babble of noise that erupted in the Pressler house.

Slowly, the conversations died down and everyone turned to look at Ellen. Someone clicked the remote control and turned off the television.

Ellen spoke as calmly and forcefully as Kathy Angleton had a few moments before. "That bastard. That scum." She turned toward Mark Pressler, who had been watching her with a detached, analytical air. "Mark, forget everything I said to you earlier. If you still want to defend that murderer, you can deal with him directly. I have nothing to do with any of it any more."

Tom looked at the faces of the crowd in the family room, estimated the number of smirks compared to the number of sympathetic looks, and felt depressed.

Thirty

The party broke up quickly after that. Tom lost Ellen in the milling crowd. For some reason, quite a few of the people gathered there seemed to be feeling friendly toward Tom and wanted to talk to him. By the time he got out of the house, Ellen's car was gone.

He got in his own car, drove home, and called the Tourneau house immediately. He got the answering machine, with Ellen's voice reading the announcement. He left a brief message and hung up.

He felt exhausted. His eyes burned and his eyelids drooped. He felt the way he had sometimes felt in his Chicago years after days without sleep, days of continued mental strain. He had made decisions involving the lives of others, on a few occasions deciding to order the ends of those lives, and it had always drained him of all physical and mental energy. But what had he done to feel that way this time?

I'm getting soft in my almost middle age, he thought. Or maybe I am getting old. Maybe this is how it begins, how you first realize it.

Or maybe I think too much.

He turned off the lights in the living room, washed up quickly, and went to bed.

The telephone woke him the next morning. It was Ellen.

"Sorry I couldn't call you back last night," she said, speaking rapidly. "I had a lot of things to arrange. I'm going away."

"You're what?" He couldn't seem to fully understand her words. He heard them, and he understood each word by itself, but the combination wouldn't hang together.

"I'm going away," Ellen repeated. "Oh, not permanently. Just for a while. I don't know how long. Mark Pressler is apparently going to be able to get Jack out of prison for now. He'll be out sometime today, and I don't want to be in the house when that bastard comes home. I don't think I'd even be able to look at him, the son of a bitch. The slime ball."

At last he felt able to understand the sentences he was hearing, but he still seemed to be missing something. "Where are you going? An apartment somewhere?"

"No! I want to get out of this town! You saw those people last night. Those are people I thought were my friends. I don't have any friends." She paused as if waiting for Tom to say something.

"You know that's not true," he said dutifully. "Most of the people last night were genuinely supportive. Yesterday afternoon, even Diane Snow told me to pass on her best wishes. She said you should call her if she can help in any way." As soon as he had said that, he thought he should not have. Did Ellen know about Diane Snow and Jack?

Apparently she didn't. Her voice turned warm and happy.

"Isn't she sweet? I can't imagine how she ended up married to a jerk like Snow."

"I was thinking the same thing yesterday," Tom said, feeling relieved.

"That marriage has aged her. She was a good–looking woman when they moved here. Marriage to a jerk will do that to you. But she's still a sweet person. Yes, I guess you're right, Tom. There *are* a few people I can count on. Anyway, I want to get out of this house. And I've got to get away from this town. I can't think here. It's filled with ghosts for me. And Jack's former lovers, like that little bitch, Kathy Angleton. Probably bunches of his present lovers, too. Wherever I go in town, I know people are looking at me and laughing. I've turned into just another aging woman whose husband sleeps with young girls for his kicks."

"That's Jack's failing, not yours."

"You're sweet to say that, Tom. That's because you're a sweet guy. I've got to hang up now and finish packing. My flight leaves Denver at noon."

"Your flight? Wait a minute! Where are you going?"

"Away from Ransom. I told you that. I'm going to stay with my cousin Liz in Portland."

"What about the rehearsals? Trying again with the opera?"

"I know this sounds weird, but all of a sudden, it just doesn't matter that much to me any more. I've got to hurry now, or I'll miss my flight. You know what that airport's like. 'Bye." She hung up.

"Wait! Oh, shit." He was too late. He dialed her number quickly, but he got her answering machine.

He didn't bother leaving a message. He pushed himself out of bed and roamed around his bedroom, finding the clothes he had taken off the night before and pulling them back on. Now he regretted having dumped the remnants of his drink down the drain the previous night. It would have made a good mouthwash this morning. Diluted though it had been by melted ice cubes, it had probably contained enough alcohol to kill the awful things the taste inside his mouth told him must be growing there. He settled for water from the faucet in the bathroom sink. He looked in the mirror and saw that his hair stuck out in all directions. He ran his fingers through it to no effect.

Christ, what does it matter? he asked himself. You're wasting time.

He was also starving. On his way to the front door, he checked in the refrigerator and found an aging bagel. He took it with him. It felt hard enough to make him worry about his teeth. He decided that he worried too much.

He arrived at the Tourneau house with the bagel half eaten and his lap covered with crumbs. He left the remaining half on the dashboard as an experiment. Would the sun soften it or make it even harder? Was it possible for a bagel to be harder than this one?

The driveway was empty of cars. Tom hoped that meant that Ellen's blue Honda was in the garage, not that she had already left.

No one answered his repeated banging on the front door and pressings of the button set beside the door. This time, there was no door key on the ledge. On the front step, next to the door, was the day's edition of the *Ransom Roundup*. It probably contained the story of Kathy Angleton's damning revelations. Probably on the front page. Probably under a huge black headline. Tom decided not to pick it up and see.

He walked all the way around the house, looking in all the windows, and saw no sign of life. The grass was soaked from the automatic sprinkler system. Tom tried to ignore the cold water soaking into his running shoes. He knocked on a couple of the windows and waited for some response from inside the house, but there was none.

As he came back around to the front, a pale gold Accura Legend was turning into the driveway from the street. Tom stood beside the driveway and waited for Jack to pull to a stop.

Jack stopped beside Tom. He climbed out of his car, stretched, and leaned back against the door. He was trying to project his old calmness and self–assurance, but his wrinkled suit, which he had obviously slept in, and his need for a shave undermined that pose. He said, "Why are you always sneaking around peoples' houses? You're just asking for someone to blow you away, you know."

"You're remarkably cheerful for someone who's facing a murder charge," Tom said. "With some damning evidence."

The good cheer left Jack's face immediately. "I didn't do it! You know I couldn't!"

Tom shook his head. "I know you could. You pointed a gun at me and threatened me."

"That wasn't serious, Tom! You could tell, couldn't you?"

"It seemed serious to me. I think you could have killed Jerry Angleton and crippled Mike Berens. That doesn't prove you did it, Jack, but there's also a lot of evidence gathering up against you."

Jack seemed to shrink and age. "I didn't do it, Tom. Christ, I'm living in some kind of fucking nightmare."

It was impossible not to feel some pity for the man. The

pity Tom felt growing in him wasn't enough for him to make any large gesture of support or friendship, though. The antagonism toward Jack that had accumulated in him during the years of their boyhood and adolescence, and that had started growing again since Tom's return, was too great for that. "Why don't you go inside your house and try to relax, Jack?" he said at last. He could manage that much. "Try to trust Mark. You know he's good."

Jack nodded. "Yeah. He's tough. You should have seen him in action against Snow. Thanks, Tom. You're a real friend. I know I haven't always behaved well toward you, but you've always been a good guy in return."

Before Tom could move out of the way, Jack grabbed him and gave him a manly, back-slapping hug, then pushed him away again. Jack seemed genuinely moved. "You're right. I'm going into my house, and I'm going to have a drink with my wife."

"Jack...Yes, you do that. That's a good idea."

Tom watched Jack begin to walk toward the steps leading up to the front door. His shoulders were bowed and he walked slowly and listlessly, as though his body lacked the strength for even that little effort.

Tom walked rapidly back to his own car, started it, and backed out of the driveway. He thought it would be best if he were well away from the house by the time Jack discovered that Ellen had in effect moved out. It occurred to him that Jack might not yet know about Kathy Angleton's interview. Perhaps he would read about it in the morning newspaper. Another reason for Tom to be in a different part of town.

Thirty-One

Tom finished the bagel on the way home. He was scarcely aware of its staleness. Other matters preoccupied him.

When he got home, he picked up the Saturday editions of the *Ransom Roundup* and the *Denver Post* that were lying in front of his door and paused to scan both front pages. The arrest of Jack Tourneau and the interview with Kathy Angleton were on the front page of the *Roundup*, as he had expected, but he was unpleasantly surprised to see both stories on the front page of the *Post*, as well—although below the fold. He tossed both papers on the kitchen table and went to his bedroom to undress and shower.

When he finished showering and turned the water off, he heard the phone ringing. He jumped out of the shower and ran for the telephone next to his bed. He was sure it was Ellen.

It was Harriet Fischer. Tom sat down on the bed, disappointed, and too distracted to keep his disappointment out of his voice.

"Is this a bad time?" Harriet asked. "I didn't want to bother you, but I'm afraid it's pretty important. I just had a call from Golden Days. They had to transfer Dad to a hospital, and they don't think he's going to make it. It's his heart. He refuses to let them do anything more to it. He always said he didn't want any more surgery. He told them he wants to see us and you. We're headed up there now."

"Oh, no. Which hospital? I'll go there right away." Selfish bastard, he told himself as he took down the information. Think how hard it must have been for Harriet to take the time to call you before leaving, and you made her feel guilty for bothering you.

"I guess we'd better forget about dinner tonight," Harriet said.

Oh, shit, Tom thought. He had completely forgotten their arrangement. "Yes, of course. I was just thinking about that. We'll reschedule."

The hospital was a large, new one, part of a national chain called Max Care Health Systems. It was in northeast Denver. Given Saturday traffic, Tom thought he could be there in about an hour or an hour and a half.

He hoped Nick would still be conscious when he got there. He had never had a chance to say goodbye to his mother. He had had no wish to say goodbye to his father. Nick Jaruzelski was the only part of his past—the only good part—that still remained. It would be simply too unfair of the fates to deny Tom the chance to say goodbye properly to Nick. Despite all of his experience with the maliciousness of the fates, Tom was irrationally sure that they would not deny him this.

It was a bright, sunny day, hot for the time of year. It seemed strange to Tom that someone so vital as Nick Jaruzelski could die on such a day.

Tom took County Line Road east to Interstate 25 and turned north onto the interstate, heading toward Denver. The highway was virtually empty and he made good time. Soon he could see the tops of the tallest buildings in downtown Denver rising above the folds of the land ahead. More life, more bustle, more vitality.

The contrast kept catching him off guard. He kept blinking his eyes to clear them of tears. Couldn't he have found some way, during the last twenty years, of keeping in touch with Nick without endangering himself? He had been so determined to keep his two lives separate so that he would have this one to escape to that he had neglected the lives of others entirely.

Harriet had cleared the way for him so that he was allowed into Nick's room despite not being a family member. This was the kind of advance preparation he had become used to having done for him in Chicago, but he had already learned not to expect it in Colorado.

Nor had he expected the sense of *déjà vu* that overcame him when he entered Nick's room. When he stepped inside the hospital, it looked and felt just like hospitals he had been in in Chicago. Nick's room, with the shrunken old man breathing shallowly and painfully in the bed, threw Tom back six months to Trager's similar death in a similar room. That time, the room had been filled with uneasy men, some of them Tom's mortal enemies, watching the dying man and each other, each calculating the odds of his own survival after Trager finally gave up the fight to live. It had been a time of muttered conferences in the hallway outside the room, of breaking old alliances and forging new ones, of plotting killings.

This time, only Harriet and her husband and Tom were

there to watch an old man die. This time, the old man knew that those watching him loved him and wished he could go on living.

Nick slept most of the day. He was awake and lucid for brief periods. During those times, he asked the three of them to speak to him because it was too hard for him to speak but he wanted to hear their voices. He listened to them and smiled. He drifted off to sleep as they spoke. At six p.m., he opened his eyes. His voice was a whisper, his words interrupted by gasps for breath. He tried to look at them, but he was having trouble keeping his eyes open.

"Joseph," Nick said to Harriet's husband, "you've been good to Harriet. Thank you. Harriet, I'm gonna say hi to your mama for you." There was a long silence, then Nick smiled and said, "Tommy, same thing for your mama." He sighed once and gave up the struggle.

Hours later, after Joe and Harriet had left to return to Ransom, Tom wandered through the visitors' waiting room just inside the entrance to the huge complex. The gift shop and drugstore next to the waiting room were both still open. He drifted through those. He needed to walk, but he didn't want to leave the building. It gave him a feeling of contact with Nick, despite his intellectual knowledge that Nick no longer existed. He was glad that Nick had had the comfort, during his final moments, of thinking he was going to meet his long-dead wife in some happy place, but Tom couldn't let himself fall into the trap of mistaking wish-fulfillment for reality. He wished he could believe that his mother's spirit still lived, that she was spending eternity in some lovely garden spot where no one mistreated her, where she waited to welcome her son.

He had only visited Nick once before the end. Why hadn't he come to see the old man more often? You have to treasure people while they're still alive, he thought.

Guilt—at the neglect of the living, the neglect of the dying, the causing of deaths. He had enough of that. He didn't think he could bear any more.

He found himself standing in front of a bank of telephones. Most of them were pay phones, but one was for in-house calls. On the wall next to it was a listing of numbers within the hospital.

INTENSIVE CARE 632

It jumped out at him. The name of the hospital had been tickling his memory ever since Harriet mentioned it to him on the telephone, but only now did he remember that this was where Mike Berens was. Ellen had mentioned that Mike had just come back from the ICU when she saw him.

From what Ellen had told him, Mike was being moved in and out of the ICU constantly. He had had a series of operations to repair the damage done by the bullet, and quite a few more would be needed. He would be at Max Care for some time yet. After that, he would presumably have to go somewhere for rehabilitation. And then? How long until he could start truly rebuilding his life? Never, Tom thought, if one meant the life Mike had been building before he was shot.

More guilt, Tom thought. For all his sympathy for Mike and

his horror at the ruining of the boy's life, Tom had never driven up here to visit him. The suffering of people in a hospital was...He admitted it to himself: Too real and immediate. Being here stripped from Tom his armor of detachment, his habitual distancing of himself. He never liked to see people actually suffering in front of him, even when it was his orders that had caused that suffering.

He had behaved uncharacteristically with Nick Jaruzelski today, but Nick was a special case. Also, when Harriet called, Tom hadn't had time to think about what he should do. He had thought only of seeing Nick one last time.

This time, though, he would force himself to do the right thing in a conscious and deliberate way.

One of the numbers in the directory was for Patient Information. He called that one and got an operator who told him that Mike Berens was currently in Surgery East, visitors welcome, just follow the yellow line, thank you for visiting Max Care Health Systems Denver, bringing you the latest in medical technology at the most affordable prices in the Rocky Mountain West.

The yellow line led him through a connecting tunnel to Surgery East, which was a separate building from the one he had been in. The line ended at a nurse's station. The young man seated there put his hand over the receiver and held it away from his face and smiled an unconvincing professional smile. "Can I help you?"

"I'm a friend of Mike Berens," Tom said. "Can I just go on to his room?"

The professional smile gave way to a genuine look of

sadness. "Sure. Visitors are good for him. He could use a lot more of them."

"He's not doing well?"

The nurse hesitated, then said, "I guess there was some brain damage. Hydrostatic shock via the CSF. He's got a lot of painkillers in him, too, so be patient with him."

Tom assured the nurse that he would be patient and walked down the hall. He stopped in the open doorway, not sure he had the right room, confused in much the same way he had been when he first saw Nick Jaruzelski. How could that thin, pale figure dozing in the bed be Mike Berens? This was someone much smaller and older.

Tom stepped closer for a better look. The man in the bed had sunken cheeks and deep shadows under his eyes. His eyelids fluttered. The veins showed blue in them. His arms lay by his side above the covers, motionless and weak. Oh God, Tom thought, it could be Berens, aged twenty years in just over a month. "Mike?" Tom said. "Mike Berens?"

The eyelids fluttered open. Suddenly, it was Mike's face, just thinner and older. "Hi. Who are you?" Whispered. The ghost of the singer's voice.

"Tom Hamilton. I came to the practice room while you were in there getting ready to..." He found that he didn't want to finish the sentence. What could he say? While you were getting ready to be shot? While you were getting ready to have some bastard destroy your life?

He needn't have worried. Mike's head rolled back and forth slowly on the pillow. "Sorry. Don't remember that." He paused for breath after every word or so, another parallel with Nick.

"It doesn't matter. I just wanted to see how you were

doing."

"Okay. Doing fine." The phrases were mechanical, obligatory. Mike seemed to gather himself and said, "I appreciate your coming. Sorry I don't remember the time we met."

There was a long silence while Tom wondered what to say and Mike relaxed after his effort at speech. Now that he was finally paying this visit, Tom had no idea what to talk about.

Mike said, "Girl out there?"

"What?"

"Girl. Outside the room. Waiting to see me?"

"Oh. No, I'm sorry, Mike. I didn't see anyone else. Were you expecting someone?"

"Hoping. Singer I worked with."

"Karen Franks," Tom guessed.

"Right. Thought she'd come."

"I'm sure she'll be here later, Mike." When you get back on your feet and miraculously recover your voice and get a contract singing at the Met. Then she'll crawl all over you, but don't expect to see her before then. Tom felt like a coward for lying to the injured boy, but he knew that telling Mike the truth would have made him feel even worse. "You know, I was supposed to bring you your lucky pen at—at the auditorium, but I wasn't able to find it. If you tell me where it is, I'll go get it and bring it with me the next time. That would be a good thing to have, wouldn't it?"

"No lucky pen," Mike said.

"You don't want your lucky pen?"

Mike's head rolled from side to side again. "That's silly. Want my teddy."

"Oh. Well, I guess I could get that for you. Is it in your apartment?"

The slow head roll. "Home. Parents. Western Slope. Pastora. Driving here tomorrow. Call them. Tell them teddy."

Tom promised that he would call Mike's parents and tell them to bring their son's teddy bear with them, assuming they still had it. In a way, he thought, listening to Mike's meandering, childish conversation was even worse than watching Nick Jaruzelski die. Nick had had many more years of healthy living behind him than Mike, and he had died with his mind intact. How many years would Mike go on like this, semi-crippled and mentally reduced to childhood?

Tom walked quietly from the room, hoping that Mike wouldn't hear him leaving. He left without seeing any sign that the young man in the bed was aware of his movement.

Thirty-Two

Pastora. Somewhere on the Western Slope, which Tom had already known before Mike said so. They raised something there. Apples? Cherries? Cantaloupes? Something else entirely? Whatever the crop was, Tom assumed that Pastora was probably the sort of place where everyone went to bed early. He checked his watch. It was after 8 p.m. already. The Berenses would be driving to Denver the next day, if Mike wasn't confused about that, which made it all the more likely that they would be in bed already or headed there soon.

He probably shouldn't call them at all. But he couldn't forget that sad request for the teddy bear. Having his beloved childhood toy might make a big difference in Mike's recovery. Tom couldn't ignore that possibility.

Tom followed the yellow line back to the hospital's main lobby and the bank of telephones. He used his calling card to get information for Area Code 970. There were three listings under "Berens." Tom chose at random and called Carl Berens.

"Mike's my nephew," Carl Berens said. "You don't want me. You want my brother Bob. How's the boy doing, anyway?"

"He's...He's not doing very well, Mr. Berens."

"Damn. He was a good boy."

"I think he still is." Although it's hard to tell.

Tom asked Carl Berens for his brother's number and tried that one.

A man's voice, thick with sleep, answered. "Hello?"

"Is this Bob Berens? Mike Berens' father?"

The man at the other end woke up immediately. "Yes, it is. What's happened? Is Mike okay?"

"He's fine, Mr. Berens. Nothing has happened. My name is Tom Hamilton. I'm a friend of Mike's. I visited him in the hospital today, and he seemed fine to me."

"Thank God!"

So much relief, so much concern in those two words. What must it be like, Tom wondered, to be a son whose father cared that much about him, loved him that much? Tom thought that he could almost trade places with Mike, take on his wound and pain and limited future, just to gain that loving relationship in return.

He could hear the elder Berens talking to someone else. He was reassuring Mike's mother, probably—a mother as worried as her husband, a mother still living at home.

"Mr. Berens," Tom said, "when I spoke to Mike, he told me you were planning to drive to Denver to see him tomorrow. He wanted me to ask you to bring his teddy bear with you."

"His what?"

"His teddy bear."

More mumbled conversation in the background. Then Bob Berens said, "We don't remember that Mike ever had a teddy bear."

"Maybe he had it when he was a kid and just kept it in his

room, and you never noticed it there. Is that possible?"

"Tom. That's your name, isn't it?"

"Yes, that's right."

"Tom, Mike never gets attached to things. He's too sensible for that. He's got both feet on the ground. He had some toys when he was small, but as soon as he outgrew them, he gave them away. Going into music is the only stupid thing the boy's ever done. Thank God that's over with now, anyway. So what is this about a damned teddy bear?" Mingled anger and suspicion were growing in Bob's voice.

Tom realized that Mike's brain must be in worse condition than his doctors knew. Tom didn't want to alarm Mike's parents by saying that to them, though. "I must have misunderstood him. Maybe it was a book he wanted. Or a videotape, or a CD."

"Wait a minute, I bet I know!" Bob laughed. "We went on a bear hunt, Mike and me, when he was about ten. I kept...uh, a part of the bear. Had it tanned and stuffed. Mike always thought it was funny. I used to use it to cheer him up when he was feeling low. Damn, where is that thing? Out in the back shed, maybe. Anyway, I'll try to find it before we leave in the morning. Thanks for letting me know about it, Tom." His voice was friendly again.

"You're welcome. Sorry if I woke you up."

"Oh, hell no. We were still getting ready for our trip."

Lying to make me feel better, Tom thought as he hung up. Western Slope politeness and courtesy. Except toward bears. Strange how otherwise good people could derive pleasure from killing things.

It was time to go home at last.

The hospital was on high ground and faced westward. There was a good view of the mountains. The sun had set while Tom was in the hospital, and the Rockies were outlined against the fading glow of twilight. In the valley between Tom and the mountains, the lights of Denver twinkled in the cold, dry air and pollution of Indian Summer.

Tom stepped away from the building and turned to look at it. The moon, just past full, must be above the horizon but behind the hospital, he guessed. The moon's glow lit the eastern sky, transforming the hospital into an ominous silhouette. It loomed over him, a huge dark mass, seeming to be not a place of refuge and healing but an eater of souls. Mike Berens had been taken there to be healed to the extent he could ever be healed, but so many others went there to die. Nick Jaruzelski had gone there to die, to end, to become nothing.

Tom looked up at the few stars twinkling overhead and wanted to believe that up there, or somewhere on some other plane of existence, Nick was saying hello to his mother for him.

Where are you, Mom? Did that bastard murder you and hide your body? Where are you?

Tom looked at the ground again and shook himself. He was accomplishing nothing. He was doing nothing with his freedom. Not knowing, he knew, was destroying him.

Thirty-Three

When Tom awoke on Sunday morning, Indian Summer was over and it was snowing. He hadn't been paying attention to the weather forecasts, so he hadn't expected the change in the weather. The first measurable snow of the year usually came in mid-September, he remembered, so this was now a perfectly average year for Ransom. If one ignored a couple of shootings during performances of Tosca.

It didn't feel particularly cold outside. When Tom stepped out his front door to pick up the Sunday papers, he stood for a while, dressed in only his robe and slippers, watching the snow fall, feeling the flakes on his face like light touches by a cold, wet finger. The first few snowfalls of winter were usually like this—big, wet flakes and an air temperature right around freezing. The grass in front of his house was still green. Tom had always loved the contrast in the fall between the green blades of grass and the white flakes landing on them.

The snow was thick enough to hide the town from him. The drop-off in front of his house looked like the end of the world, with nothing beyond it but a wall of mist. His house was in a world of its own, a new and peaceful world. Ransom and all its troubles and memories had vanished.

You'd like to think so, he told himself.

He picked the papers up and went indoors for the hot drink Mr. Coffee had prepared for him.

That afternoon, Tom and Janice Sheridan went to a movie.

He no longer thought about the strangeness of Tom Hamilton having lunch dates and now a movie date with Janice Sheridan. With Janice, there was none of the edginess that there always was with Ellen Tourneau, none of the ghosts of past desires and longed-for relationships hovering at his shoulder and whispering in his ear. Janice was Janice as she was now, and when he was with her, Tom was the Tom of today. They were two friends who spent occasional pleasant times together, and that was all. He looked forward more and more to seeing her.

When she called him up in the morning to ask if he wanted to go to a movie, Tom had said, "Great! There's a new French movie playing in Denver that I've been reading good things about."

Janice had laughed. "I don't have to drive to Denver and pay the price of a movie ticket if I want a nap! I can do that at home. The new Schwarzenegger movie is showing right here in Ransom. That's what I had in mind."

Tom groaned. "You're getting revenge on me for something, but I don't know what. How do they explain away his accent in this one?"

By having the hero be a German defector flying for America during World War I, as it turned out. Highjinks and one-liners and terrifying stunts on the Western Front in 1917.

"This must be one of Arnold's serious movies. No high tech

at all," Tom said as they were sitting in Ransom's one and only coffee bar. This was its second day in business. The snow had stopped and the sun had come out. Down here in town, the temperature had stayed above freezing, and the streets and sidewalks were wet, with no sign left of snow. It was now cool, damp, and sunny in Ransom. The two of them had draped their winter coats over their chairs. The hot drink felt good to Tom in a way it never did in summer.

Tom sipped his latte and said, "I guess this beats driving all the way to Denver for good coffee, but I'm not sure."

"So you're an expert on coffee, too?"

Tom grinned at her. "I didn't spend the last twenty years in Istanbul for nothing." His whereabouts for all those years had become a joke between them. She no longer tried with any seriousness to pry the secret out of him, and he threw in whatever unlikely city or country popped into his mind at the moment. "Poor Arnold! I wonder how they managed to squeeze him into those cockpits. Probably built an extra-large mockup just for him."

"Admit that you enjoyed it," Janice said. "You cheered when the bad guy got shot down." Janice was drinking ordinary coffee. Just coffee: no flavored syrup, no steamed milk, no foam on top. In Tom's opinion, it was only by adding such ingredients that one made coffee drinkable.

"I didn't cheer. I said, 'Nicely foreshadowed.' Okay, it wasn't a bad way to spend two hours, I admit. Quite good as mind candy goes."

"I could have done with more explosions," Janice said. "I like it when Arnold really goes over the top in his movies. This one was kind of tame. But I'm not as sophisticated as you."

"I've been doing it again, haven't I?"

Janice nodded. "You've improved a bit since you came back to town, but you've still got a ways to go."

Because it's not just a habit I have to learn to break, Tom realized. The kind of cultural education I've given myself is more than a way of distancing myself from my childhood. It's also a way of distancing myself from guilt over my work in Chicago. See what a superior, fine creature I am? Doesn't that compensate for what I've done?

"I thought the clothes were pretty nifty," he said.

"Cool, you mean."

"Pretty cool. The scarves the pilots wore, especially. Having Arnold's scarf be the only red one was just a bit extreme."

"He's the hero. I liked the scarf. It reminded me of the ones we all wore when we were juniors."

"We did?"

"No, not the boys! All the girls at Ransom High. You don't remember that? Maybe you never looked that high. It was the short skirts you used to look at mostly. I remember that about you."

"Christ, was I that obvious?"

Janice laughed. "All teenage boys are that obvious. Anyway, during junior year, all of us started wearing red wool scarves. Had to be red, had to be wool."

"Why?"

"Who the hell knows? That's the way teenage girls are. If you were part of the crowd, that's what you did. The losers didn't. If they tried to, we made sure they stopped."

"And I thought the boys were cruel and heartless."

"You were amateurs. Hold on. I've finished my coffee." She

took her empty cup to the silver coffee machine standing on a shelf at the far end of the shop and refilled it.

Tom watched her and tried to visualize her as she was and then to add a red scarf. He couldn't fabricate the image. It was true as Janice said that he had concentrated on girls' legs when he was in high school, but he was surprised that he hadn't noticed the red scarves at all. Surely he had noticed them. That meant that he had forgotten about them. He had always thought that every tiny detail of his childhood and adolescence was permanently etched into his mind, but here was proof that that wasn't the case. The realization was disturbing.

Janice came back, put her cup down on the table carefully, and then fell into her chair. "We're the only people in here," she said. "Ransom isn't ready for sophistication."

"I noticed that. I hope business picks up. I always hate to see small businesses go under. So what happened with those scarves? Did you girls wear them all through school?"

"Nope. I told you, junior year. I guess it only lasted for a couple of months. Must have been during the winter. Then we all stopped."

"Why?"

"I don't remember." She sipped her coffee and seemed disinclined to say more. Finally she spoke again. "I'm lying. I remember damned well. I can't forget. It was Chernikov."

"Ellen, you mean?"

She nodded. "Yeah, Ellen. The rest of us could be bitchy, but she was Superbitch. Turned out she had a really bad allergy to wool, and the scarf irritated her a lot. None of us knew about it. She managed to wear it sort of draped around her shoulders, so that it didn't touch her. Or if it did, she bore it for as long as she could. Anyway, after she had enough of that, she declared that the scarves weren't cool any more, and we were all supposed to stop wearing them. Damn, I loved that scarf! It looked great on me! But all the kids stopped wearing the scarves. The cool kids. Some of the losers started about then, and of course we just let them. But that meant that I couldn't wear mine. That's the whole story."

She raised her cup and bent her face over it, but Tom could see the tears in her eyes. He realized that she was showing more emotion, more pain over this than she had when telling him about her abortive marriage.

Thirty-Four

Monday and Tuesday were gun shop days. Tom managed to get to another ten of them in Denver on Monday and ten in Colorado Springs on Tuesday.

He learned nothing new at any of them. No one remembered seeing either Karen Franks or Jack Tourneau, and in both cities a few of the stores he went to tried to sell him a handgun or a rifle as a gift for the supposed couple.

Worst of all, Tom feared that he didn't need any more information. He was afraid that he knew enough already.

On Wednesday morning, Tom called the Tourneau house. Jack answered. Tom had been hoping against hope for Ellen. "Hello, Jack. I didn't think you'd be at home. Thought you'd be on the campus."

"I don't have anything to do on the campus," Jack said bitterly. "Fucking department chairman gave all my classes to other people. Doesn't want any embarrassment until 'all of this is settled,' as he puts it. He'd fire me if he could come up with an excuse, the bastard."

"Is there any real danger of that?"

"Mark doesn't think so. Pressler, I mean. He says they don't have anything they can use against me. I've been careful."

"What about Kathy Angleton?"

"I didn't touch her while she was my student! Christ, Tom, how stupid do you think I am? I waited until the semester was over. Anyway, Mark says the real danger will be if that bastard Snow manages to get me convicted of murder. The department will be able to chuck me out then, of course."

"Um, don't you think you'll have bigger problems than losing your job in that case?"

"Shit, yes. Of course I will. But this job means a lot to me, Tom. You don't realize. If I lose it, I can just hear my damned father cackling. Everything was going so nicely for me. Then suddenly it's all being taken away from me. It's like some outside force fucking up my life. And you know, it all started when you moved back to town."

He slurred the last few words. Until that, Jack's speech had been so clear and precise that Tom had assumed he was sober. Now he realized that Jack was far from sober. He was just more self-controlled than was usual for him when he had alcohol in him. Tom didn't like the idea of Jack sitting at home, unoccupied, drinking, stewing over his grievances, and thinking of Tom as the cause of all of his problems. It was a good thing that he had something in mind to distract Jack with.

"I was trying to reach Ellen. I guess she's not home yet?"

"That bitch. She's left me! Can you imagine that? Oh, hell, of course you can imagine that. Those problems also started when you moved back to town. Is she there with you now?"

"Jack, calm down. No, Ellen's not here with me. And I didn't have anything to do with her leaving you. Your affairs had a lot more to do with that."

The anger left Jack's voice suddenly and he began sobbing. "Oh, God, you're right!" The words were barely understandable. "I've really fucked up my life, haven't I? I've destroyed everything."

"I wouldn't say that." Your life is never so fucked up that you can't fuck it up more, if you really try. Where there's life, there's hope. "She said something about getting away for a while."

The sobbing stopped and the anger returned. "Not just a while. When I got home, there was a note waiting for me in the kitchen, taped to one of the cabinet doors. It said she was going away to settle her emotions, or something idiotic like that, and when she came back, she was going to file for divorce. Pressler better not handle it for her, that son of a bitch."

Tom thought about how to phrase his next question, but he couldn't come up with a good way. "Since Ellen hasn't come back yet, I wonder if I could get her phone number from you."

"Are you brain dead? I don't know where she is."

And I shouldn't be telling you where she is. I don't want to be an unwilling accomplice to a murder. But how else can I track her down? "She left me a message saying she would be staying with her cousin Liz in Portland."

"Oh, yeah. Elizabeth. I should have guessed. Boy, that Elizabeth is a knockout. You should see her. Makes Ellen look plain." Jack's voice trailed off as he thought about Ellen's cousin.

"Jack. I'd like this cousin's phone number."

"Yeah, sure. Let's see here. Jonas," he muttered. "Jonas. Jesus, the silly bitch can't even put these cards in alphabetical order. Can you imagine that? Hey, why should I give you the number? Why should I help you steal my wife?"

"Jack, I haven't made any attempt to steal your wife. I have no such intentions. I'm not your enemy." Now that Tom knew the cousin's last name, the chances of his being able to find the telephone number on his own had improved greatly. Still, it would be so much easier if Jack simply gave it to him. "Maybe if I spoke to Ellen, I could convince her to come back again."

"Yeah, maybe. I guess she wouldn't really want to speak to me right now, would she? That stupid Angleton girl made sure of that."

"No, I don't think she'd want to speak to you. I don't think it would be a good idea at all for you to call her."

"Okay." Jack read out the Portland telephone number. Suddenly, he began sobbing again. "Tom," he blubbered, "I'm counting on you! Save me, Tom!"

"I'll do my best, Jack." Tom managed to keep his voice calm, but he was shaking when he hung up. He was tempted to clean the telephone with a strong disinfectant.

I need a vacation from my retirement, he thought.

Instead, he gave himself five minutes. Then he called the number Jack had given him.

"Hi! Liz and Hugh are busy with their lives right now, but they really value your call! So when you hear that cute-sounding tone, why don't you leave—"

Tom hung up and decided it wasn't too early for a large drink. Then he thought about Jack and decided to stick to water. But a large water, he told himself.

He tried twice more and got the answering machine both times. He gave up at noon because he had to drive to Denver for the memorial service for Nick Jaruzelski.

A few days before his death, Nick had instructed his daughter to have his body cremated. He couldn't stand the idea of it rotting in the ground, he said.

"I can understand his feelings," Tom said. He and Harriet and Joe were standing in the scrupulously non-denominational chapel attached to the funeral home where the cremation had taken place that morning. Tom wondered how a religious person of any religion could find emotional comfort in a non-denominational chapel—a phrase which struck him as oxymoronic.

"Oh, so can I," Harriet said. "Me and Joe have talked about having it done to us, too. But you know, my mom's buried in Ransom, and I thought Dad would want to buried next to her. I visit her grave about once a month or so. It's comforting. I wanted to be able to visit both of them."

"What about the ashes?"

"He wanted them spread in the mountains. Joe's going to take care of that. He said..." She hesitated, looking back and forth at the two men as though unsure whether she should say more. "He said the main reason he wanted to be cremated was because he was pretty sure your mom is up there in the mountains somewhere, and this was the only way he could end up close to her. I didn't know if I should tell you that. You aren't insulted, are you?"

Tom shook his head. "Of course not, Harriet. I'm touched. I wish it had worked out between them." He smiled at her. "You'd be my step-sister. And Joe, you'd be my step-brother-in-law, I guess."

"I'd like that," Joe said.

Harriet said, "I feel like you're my kid brother anyway."

"Listen," Tom said, "I know it's very soon after Nick's death, but I'd really like it if you could both come over to my place for dinner on Saturday. The dinner we were supposed to have had last Saturday."

Harriet looked doubtful. "It *is* a bit soon," she said. She looked at her husband.

Joe said, "I bet Nick would say it's a damned good idea."

Tom had dinner in Denver and got home around seven p.m. He called the Portland number again. This time, Liz and Hugh were able to take a long enough break from their busy lives to answer the telephone.

Tom couldn't form a picture of Liz from her voice, so he couldn't tell if she was the knockout Jack claimed. But he certainly could tell that she was chipper despite being so busy.

"Oh, Ellen's not here," she said. "She's out."

"Do you know when she'll be back?"

"No idea."

"Well, I could call again this evening. When would be too late for me to call?"

"No, I mean I don't know what day she'll be back."

"You mean she's staying with someone else now?"

Hesitation. "Who is this?"

"I'm a friend of Ellen's. My name's Tom Hamilton."

"Oh! Tom Hamilton! Yes, Ellen's talked quite a bit about you. I was afraid you might be a friend of Jack's trying to track her down. I don't mind telling *you*. After Ellen got here, she decided she needed to really get away. She wasn't able to recover here. The kids always like seeing her, and they were bugging her a bit. So she borrowed Hugh's Cherokee and some camping gear and left for a few days. She was heading for the Olympic Peninsula to do some hiking and camping."

"Alone?"

Liz chuckled. "You don't think Ellen can take care of herself? I pity the man or beast that tries to bother her! Anyway, when she does get back, I'll tell her you called."

"Have her call me, please." Tom gave her his number. "Tell her I said that things might be coming to a head here. Tell her I think I've figured out some things, and she needs to know about them for her own safety. Tell her it's turned chilly here. I've had to put an extra wool blanket on my bed."

"Your bed, huh? My, my. I got that part, but repeat all the rest of it. I was writing it down."

Tom repeated everything more slowly.

"Okay, got it. It's been nice talking to you, Tom. I hope I'll get to meet you in person some day. Ellen's told us a lot about you. If you're ever in Portland, I hope you'll give us a call."

Portland was one of the cities he would never be able to visit. One of Trager's main business associates—as they liked to call each other—lived and had his headquarters there. Tom had met the man and some of his underlings when they were visiting Chicago. So Tom—or Jimmy Nicholson—had best stay away from Portland if he valued his life.

"If I'm ever in Portland, I certainly will," he said.

Thirty-Five

Tom kept hoping for a call from Ellen. He assumed she was still away on her camping trip. He considered calling up her cousin again, just to check, but decided that would be silly.

Instead of sitting at home waiting for the telephone to ring, Tom did gun shops again on Thursday and Friday. He was still hoping against hope for a reported sighting of either Karen or Jack, but he remained disappointed.

He worked Denver on Thursday and Colorado Springs on Friday like a zombie. He repeated his lie about the couple he wanted to buy a deadly present for, and he scarcely understood his own words. They had become sounds that elicited a certain response from the people he spoke to, and that was all that mattered.

On Saturday morning, Tom struggled awake when the radio came on at 7:01 a.m. NPR was giving him the news with a chipperness worthy of Liz Jonas or Julie Pressler. He raised himself on one elbow and turned the radio off with the other hand.

Why the hell did I set that? he asked himself.

Then he remembered that he had planned yet another day of going to gun shops, and he groaned and fell back onto his pillow.

If he stayed in that position for more than a second or two, he knew, he would fall asleep. He pushed himself out of bed, pulled his robe on, and went into the kitchen. Coffee was just finishing dripping into the pot, and the bagel he had wisely sliced the night before was in the toaster. He pressed the lever down on the toaster, pushed on the thick bagel to force it down, poured coffee into the cup he had put on the counter the night before—milk and sugar already in it—and told himself that he'd rather slice his wrists open than go to one more gun shop. He stood at the counter drinking coffee and feeling sorry for himself.

The coffee finally woke up the necessary brain cells. Tom remembered that this was the evening Harriet and Joe were supposed to come over for dinner. He had no gun shops scheduled for today. That was simply a leftover nightmare from earlier in the week. He now remembered that when the radio turned on, he had been dreaming about an endless street lined on both sides with gun shops. The fading memory of that nightmare had confused him. The real nightmare was that he had eleven hours to prepare a dinner for three.

Or buy one. If he bought gourmet food, Harriet and Joe would feel uncomfortable, if his judgment of them was correct. Or he could buy cheap food, and then it would seem as though he was sneering at them.

No, he really had to cook this meal. That means, he calculated, that I have about eight hours to learn to cook.

He smelled burning bagel. He pushed up on the toaster

lever, but the bagel was firmly stuck to the glowing element. He grabbed a knife from the drawer and tried to dig the bagel out. By the time he succeeded, all he had was a counter covered with black, smoking pieces of charcoal.

I don't think I can learn to cook in eight hours, he thought.

The only telephone directory he had in the house was the one for Ransom. It was a small book, combining white and yellow pages. In the yellow pages section, under Catering, he found no listings for businesses in Ransom, but he did find two in Denver. Heartened, he ate breakfast, read the Ransom and Denver newspapers, showered, shaved, and called the first Denver number, a company called Your Own Chef.

They had obviously dealt with his kind before. The woman he spoke to suggested their Number Five, a prime rib dinner for $25 a person, and guaranteed to make his guests think he had prepared it himself. He could pick the food up two hours in advance. Along with the food, he would be given detailed printed instructions about heating it up so that it would be ready in time and would give the impression of having been freshly prepared.

So I would actually have the time to do a few gun shops in Denver before picking up the food, Tom thought. Or I could clean the house in preparation. Or do something else productive and Puritan-ethical.

Or I could go for a walk.

He went for a walk.

Later in the morning, Tom did do a bit of desultory cleaning up. Then he drove to Denver hours early and indulged himself in some idle sightseeing, coffee and a sandwich, and a couple of hours in a bookstore.

By then, it was time to drive to Your Own Chef and pick up the home-cooked dinner for three. For $75, he got three plastic shopping bags with the caterer's logo on them, all of them sealed with heavy tape, and two photocopied pages of instruction. He was waited on by a man wearing a chef's hat and apron who looked at him doubtfully, shrugged, and took his money.

"You know," Tom said to him, "I was going to cook something myself." He told him about the incident with the bagel. "That's when I changed my mind."

"Good way to electrocute yourself," the man said. "Next time, unplug the toaster, then push down on the lever and down on the bagel to loosen it. It'll pop up."

"I didn't even think of that!"

"Of course you didn't."

The moon rose during Tom's drive home. It was just past three-quarters full. It was pale against the blue sky, but it grew brighter as it rose higher and the sun dropped lower. By the time he reached Ransom, the sun had set. The air was dry and cold, and the sky was cloudless and filled with the glow of the moon. Between that and the lights of town, Tom couldn't see any stars at all.

He noticed a dusty off-road vehicle of some sort parked in the driveway of the empty house next door.

Neighbors at last, Tom thought. I suppose I ought to go over and welcome them. Do the small-town thing. No time tonight. Perhaps tomorrow morning.

He parked in his driveway, took one of the plastic bags

from the trunk, unlocked his front door, and headed for the living room. It was surprisingly cool in the house. He flipped on the light switch just inside the living room doorway.

His picture window was shattered. Glass shards covered the hardwood floor.

He let the bag fall to the floor. Turned to run from the house.

Ellen Tourneau was sitting on the couch, watching him.

"What a mess you've made," she said.

"My God, what are you doing here?"

"I got your message. The cryptic one."

"I meant that as a warning, Ellen. I meant for you to stay away."

"And do what? Move somewhere, take on a new name, a new identity, start all over?"

"It can be done."

"Not by me. That's the sort of cowardly thing you'd probably do. But I'm tired of being a victim. I've decided to control my life, Tom."

Tom gestured over his shoulder with his thumb. "Does that include smashing my window?"

"I had to get in. Good thing you've got so many rocks lying around there instead of a lawn. Don't you hate people who pay lots of money for a house in the mountains and then put a lawn in front of it? If you had left your door open, the way we trusting small-town folks are supposed to, I would have walked in without doing any damage."

"You could have waited until I got home. I have company coming in a little while. I'll have to clean up the broken glass and get ready for them. I don't suppose there's any place in Ransom that will come out on a Saturday evening and replace a big window like that. Have to wait for Monday morning."

Ellen jumped to her feet and shouted, "Stop talking so much! Jesus Christ! I don't give a shit about your company or your window! Do you think it matters now?" She stood close to him, staring down at him, her face white and drawn with anger.

He had hoped that his talking about trivia would distract her, calm her, enable him to tilt the balance of psychological control in his direction. Now he was afraid it had had the opposite effect. He tried a different tack. "Do you need a ride to wherever you're staying? I suppose you took a cab here from the airport."

It worked to a degree. Ellen stepped back, and her coloring returned to normal. "Oh, that's what you think? It's a bit more complicated than that, Tom. I drove."

"In your Honda? Where did you park it?"

She shook her head. "You still don't understand. I mean that I drove here from Portland.

"I called up Liz and Hugh from Port Angeles on Wednesday night, just to let them know I was okay, and they told me about your phone call. Liz told me about you adding a wool blanket to your bed. She was giggling about it, the silly bitch. She thought you were inviting me to come live here with you. So I told them I'd keep on camping and hiking, but instead I set out for home. I had Hugh's Cherokee. It's in the driveway next door. I've got his camping gear in it, so I was able camp along the way instead of using motels. And I've got lots of cash for food and gas. There are no records of my trip."

Sick dread filled him. He thought he knew what she must be planning. Now he spoke to distract her and gain time. "Where did you get that much cash?"

"From an ATM machine here in Ransom, before I left town. I didn't want to wait till I got to Portland in case Jack did something to freeze me out of the account. That's just what that bastard would do, you know? So I beat him to it. I knew I'd need lots of cash for the trip back here."

"So you were planning to drive back to Ransom from the beginning?"

"Not exactly," Ellen said. "I hoped that wouldn't be necessary. I just wanted to be prepared for any eventuality."

"Does that include a house that will soon be filled with dinner guests?"

"Well, let's see," Ellen said. "You obviously thought you'd have a lot of time before they arrive—time to drive me somewhere and come back, and clean up the glass, and fix the food. Oh, it's prepared, isn't it?" She pointed to the sack Tom had dropped.

He hadn't even been aware that it had burst on landing, spilling the serving of prime rib and accompanying salad, vegetables, and dessert. Gravy had splashed on his shoes and pants legs. He stepped away from the mess, feeling regret that so much food and careful work and had gone to waste.

"I figure that you're not expecting your guests for a while yet," Ellen said. "Plenty of time for me to do what I have to do. In fact, I see only one serving of food. Maybe it's for you, and there aren't any guests coming at all."

"The rest of it's in the car. I should get it in before it spoils."

Ellen laughed. "You just keep on trying, but it won't work. I want to show you something." She bent and picked up her purse, which she had placed on the floor beside the couch. She opened it and rummaged inside. "It's a present for you. Now where—? Oh, yes."

Tom relaxed at the word "present." But when Ellen's hand came out of the purse, it was holding a gun. She pointed it at his chest.

Thirty-Six

"Isn't it a beauty?" she said. "It's called the Black Widow. I had to have it just because of the name. And because this one fires 22 Long Rifle bullets. That made it easier for me to buy the ammunition I needed. It would have been best to take the ammunition from Jack's desk drawer, but the idiot keeps it locked. I didn't want to break the lock. That would make it look like someone broke in and stole the ammunition, and that would have diverted suspicion from Jack. So I had to buy some myself. I suppose I could have just bought the bullets in Denver, and no one would have thought anything of it. But I really liked this gun, and I just knew it would come in handy. Just in case someone figured things out, I wanted to be able to eliminate him with the same kind of bullets that were put into the rifles in the opera. Did you know that you can't tell from the slug whether it was fired from a rifle or a handgun?"

For the first time since seeing her in his house, Tom felt calm. One of Trager's men had told him of experiencing a similar calmness when he thought he was about to be murdered and knew he could do nothing to prevent it. Until now, Tom hadn't quite believed that story. "I wondered how you could have done so much target shooting and hunting with your brothers and yet be so ignorant about guns and ammunition," he said. "I wanted to ask you about that, but you left town too quickly. I guess that *was* you that the man in the gun shop was talking about. I wasn't completely sure. It did fit with the rest, though."

"Like the wool, you mean? How did you figure that out?"

"Yes, the wool. Janice Sheridan told me about the scarves you girls wore for a while in high school, and how you were so allergic to wool."

"That bitch. I ought to kill her, too."

"That night at the school, when you were obviously hot. You had Jack's wool suit jacket inside your coat. You were wearing both at the same time. The wool cuffs were touching your wrists. That's why they were red the next day, when we had lunch. That whole thing about Jack tying you and up and forcing you to have sex, that was all made up, wasn't it?"

She grinned. "Not entirely. We used to do that when we were young. Kind of a game we played."

Her face paled again. "That idiot Snow screwed things up for me. I was going to come back the next day and put the blank cartridges in the jacket, and then one of the singers would have found it at the next performance. But Snow's men thought it was one of the props and locked it up backstage with everything else, so I had to get rehearsals started again right away with that miserable so-called tenor, Hillerman. It would have been a pleasure to see him get shot, if I'd had to do it a third time. I switched to doing the opera in Italian to make sure Hillerman would throw in the towel and I could send everyone home and go home with the jacket. Then you decided to do your duty and show up, so I had to make up a reason to send you away. I knew none of the kids would notice me putting the jacket inside my coat so that I could put both of them on together. They were too nervous about what they were supposed to be doing. But I wasn't sure about you."

"You had no reason to worry about me. I'm on your side, Ellen. That's why I tried to warn you with that phone call to Portland."

"Oh, I do worry about you. I think you're a very ethical little guy. I think about you a lot. I've been thinking that it would be fun to play the bondage game with you, but with me doing the tying up. I didn't lie about that part, you know. I really have been thinking about what it would be like if I left Jack and moved in with you. You're so interestingly small and weak." She gestured at the room with the gun, then aimed it at him again before he could react. "And this is such a beautiful, expensive place. It'll be a real shame to mess it up with your blood.

"It's dangerous for me to be in town. Someone might see me. I tried calling you from the highway a couple of times. I thought I could get you to meet me out in the mountains somewhere, and I could do it there. But you didn't answer, so I just decided to come on over."

"And then what? You'll still have to go on the run and live under an assumed name."

"Of course I won't, Tom. I'm going to kill you with this gun, and then I'm going to drive back to Portland. No one will know I was ever out of the Northwest. When they find your body, they'll think you were killed by the same person who set up the two shootings during the opera. Jack will be the obvious suspect."

"The confrontation in your house, the night you sent me there."

"Exactly. That worked out even better than I hoped. I was afraid Jack might have left the house and gone catting around. Or if he was there, it was possible that he was sober for a change. But it was perfect. In Andy Snow's mind, what happened that evening will be one more piece of evidence against Jack when your body is found."

There was a clock over on the wall beyond the bar, but Tom couldn't see it from where he stood. He wondered how he could move so that he could see it. He had no idea how much time had passed in this otherworldly conversation and therefore how much time remained before Harriet and Joe arrived. Then it struck him that if they did arrive, Ellen was quite likely to kill them, too. Like others in the past, they would die because they were too close to him. To save them, he had to get her to shoot him now and leave.

"You didn't plan everything well," he said. "You made up that stupid story about Mike Berens' lucky pen. He has no such thing."

"I had to do something to get you out of the theater so that I could reload the rifles, and that's what came to mind. Besides, I was assuming he'd be dead in a few minutes, so you'd never know there was no lucky pen. Bad luck that he survived. That's why I visited him in the hospital, you know—to see if I needed to finish the job on him somehow. But I decided that his mind was so permanently fuzzed that he wasn't a problem. Okay, so I was wrong about that and you found out about the pen. That's okay. No one else knows about that story."

She was staying surprisingly calm. A few minutes earlier, she had seemed on the edge, but now Tom's words didn't seem to be upsetting her. Perhaps movement would do it. He had been standing almost frozen all along. If he simply left, or tried to, wouldn't that make her shoot?

"All very interesting," he told her, "but now I'm going to leave." He took one step toward the doorway.

She was surprisingly fast. She whipped her hand to the left and then back, slashing the barrel of her gun across his face.

He staggered back and fell to one knee. The gun's sights had cut across his forehead, slicing it open. Blood filled his eyes. He rubbed his eyes, trying to clear them. He could feel the skin of his forehead sliding around horribly as he did so. He felt dizzy and nauseated, and yet he felt little pain.

It will come, he thought. If I live long enough.

"You're supposed to ask for a pen and paper now. To write me one final letter."

"What?" He could make no sense of her words.

"Like Mario in the last act. You're even a tenor. Lyric, right? Never mind. Don't answer. How would you know? I bet you've never tried to sing anything. I bet you just listen all the time, the way you've always watched instead of participating. I used to think you were pretty creepy, back in high school."

"Participating now," Tom gasped. "Rather be watching." He sat down carefully on the floor. The movement made his head swim. His forehead was burning. He had a headache, a growing pounding inside his head. "Ellen, get it over with."

"Why should I? I'm enjoying this, controlling the final minutes of your life. This is total power over someone else. I felt it with Jerry and Mike as well. But this is even better because you know what I'm doing. This is even better than sex. You have no idea what it's like."

"That's what you think." He had never enjoyed it, though.

He thought that he shouldn't have said that, shouldn't have revealed that about himself to her. But then he realized that it didn't matter now what he revealed.

He was able to think more clearly—clearly enough to understand that the odds were growing that Ellen would still be here when Harriet and Joe arrived.

Got to try to run again, Tom thought. Make her shoot me so that she'll leave.

He tried to rise. He couldn't see properly. His head spun and he was filled with nausea. He could barely make out Ellen, silhouetted against the moonlight.

So clear, he thought. Window must be really clean. Then he remembered that the window was no longer in the way. The cold evening air flowed through the room. "Chilly," he muttered. "Close the window."

Ellen laughed. "I was right. This *is* better than sex."

"Took you this long to decide to get rid of Jack," Tom said. "Why did you wait? Such a complex plan. Convicted of murder. Killed for you by the state."

"I was waiting for you, Tom. It was your arrival that started everything going."

"No!" Tom shook his head vigorously. That was a mistake. He had to wait for the spinning to stop before he could speak again. The pounding in his head didn't stop. It just kept increasing. "Planning for the opera and killing Jerry Angleton—that was all in place before I got here. Someone else's idea? A Mark Pressler idea. Were you having an affair with him? Is that why you put up with Jack?"

Ellen hit him again. With her open hand this time, not the gun, but in his state, it was enough. He fell heavily on his side and lay unable to move. He closed his eyes and fought against vomiting.

"It was all my own idea." Ellen's voice sounded muffled and distant.

I'm dying, Tom thought. Must be. Be over soon, even if Ellen doesn't get around to it. Didn't remember she liked to talk so much. Poor Jack.

"What have you been reading during the last twenty years?" Ellen asked. "You're out of touch with reality. I've had all the sex I needed or wanted. There are lots of available, discreet men in Ransom, and lots more of them in Denver. No, Tom, I wasn't planning to replace Jack with anyone. I got tired of the double life *and* the dependence. You have no idea what it's like to always wear a false front while you're doing things you hate for a man you despise. At the same time, you're dependent on him for your survival."

"I know."

She didn't seem to hear him. "This way, I'll end up with the house and generous amounts of money from Jack's parents, I'm sure. And I can still spend weekends in Denver enjoying myself. I think it'll work out pretty well, don't you?"

"Why Mike Berens?"

"Well, yes, that was an unforeseen difficulty. I thought I'd only have to go through it once, and that would take care of Jack. I certainly didn't imagine doing the whole thing again. It was very stressful the first time, you know. But then Snow seemed to be focusing his attention on Mike, and I was afraid that he'd be able to make a case against Mike, and Jack would get off. So I had to do something to remove suspicion from Mike. That's why I did it all a second time. Pretty clever of me, if I do say so myself."

He blinked at her silhouette and saw the girl he had yearned for in place of the grown-up killer. "Always you," he muttered. "Only one."

"That's right. It was always me. I took out the blanks and put in the live ammunition. I planted all the suspicions. And now it's time to clean up the only evidence that could point to me. By which I mean you, Tom. I'm really sorry."

Her vague shadow grew, blocking out the moonlight. Something hard pressed against his head.

"This should work really well from close up," Ellen said. "It'll be really interesting to see this."

Tom thought about twenty-two caliber bullets ricocheting inside a man's head, bouncing off the inside of his skull, reducing the brain to mush.

At least it'll be quick and painless, he told himself. Be nice to get rid of this damned headache. He closed his eyes.

He heard voices, yelling, an argument. He felt Ellen pull the gun away from his head. Tom opened his eyes. Ellen was turned away from him, toward the front of the house, tensely alert.

She said, "Damn!" and turned back toward Tom and pressed the muzzle of her gun against his head again.

Someone moved behind her. "Freeze!" Andy Snow stepped into Tom's field of vision and up to Ellen's side. He, too, held a pistol. It was aimed at Ellen's chest. "Give me your gun, Mrs. Tourneau."

Ellen turned her head and looked at him over her shoulder. "Why, Lieutenant," she said. Her tone was relaxed, friendly.

It seemed to catch Snow off guard. He hesitated, let his gun drift slightly to one side.

Again, Ellen moved with remarkable speed. She flicked her

wrist, whipped her pistol away from Tom, aimed it at Snow, fired.

Snow gasped and collapsed on the floor. He lay immobile. He breathed heavily with a gurgling sound.

Ellen stepped toward him.

The front door slammed open and three uniformed policemen burst into the living room. They were all pointing pistols at Ellen and shouting incoherently.

This time, Ellen froze. Tom saw her gauging the odds. Then she opened her hand and let her Black Widow drop. It landed on the floor with a bang. She looked at Tom, smiled slightly, then pursed her lips in a kiss.

She spun about and in three long leaps was out through the shattered window. One more leap took her over the cliff and into the darkness.

Thirty–Seven

After the ambulance crew from the Phillipot County Fire and Rescue Unit had stabilized him, Andy Snow was driven with lights flashing and sirens screaming to Max Care Health Systems in Denver for more extensive patching, sewing, and replacement of lost fluids.

The crew urged Tom to come with them, but he declined. His headache was fading and he was sure he could find whatever treatment he needed for his forehead in Ransom.

He turned out to need only three stitches, which surprised him considering how much the injury had affected him at the time, and he had none of the symptoms of concussion. In retrospect, Tom felt embarrassed at having been so incapacitated when Ellen struck him.

He got his window replaced, and he cleaned up the last pieces of glass.

He removed all traces of the spilled food.

Those were the easy repairs.

Harriet and Joe had arrived for dinner to find policemen with guns drawn at Tom's front door. Joe had insisted that they be allowed to pass, and an argument had ensued—the voices Tom had heard, the distraction that had kept Ellen from shooting him for just long enough.

Tom reinvited Harriet and Joe for Monday evening. That made their third attempt at having dinner together, and this time it went well.

Harriet had deduced how Tom had planned to provide the food. This time, she insisted on doing the cooking for the three of them in Tom's kitchen, but with Tom watching and helping. She told him it was just the first lesson. The next one would be in her kitchen, the following weekend, when Tom was ordered to show up at their house for Sunday dinner.

During the dinner at Tom's house, he managed to fend off their questions about what he had been doing for more than twenty years. He still didn't have any good lies dreamed up.

Finally, on Wednesday afternoon, when the automated phone system at Max Care told him that Andrew Snow was now allowed visitors, Tom drove up to Denver to thank Snow for saving his life.

Snow was a few doors down from Mike Berens. Mike was no longer there, however. The same male nurse Tom had spoken to before told him that Mike's family had had him moved to a facility on the Western Slope where he would be given long-term therapy. The nurse volunteered that the prognosis wasn't good. Tom thanked him and went to Snow's room.

Snow was awake and alert, and his wife was with him. She was leaning over the bed and seemed to be kissing her husband's forehead. "Sorry to interrupt," Tom said. "I'll come back later."

Diane Snow straightened and smiled happily at Tom. "Don't be silly! I was just trying to fix Andy's hair a bit. It gets to be such a mess when he can't shower regularly. Please come in. It's good for him to have visitors."

Andy Snow glowered from his hospital bed, communicating clearly that he didn't think it would do him any good at all to have this visitor.

The covers were pulled up to Snow's chin. His face seemed perfectly normal. Whatever dressings he had were hidden by the bedclothes.

Tom stood at the foot of the bed. "I came here to thank you for saving my life. In the end, I did need you to pull my fat out of the fire, didn't I?"

The aura of ill will that Snow was broadcasting seemed to fade a bit. "Hah!" he said. "Damned right. Maybe I should have waited a few seconds longer. Let her blow your brains out."

"Andy!"

"Okay, okay. Protect and serve. That's what I was doing. Don't thank me, write a letter to the chief."

Tom laughed. "I'll probably do that. What were you doing there?"

"Preparing to arrest you."

"Me? For what?"

"Accomplice. First degree murder, attempted first degree murder. Tourneau's accomplice, I mean."

"You have to make up your mind, Lieutenant. Was I..." Tom hesitated, looked at Diane Snow, then decided to continue. "Was I screwing Tourneau's wife or was I helping him to murder his lover's husband? Doesn't seem I'd be doing both, does it?"

Snow looked uncomfortable at this twist in the conversation. "Well, I was wrong on both counts, obviously."

"Come to think of it," Tom said, feeling the need to see Snow squirm a bit more, "maybe the two aren't incompatible after all. If I had been screwing Tourneau's wife, then it would be in my interest to help him free his lover from her marriage so that Tourneau's attention would be focused on her, and Ellen would have that much more freedom. Gee, maybe you're onto something there."

"Christ, give it a rest," Snow said. "I admitted I was wrong. After what I heard Ellen Tourneau saying to you, I've asked the D.A. to drop all the charges against Jack Tourneau, and you're no longer under suspicion for anything."

"I should think not," Diane Snow said.

"You were in my living room listening for that long?" Tom said in amazement. "Ellen could have killed me at any time, and you just waited?"

"She didn't, did she?"

"I'm sure she didn't really mean to hurt you," Diane said. "It wasn't in her, you know."

"Jesus, Diane," Snow said, "she meant to hurt me! She meant to *kill* me! And she did kill one guy, Jerry Angleton, and crippled one other."

"But why did you think I was involved?" Tom asked.

"For one thing, I found out that you and Tourneau were thick as thieves when you were kids. You hung out together at school and you were over at his house all the time. Second, I had a tail on you. You spent a hell of a lot of time in gun stores all over the area. Had a tap on your phone, too. Don't worry," he added quickly, "it's gone now. You sent that message to Ellen Tourneau about a wool blanket. I didn't know what it meant, but I knew it had to mean something. I got a warrant to search your house as well as arrest you. I wanted to find that blanket and see what part it played."

Tom shook his head. "Amazing. A policeman who thinks too much. You need to learn to rush in faster and spend less time inventing fantastic links, Lieutenant. How did you get authorization for a wiretap, and a search warrant, and an arrest warrant on such a flimsy basis?"

"Friendly judge. We play golf together. The judge, the D.A., and me. Couple of Sundays a month."

Tom shivered. He had realized anew how exposed he was here in the small town where he had expected to feel safe, anonymous, and protected. In Chicago, he would have known about the request to the judge almost as soon as it was made. And probably about the tail, too. "So you weren't really there to serve and protect me at all."

Snow shook his head. "Nope. Just turned out that way. My men were at the front door. I went around the house to see if there was another way out that we needed to cover. Found the big window smashed, heard the conversation inside. Mrs. Tourneau was so occupied with you, she didn't hear me climbing in. I listened. Good thing for you I did. That's why you're in the clear now."

"Along with Jack Tourneau."

"Yeah, him too. We know who did it, and she took care of her own punishment."

The beautiful woman, the object of Tom's yearning for so long, changed in an instant to a shapeless mass of torn flesh and broken bones. He had seen it in the lights of the policemen's powerful flashlights. He had stood wavering on the edge, barely able to keep his balance, in danger of toppling off the cliff himself, and he had wondered how that could be Ellen. And he had longed for some way to undo what had happened, to make it so that it had never happened. He had stood there whispering her name like a charm, a defense against what she had done and what she had destroyed.

One of the policemen had finally pulled him away and led him back inside the house.

Snow was still talking—more for his wife's benefit than Tom's, Tom realized. After all this time, Snow still needed to shine in her eyes. "Then she heard Hamilton's friends arguing with my men at the front door," he was saying. "That made her hurry up. She stopped talking and was going to shoot Hamilton. So that's when I knew I had to do something right away to stop her."

"And you did, Andy," Diane said.

"And I got shot," he said in disgust. "By a woman! Bitch shot me through my right lung. I almost didn't make it."

"You were lucky," Tom said. She specialized in hearts.

"How could she have done it?" Diane cried out. "How could she do this to us? I thought she was my friend!"

Tom stared at her. "Don't blame her too much. When you come down to it, all the bad things that have happened were Jack Tourneau's fault, weren't they?"

Neither Snow said anything.

Finally, Tom said, "I think I'd better be getting back to Ransom. I'm glad you're okay, Andy."

"I'm okay, and I'll be back on duty before the end of the

month," Snow said. "At which point, I'm going to take up my investigation of you again."

"But you said—"

"I said you were innocent in the murders of those singers. What you were doing for the last 22 years before you came home to Ransom, that's another matter. That's what I'm going to be concentrating on."

Tom sighed and went to the door. "See you around town, Lieutenant."

About the Author

David Dvorkin was born in 1943 in Reading, England. His family moved to South Africa after World War II, and then to the United States when David was a teenager. After attending college in Indiana, he worked at NASA in Houston on the Apollo Project, then at Martin Marietta in Denver on the Viking Mars lander project. His aerospace career ended in 1974. Thereafter, until 2009, he worked as a software developer and technical writer. He and his wife, Leonore, and their son, Daniel, have lived in Denver since 1971.

In addition to non-fiction, David has published many science fiction, horror, and mystery novels. For details, as well as quite a bit of nonfiction reading material, please see David's website: http://www.dvorkin.com/

David is on Facebook at
http://www.facebook.com/DavidDvorkin
and on Twitter at http://twitter.com/David_Dvorkin
His blog is http://eyeblister.blogspot.com/

For information about the self-publishing service that David operates with his wife, please see https://www.dldbooks.com/

David in 2019.

www.ingramcontent.com/pod-product-compliance
Lightning Source LLC
Chambersburg PA
CBHW070834020826
48982CB00019B/1124/J

* 9 7 8 1 7 3 6 2 8 8 6 0 3 *